James E Mack wa   s
childhood abroad, ...ure, the outdoors
and wildlife. He became a Commando in the late 1980s and
a member of a Special Operations unit, with a 22-year career
serving in many of the world's troubled hotspots. James
subsequently specialised as a Counter-Terrorism adviser
and assisted in capacity building operations in support of
UK and US Government initiatives.

His passion for wildlife led James to assist in the
development of counter-poaching programs in Africa. This
passion remains and James spends much of his leisure time
photographing the very animals that he strives to protect.

When time allowed, James began writing novels based upon
his experiences in Special Operations and conflict zones
around the globe. *Only the Dead* is his first novel.

James lives in Northern Scotland where he enjoys the
surfing and the mountains nearby.

Published by Achnacarry Press

ISBN: 978-1545251775

ONLY

THE

DEAD

JAMES E MACK

My thanks to everyone who supported me through this process. From the friends and colleagues who offered fair criticisms, to the many independent forums and the support that they too provided this nascent author. I must also acknowledge Brian Carter's Lundy's War, a beautiful book that provided the inspiration for my own. Once again, I am humbled by your support and good wishes.

James E Mack

Also by James E Mack:

Fear of the Dark
The Killing Agent

'Only the Dead have seen the end of war'

Attributed to Plato

I

Finn walked around the position, ensuring everything was up to scratch. The heat was intense, no shade or respite from the soaring temperatures. His troop was strung out along the road at irregular intervals, the standard formation of the vehicle checkpoint, each man watching the area around him with well-practised vigilance. He spoke softly into his radio microphone, informing Company Headquarters that his position was ready. The reply came back; a squelch of static followed by a monotone acknowledgement from the signaller back at the Forward Operating Base.

Walking along the road Finn stopped to talk with each of his marines, taking the time to ensure that they knew their roles and indulge in some aimless banter, keeping the morale up. As the Troop Sergeant, Finn Douglas was the linchpin in the effectiveness of his men; manager, father, brother and mother all rolled into one. As he patted a young marine on the shoulder on his way past, he reflected upon how even the more youthful soldiers had aged over the past few months. His nineteen-year-olds easily passing for men in their early thirties, the stress of the war etched in every deep crease and crow's foot of their craggy faces.

The heat here was even worse than in Afghanistan. It reminded Finn of being in a sauna where the inside of your nose stung from the dry heat that hit you like a physical blow. The fighting in Libya was also harder than he had experienced in either Iraq or Afghanistan, the enemy here having the benefit of being seasoned veterans from the ISIS battlefields further east as well as receiving training and support from Iranian Special Forces, the latter fighting a war by proxy against their western foes. Finn had lost three of his guys early on in the tour to a huge IED strike while they were inserting into a village during a clearance operation. They had been pinned down for two hours before they secured some close air support that gave them some room to manoeuvre and get the casualties out. Every contact that Finn and his men had experienced on the ground had been a tough one. There was none of the 'shoot and scoot' tactics that they had experienced in other theatres. The enemy here fought like professionals, dominating the ground, holding their positions, using flanking manoeuvres to close with the marines.

The marines, for their part initially held a grudging respect for the enemy, that age-old acknowledgement of kudos for any fighting force that met the threat with strength and commitment. Over the months that respect evolved into a resigned acceptance of the enemy's capabilities, then to downright hatred of them and their unwavering willingness to take on the marines at every opportunity. The strain of this relentless pace of operations was clear to see on the faces of all his guys, young and old, fresh or experienced: A tension in their expressions and the way in which they carried themselves. One of the corporals from two troop told Finn that his wife worked for a charity that helped ex-prisoners and their families with re-integration into normal life. She had told her husband after a unit barbecue one evening that his soldiers reminded her of some of the prisoners she dealt with; that they shared the same attitude of almost seeming coiled, unable to relax fully. The corporal had laughed it off until he had been in Libya for a few months and identified the same thing himself.

Finn made his way towards the first men of the checkpoint, the marines who would signal for the vehicles to slow down, stop and the occupants to walk forward. There were two marines and one interpreter here, the extra marine acting as cover for his colleague while his attention was focussed on the vehicles he was dealing with. The small village in the distance was lost in the heat haze, barely visible through the rippling effect of the rising thermals. A whirling red dust devil twisted across the road in front of him and danced gracefully across the desert, leaving the men to their static commitments. As he was approaching the small group, one of the marines turned and nodded to Finn, the gleaming white smile of the man a stark contrast against the tanned, weather-beaten face. Finn nodded back and continued along the road until he reached the interpreter and the second marine.

Ali, the interpreter, saw Finn and barely managed to repress his scowl. There was no love lost between Finn and Ali as on many occasions Finn had been forced to address Ali's laziness and unwillingness to go on patrol. He had tried several times to have Ali replaced but there was such a shortage of interpreters that HQ was adamant that Ali remain. Even yesterday when Finn had put out the warning order for the operation, the marines could not locate Ali to tell him that he was loaded on to the Op. Finn had found him hiding out near the civilian compound that housed the locally-sourced cleaners, cooks and contractors. Finn had grabbed Ali by his neck and dragged him from the bunk where he lay. The interpreter had squealed and threatened to have Finn charged for assault and racism. By closing the grip on Ali's throat, Finn had secured a silent nod of agreement that the incident would not be repeated to anyone and that Ali would be ready to deploy with the rest of the troop at the given time.

The interpreters that worked with the marines seemed to fall into two clear categories: really good or really bad. The good ones worked hard to provide the best service that they could, often supplying valuable cultural advice in addition to their linguistic role. These men were welcomed and assimilated into the marines' close-knit sections, part and parcel of the fighting unit. The bad ones brought nothing but trouble: Malingering, stealing, bullying local employees, giving wrong advice and regularly placing unfounded accusations of racism against the marines that they worked

4

with. The problem as Finn saw it was that they were in such short supply that they were well aware of their value and exploited this as much as they could. And Ali was one of the worst. An Eritrean national, he had studied English at university and worked in most countries in the middle east, exposed to many of the dialects and aspects of the language. On paper his qualifications were impressive. In real life less so.

Tommo, the troop's youngest marine, turned and smiled at Finn. "Hot enough for you Sergeant Douglas?"

Finn returned the smile and patted the soldier's back. "Yeah Tommo. Hot enough and then some. Don't think I'll ever drip about British weather as long as I live." Finn watched as Ali skulked off to the side of the road, squatted down and lit a cigarette. Finn indicated with his head towards the interpreter. "How's he holding up Tommo?"

The young marine looked in the direction of the interpreter and shrugged. "The usual: Tired, moaning, sulking, dragging his feet. Least he's not talking much."

Finn sighed and shifted his rifle to the other hand as he took out the mouthpiece of his hydration system and sucked down a drink. Once finished he opened the collar of his body armour in a vain attempt to circulate some air around his sweating torso. "Okay mate, I'm heading back up to check on Overwatch. Keep an eye on that slimy bastard and let me know if he causes you any dramas."

"Yeah, no worries, I'll make sure he's up to scratch."

5

Finn walked back along the road and spoke once again into his radio, confirming that the fire support team watching over his men were in position and ready. Satisfied, he continued making his way to the far end of the checkpoint, feeling the searing heat rising from the black road surface and into the air around him. They had another two days of this before their return to the FOB, another two days of bouncing between locations, setting up VCPs, gathering atmospherics, trying to win hearts and minds. *Hearts and minds*; that was all well and good where there were some hearts and minds to win over. In Libya, Finn and his men were neither welcomed nor accepted, the local populace seeming to sit on a sliding scale somewhere between grudgingly indifferent and openly hostile.

The other factor that fuelled the local population's hatred of the marines was the regular night raids by the Special Forces units. It was a constant frustration to the marines that they could be making headway with the locals in an area, turn up a week later and be attacked by the same people they had been breaking bread with. Inevitably a night raid would have taken place during the marines' absence from the region and the locals would vent their fury on the only targets that they could; the conventional troops who remained in the region. Finn was well aware of the necessity for these raids but the sheer volume and the negative impact of these operations left many questioning the validity of their effectiveness. This had led to some friction between the SAS squadron and the marines back at the FOB and several fistfights had broken out before the hierarchy stepped in and quelled the dissent. To Finn, it seemed as though there was little or no cohesion to the coalition's efforts. The Special Forces' raids would undo much of the work that the marines had carried out over long, painful months of winning the trust of the local populace. The American Special Forces would kill a tribal elder that the British had been communicating with, the SAS would detain an elder confirmed to be an insurgent only to have the spooks walk in and claim him as one of their 'assets' and the Italians, well, their SF just seemed to kill anyone they liked. *Surely this was no way to fight a war.*

Finn's thoughts were interrupted by a call on his radio from the Overwatch commander. As he listened, he turned to face Tommo and Ali's position, bringing his rifle up and looking through the optical sight to the road beyond the marines. He let out a soft grunt as he saw the movement through the shimmering heat haze: A kid with a wheelbarrow walking from the village towards the checkpoint. Finn couldn't make out many details at this distance but spoke into his radio. "Yep, got it. Kid with barrow approaching checkpoint from south, Tommo acknowledge." The young marine's reply came through and Finn watched as Tommo raised his own rifle and monitored the progress of the boy.

Finn continued with his walk to the men at the northern end of the checkpoint. The marines were accustomed to kids approaching them, looking for sweets, gifts or just through sheer curiosity. They kept a close eye on them however, all too aware that some of them would have been sent by the enemy to gather intelligence or steal kit and equipment. A patrol from Yankee Company had recently lost a valuable piece of ECM; the Electronic Counter Measure equipment that identified and blocked the frequencies used to detonate IEDs. That had been a serious incident as this equipment was highly classified and the impact of the enemy having access to it meant that they could adjust their frequencies accordingly, rendering the equipment useless. It had been stolen by a couple of youngsters, lifting the equipment while the marines had been distracted by the antics of the smaller kids. The officer and troop sergeant had been taken off the ground almost immediately and returned to the UK in disgrace as a result of their loss. Finn continually reminded his guys to keep an eye on the kids and make sure they did not get anywhere near any sensitive equipment.

He had almost reached Smudge, Frank and Majid, the two marines and the interpreter responsible for the northern end of the checkpoint, when his radio squawked with a transmission from Tommo at the other end.

"*One Zero Bravo, be aware young boy approaching my location with bread and food, over.*" Finn stopped and spoke into his radio, connecting with the Overwatch commander. "One zero Charlie, do you have eyes on the kid, over?"

There was a brief pause before the Scottish burr of Corporal Darren Shepherd came over the net. "*One Zero*

Bravo this is One Zero Charlie, we have eyes on but no details due to heat haze, over." Finn understood: The heat haze would obscure all but the most general of details visible to the Overwatch group's position almost a kilometre away. Finn began walking back down to Tommo's location. As he passed the other marines, he was gratified to see that each man was covering his arcs, their individual areas of responsibility, well aware that the kid could be a diversion. He felt a lump come to his throat as a sense of proprietary pride welled up within him. They had become a very tight unit, each man loyal and committed to the next. Finn loved his guys and was constantly humbled by their faith and trust in him as their troop Sergeant and was determined that he would get them all home. Repay their faith by doing his job as best as he could.

Reaching Tommo, Finn saw that he was having a heated discussion with Ali, the interpreter's voice carrying its angry tone through the desert air. He stopped talking as he saw Finn approach and moved slightly to one side as Finn addressed the marine. "What's the problem?"

Tommo pointed at the interpreter, his face full of anger. "It's this fucking clown, wanting to go to the kid and buy some bread. I've told him he can't, he has to stay here until we clear the kid but he's not having it."

Finn turned to Ali and caught his attention. "Hey, Ali. You do as you're fucking told; do you understand? You do NOT follow your own routine when you are out here with us. Everything we tell you to do is about keeping us safe, all

9

of us. You get grabbed or wounded and it's my guys who will have to deal with the shit of getting to you. So wise up dickhead."

Ali stared at the troop sergeant with undisguised hatred. He would be happy to see this marine die. He had no respect for Ali, for his qualifications, his status, his clan or his family. Ali had thought about leaving many times before, try to get a position in keeping with his status, maybe as an adviser to the general or something similar. He learned however that the poor performance reports that Sergeant Douglas had written about him meant he would never be considered for such a role. He had formally complained about Sergeant Douglas on several occasions but nothing was ever done and Ali got the impression that Sergeant Douglas was well liked by the command staff as well as his own men. *Ridiculous; the man was nothing less than a devil clad in his country's uniform.* Ali spat and glowered at the approaching boy, watching as the child staggered with his unbalanced road.

Finn looked through his sight at the boy. The kid was dressed in traditional garb and was smiling as he tottered up the road balancing his barrow. Finn could now make out the flat breads and fruit that appeared between the bouts of heat haze. He lowered his rifle and turned to Tommo's support, Marine Daly. "Make sure you cover his arse when that kid approaches, don't want to be caught by any surprises okay?"

The marine nodded and Finn knew that he had not needed the reminder but it didn't hurt to make sure. Turning again to Tommo he addressed the marine as he continued to watch the boy's approach. "Tommo, usual drills mate. Get him to stop short and walk forward a bit, raising his shirt and turning around. Ask him what he wants and then tell him we don't carry any money so can't buy anything from him. If he just wants to pass through get him to unload his barrow at a distance and check it out with your scope before he comes through." The young marine did not divert his attention but nodded to show that he understood. Finn walked away and spoke into the radio again.

"Charlie this is Bravo, anything suspect, over?" Finn knew that the Overwatch team would have been monitoring the area looking for any indication that the boy was part of an enemy initiative. The familiar Scottish burr came over the airwaves.

"Bravo, Charlie, negative. All quiet so far."

Finn stopped and took another drink. The baking plain silent around him as his men quietly concentrated in silence on their individual responsibilities. He took off his goggles and rubbed his eyes with the back of his glove, feeling tired already. Just as he was replacing them, he heard the raised voices of Tommo and Ali drifting up the road. He watched as the marine and the interpreter communicated with the boy and heard the higher notes of the boy's singsong voice replying. The exchange seemed to go on for longer than Finn would have expected and he was just about to get on the radio when the tone of the voices changed and he registered the urgency of the commands. Frowning, Finn strode back down to the marines' position, the voices now raised and insistent. He spoke into the radio as he made his way along the road. "Tommo, what's going on?"

"Bravo, the kid's not listening. He's not stopping, just keeps coming towards us fucking grinning. Ali thinks he might be a bit simple, over."

"Roger that Tommo. Keep at him but if he gets within thirty feet fire a warning shot, over."

Finn felt the tension rise within him. He hated this shit: The way an innocent, innocuous event could suddenly spiral into a completely different scenario. It was the unknown element of it that tortured him, that limbo between identifying something wrong then dealing with it. Once an incident was triggered, the training and experience kicked in and you dealt with it. It was that bit in between, the waiting and uncertainty that all soldiers hated.

He had just reached Marine Daly when Ali yelled another series of commands to the boy and Tommo fired a warning shot, the noise splitting the still desert air. The boy did not even flinch but kept walking in his odd manner as he counter-balanced the shifting contents of his barrow. Finn now stood beside Tommo and raised his own rifle, staring intently through the optic, using the magnification of the sight to study the boy as much as he could. He cursed as the boy wavered in and out of focus in the heat. "Fire again Tommo."

The young marine fired another shot and Finn winced at the shock to his hearing, his eye drawn to the ejected brass cartridge as it spun and tumbled through the air. Finn saw that the boy continued to move without any hesitation. Ali was shouting something and Finn looked over at the interpreter who was gesticulating wildly.

"Stop shooting, stop shooting, he is only a child, you understand? A CHILD!"

Finn pointed at Ali and shouted back. "Tell that kid to stop right where he is and step away from the barrow. NOW."

"Are you blind Sergeant? Can you not see with your own eyes that the child is simple? He does not have all his brains, does not know what he is doing and you are shooting at him? I will be reporting this when I get back."

Finn fought back the urge to march across and physically grab the interpreter but settled his concentration on the boy once again. He laid the sight's focus over the boy's jacket looking for any signs that he might be wearing a suicide vest beneath his shirt and waistcoat but could see nothing to indicate that this was the case. His attention was diverted by a shout from Tommo. Lowering his weapon, Finn turned to see Ali striding down the road towards the boy and Finn swore.

"Ali, get your arse back here NOW!" Finn felt his anger grow as the interpreter studiously ignored him, his receding back radiating disrespect for Finn's authority. "Ali, stop what you're doing and get fucking back here." This time the command was acknowledged by an indifferent wave of the hand above the interpreter's head. Finn saw that Ali was rapidly closing the distance towards the boy and Finn studied the kid once again. As he was traversing the sight down the front of the boy's shirt, his eyes picked out something unusual. Through the shimmering waves of the heat haze Finn noticed something strange about one of the wheelbarrow's handles. His eyes strained as he stared through the sight, seeking confirmation for the worry already chewing at his stomach. Before he could determine whether his suspicions were correct, he was once again distracted by a yell from Tommo. Finn lowered his weapon in time to see the younger marine sprint off in pursuit of Ali.

A sudden sense of despair engulfed Finn and he raised the rifle once more and looked through the sight at the approaching boy. He followed the line of the boy's arm down to the handle he had been examining earlier and gave a sharp intake of breath. He could now see that something was attached to the handle by black electrical tape and that a pair of wires ran from the handle into the contents of the barrow. Time seemed to slow for Finn as he took his eye from the sight to see how far Ali and Tommo were from the boy. The interpreter was only a matter of metres away while Tommo still had some distance to go. Finn trained his sight back on the boy while speaking into his radio. "Tommo, Stop, Stop, Stop, the kid's got a bomb."

He watched the young marine raise a hand to his earpiece but continue with his chase, Finn's transmission obviously not coming through. Tommo was now less than ten metres from the boy and Ali had slowed to a walk and was talking to the kid, arms open and smiling. Finn looked at the boy's smiling face, clear now through the magnification of his rifle sight. His breathing quickened and his mind raced as he attempted to assimilate the unfolding events and come to a decision that would save the lives of his marine and the interpreter. Another look over his sight showed him Ali fast approaching the boy with Tommo rapidly closing the distance between himself and the interpreter. A brief surge of panic swelled up within Finn as the hopelessness of the situation and the potential for the deaths of his men became reality. His breathing hitched and his hands trembled as he sought to justify the horrific action that he was now forced to contemplate. Fighting the panic, he swallowed hard and settled the point of the sight in the dead centre of the boy's face. With a strange sensation of detachment, he flicked the weapon's safety catch to the fire position, steadied his breathing and pulled the trigger. The boy disappeared from the confined view of the sight as though snatched away, and Finn registered the recoil of the rifle against his shoulder and the ringing in his ears. The sharp tang of cordite lingered in the still air as he lowered the weapon and looked down the road.

Ali was stood, stunned and staring at the dead child now collapsed behind the upright wheelbarrow. Tommo had also stopped but had turned to face Finn, a quizzical expression visible on his shadowed face beneath his helmet. Finn could hear the thumping of boots on the tarmac behind him as some of the nearer marines approached him to see what was going on. A shrieking noise reached Finn, dim initially after the sharp retort of his shot but becoming louder as his hearing returned. Ali was facing back up the road and screaming at Finn in Arabic, pointing wildly at the dead boy behind him. Finn beckoned with his arm for Tommo and the interpreter to return to his position.

Tommo stood for a brief moment, weapon hanging by his side looking at the body of the dead boy. He was unsure of exactly what had happened and struggled to come to grips with the sight of the small corpse sprawled behind the wheelbarrow. He shook his head and turned back towards the troop sergeant walking with his head lowered.

Tommo did not know what had happened. He found himself on his back, staring at the sky and blinking rapidly. His head was filled with a strange noise, almost like a loud, deep hum. Confused, he tried to sit up but found that his arm wouldn't work, no response whatsoever to his efforts. He tried using his other arm and succeeded in pushing himself into a sitting position. He found that he was sitting on the road facing towards the village. There was a large plume of smoke and dust in the air and as he watched he saw the shape of a gaping hole in the tarmac emerge from the dissipating veil. Tommo was confused: The hole hadn't been there moments before; he surely would have noticed

16

it. *Had they called in air support for something?* He blinked rapidly as he tried to remember where he was and what he was doing. There was something wrong but he just couldn't put his finger on what it was. He looked down at where he was sitting and saw the saturated trousers covering his legs. He was bleeding heavily. With almost clinical detachment the young marine began running his hand up and down his legs, looking for the nature of the injury. When there was no apparent reason for the blood, he tried to use both arms to check underneath his legs but again, only his right arm responded. He turned his attention to his left arm, annoyed at its lack of support for him in his time of need. He cocked his head to one side and opened his mouth as he tried to process what he was seeing. His left arm was gone. From the elbow down was just a space, a void that was all wrong. Above this was a mess of jagged remnants of muscle and tendons and ripped pieces of his UBACS sleeve, all coated with a viscous varnish of his blood, which continued to flow freely down the side of his body armour, pooling in his lap.

Finn and the other marines reacted instantly to the blast and reached Tommo before he passed out from blood loss. There was no panic; each man well practiced in what was required. Two of the marines tended to Tommo's wounds: tourniquet, quick clot, morphine and IV fluids. Finn was on the radio getting the MEDEVAC and pushing out the Nine Liner; the official formatted report for any incident that the troops encountered. With no time to reflect on the incident he managed the situation at hand. He ensured the remainder

17

of the troop were alert and monitoring the areas around them in the event that the enemy attack while they were distracted. He spoke to the Overwatch commander and directed him to secure and mark an LZ, a landing zone for the MEDEVAC chopper. He briefed Corporal Waters to find out if there was anything left of Ali's body that they could bag and take back with them. They would also look for any remnants of the IED to collect for analysis and photograph the scene.

The blast had aroused interest from the village and the Overwatch commander informed Finn that a mob of people was heading up the road, most on foot but several FAMs or Fighting Aged Males were on motorcycles. Finn relayed this information back to Company Headquarters and recommended that the troop also be lifted out of the area. Another transmission told Finn that the MEDEVAC chopper was inbound and he was heartened to hear that it would be an American 'Pedro' call sign. These guys were renowned for coming in to the hottest of LZs and lifting out the casualties. The marines loved them and would often muse that if they were to be wounded that they hoped it would be 'Pedro' that came to get them out.

Corporal Waters' team had done what they could. There had been very little left of the interpreter's body as he had been so close to the bomb but they had found some pieces of him that they had secured in one of the bags the troop carried for this purpose. Finn redeployed some of the troop to the southern end of the checkpoint where the villagers were now starting to arrive. He watched as Majid began ordering them to stay where they were and the marines held their rifles in the shoulder, not aiming them but ready to do so should the situation escalate.

Shep's Scottish burr came across the airwaves and informed him that the landing zone had been identified and that some of his men were securing it now that they had swept it for potential IEDs. Finn relayed the coordinates back to headquarters and was informed that MEDEVAC was two minutes out and their own pick up five minutes. He sighed with relief, knowing that if the troop had been ordered to remain in the area, they would have been fighting hard for the next twenty-four hours.

He could hear the raised voices of the villagers and Majid's plaintive attempts to calm them. Finn couldn't understand the Arabic but he could read the body language and expressions of the villagers. They were blaming the marines for the death of the boy. Only now that there was a brief pause in his duties could Finn begin to reflect on his actions. He had killed a child. A boy of no more than twelve years old and he had killed him. Whoever had sent the boy must also have put a remote-controlled device in the bomb as a secondary or back up detonator. This was standard practice for the enemy, ensuring that if the deliverer wavered or the primary detonation method didn't work, they could fire it themselves from a position of safety. Finn experienced a surge of rage course through his body. *Who the hell sent children with bombs hidden under bread and fruit? These*

fucking savages who thought no more of a child's life than they did for
that of a dog or a goat.

He felt his breathing hitch as he replayed the shooting in his mind, saw once again, the boy's smiling face disappear from view as though yanked aside by something outside Finn's field of view. The rage dissipated and he now felt a sense of self-loathing, bile rushing up his throat and tears rolling down his face. He bent over and vomited onto the hot tarmac, retching again and again until nothing was left. He stood upright and spat the waste from his mouth and wiped his lips with his gloved hand. Over the raised voices of the village mob he heard the distant whump of approaching helicopters and soon after received the confirmation on the radio that the Pedro call sign was at his location.

Finn briefed a team to get Tommo to the chopper while the remainder of the troop dealt with the escalating hostility from the villagers. The helicopters were louder now and he saw the green smoke from Shep's team as it marked the LZ for the MEDEVAC. One of the helicopters remained high above the area, giving supporting cover to the team that would be picking up the casualty. As the second chopper flared for landing, Finn watched as the door gunner trained the M60 machine gun on the group of villagers, ready to engage if they turned their attention to the helicopter. The noise of the helicopter's blades, and the clouds of dust and debris that pelted the marines and villagers alike drowned everything out. In less than thirty seconds the MEDEVAC was complete and the helicopters banking east and out of the area.

Monitoring the villagers' antics, Finn raised Shep on the radio and directed him to locate another LZ for the troop's extraction. While it was only minutes away and they could possibly have used the same LZ as the MEDEVAC, Finn was leaving nothing to chance. The enemy would have watched the MEDEVAC and taken note of the LZ's location, probably bedding in their mortars even now, ready to take on any other helicopters that landed there.

Finn walked down the road to meet the marines who had treated Tommo and taken him to the helicopter. As he approached, Marine Daly spoke.

"Think he'll be fine Finn. He was still conscious when we got him on there and we got a line into him so hopefully the blood loss wasn't too much."

Finn nodded his thanks and patted the marine's shoulder as he walked past. The villagers were now becoming aggressive and several had picked up stones from the blast crater. Finn was more concerned with the three individuals who had arrived on motorbikes. Young, lean men whose faces were obscured by chequered scarves that covered their mouths and jaws. These men remained at the rear and sides of the village mob, watching with a detached interest as the proceedings unfolded. Finn had no doubt that these were enemy fighters, probably the same ones who had primed the kid in the first place. As he watched, one of the men answered a mobile telephone and spoke into it. The man continued with his conversation nodding now and again and on one occasion looking up directly at Finn. As their eyes met, Finn saw that the man was looking around at the whole troop while talking on the phone and Finn realised that he was counting the marines and relaying this information back to someone. Battle Damage Assessment or BDA: Checking to see the impact and effect of your attack or strike. Finn grunted in recognition of the enemy's use of the same tactic that the coalition used. He was distracted by the squelch on the radio and the information that followed. *Helo extraction inbound in one minute.*

Finn grabbed his Corporals and briefed the extraction plan, simple but ensuring there was always cover while teams were moving. The Corporals dispersed and briefed their sections and the helicopters arrived, following Shep's signal once again to the LZ. In a matter of minutes Finn's whole troop was loaded and, as he had briefed the Corporals, he jumped on as last man onto the last helicopter, ensuring all his men were clear. As the Black Hawk rose fast into the sky and the G-forces pushed Finn hard against the floor, he looked at the villagers below throwing their stones at the flying machines as they expressed their rage. He locked his gaze onto that of the man on the motorbike he had been watching on the ground only moments before. As if seeing this, the man on the motorbike mimed a gesture of putting an RPG on his shoulder and firing at the departing aircraft. An instant later he was gone from view as the helicopter changed direction and only the desert and the deep red wadis were visible from the open doorway.

II

Finn saw the dead boy as he left the showers one evening, a couple of weeks after the incident. He was walking back from the ablutions block, towel around his waist and bare feet slipping in his untied boots, a vain attempt to keep his feet clean and free from the powder-red dust that clung to everything. As he passed one of the big generators the small figure walked between the tents and out of sight. In shock, Finn dropped his wash bag, shampoo bottle and toothpaste tumbling out onto the sand. His heart was hammering in his chest as he recognised the child. On stiff legs, Finn turned the corner and looked along the thoroughfare between the rows of dun-coloured tents. Nothing. He released a breath he was unaware that he had been holding and rubbed his hand through his hair, feeling shaky. He retraced his steps and picked up his toiletries then made his way back to his tent. He was grateful that the other occupant of his tent was on an operation up north, as Finn knew his fellow sergeant would have noticed something wrong.

The incident spooked him. Finn had never experienced anything like this before. He thought it through in an attempt to rationalise what had happened. He knew he was exhausted, hadn't been sleeping well for weeks now, so potentially it could just be a hallucination brought on by tiredness.

He'd thought a lot about killing the kid. On his return to the FOB the Company Commander and the Ops Officer had debriefed him. They'd both agreed it had been a terrible situation for Finn and his men to have been involved in but that Finn's judgement had been sound: Child or not, the kid was a suicide bomber and more of Finn's troop might have been killed if he had not taken such decisive action.

The Padre had also popped his head into Finn's tent in that first week after the shooting. Finn had nothing against the sky pilot as such but preferred to just get on with things, deal with them on his own. The workload had helped: With the troop commander on leave, Finn had stepped up and taken on his role in addition to that of troop sergeant. The relentless pace of operations, taking their turn on FOB security, his spells as watch commander in the TOC, the Tactical Operations Cell, meant that Finn had no time to dwell on matters other than those directly related to what he was currently doing.

The next time Finn saw the boy was two days later when he woke from a sweaty, fractured sleep and turning his head, saw the small form standing in the shadows of the corner of the tent. Finn had gasped and sat bolt upright, grabbing his torch and shining it into the darkness. There was nothing, no sign that the boy had ever been there. He'd dragged his knees to his chest and sat huddled and strangely cold in the darkness, adrenalin surging through his body, and waited for the light of dawn before moving. Over the next few weeks, the boy would appear at regular intervals in various locations, half hidden in the shadows or corners of the FOB. Each time he regarded Finn with the same soft smile and sad, brown eyes. The personification of an innocent child ruined by the ragged bullet hole in the centre of his forehead. Finn slept less than before and his appetite waned. He would find himself thinking about something and then minutes later, realise with a start that he had been sat staring into space with no recollection of what he had been thinking about in the first place.

He'd thought about talking to someone about it but then the eight guys from Three Troop had been killed and the focus of the company became taking the fight to the enemy. Finn welcomed this and diverted all his energy into the operations that followed, pushing himself so hard that he would drop into a deep sleep the moment he climbed into his sleeping bag liner. The frenetic pace of patrolling, fighting and defending positions provided him with no opportunity to either think about his issues or deal with them in any other way.

Which was fine by him. Since being out on the operation he hadn't seen the boy again. Finn and his troop had one more week left on the hyper-aggressive Op Sharpen, one more week where he could be the old Finn, the one that didn't see dead kids hanging around him. One more week then he'd be back at the FOB, hopefully without the unwanted companionship of the child he had killed.

III

From the moment the boss had asked him to take a walk around the Hesco perimeter Finn had known bad news would follow. He wondered if it was something to do with the boy, maybe a late complaint from the family. The boss wasn't a bad bloke, all things considered, but he was young, inexperienced and ill prepared for dealing with matters of personal consequence. For the past six months that he and Finn had been working together, Finn had come to like the new lieutenant and his attitude to the men. They had a good relationship as officer and sergeant but the obvious unease contorting his superior's face brought a hollow feeling of dread to Finn's stomach.

The pair walked in silence along the wire-encased defences of the base, the baking heat a physical entity, the powder dust smoking from the earth under their footsteps. Lieutenant Bucknall took the opportunity to glance at his sergeant, a man he had the greatest respect and admiration for, looked up to by both men and command alike. His own nerves at the prospect of the task at hand were starting to get the better of him and he stopped, turning to face his sergeant. He ran a hand through his mop of blonde curls and sighed before looking Finn in the eye.

"Sergeant Douglas, I have some awful news to give you and there's no easy way of doing this so I'm just going to go ahead and say it." He took a deep breath before continuing, looking the sergeant in the eye and keeping his voice as steady as he could.

"You will have heard about the bombing in London yesterday morning. Well, just about an hour ago I received a call from company headquarters informing me that your mother and sister were killed in the blast. I'm so, so sorry Finn, I know this must be the worst thing in the world to hear."

Finn stood still, a strange buzzing in his ears and a feeling of disassociation overwhelming him. He heard himself speaking, almost unaware that he was making the sounds he could hear.

"There's no possibility this is a mistake boss?"

Lieutenant Bucknall placed a hand on his shoulder and shook his head.

"No Finn. They were both positively identified. I'm sorry mate, I really am. Look, we're getting you out of here tonight. There's a chopper inbound from Tripoli and you're on it. You've got a slot on the 2100 flight out of there and back to Brize Norton. You'll be met there by the Welfare Officer who will take care of you from that point." He could see the shock in the sergeant's paleness, the rapid blinking of the eyes and the glazed, unfocussed expression. He increased the pressure of his grip and leaned in to meet Finn's eyes. "Go pack whatever you need. Corporal

Matlock is stepping up to cover you so don't worry about a handover, he's well capable and up to speed with everything. You just concentrate on getting the hell out of here, okay?"

Finn nodded out of reflex, numbed and detached from the moment. He turned and walked back towards the tented accommodation, his gait stiff and awkward, as he struggled to process the horrific news. Lieutenant Bucknall watched him go. *Poor sod*, he thought, *you're out here fighting in the sand against the very same bastards who are blowing up your people at home. You accept that out here you might catch it up, but you could never believe that your loved ones back home would be the ones to die at the hands of these fucking lunatics.* He made his way back to the operations room to continue with his duties monitoring the UAV coverage in the eastern sector. While watching drone footage was not a prospect that filled him with joy, it was at least cooler there thanks to the air conditioning.

1

The journey from Libya back to RAF Brize Norton was a blur of noisy aircraft, the sharp tang of aviation fuel, fractured sleep and the smell of soldiers who had been in the same clothes for too long in the heat of North Africa. The Welfare Officer was waiting for Finn and after the initial introductions and condolences the pair spent an awkward twenty minutes waiting for Finn's luggage to appear on the carousel. Around them Finn could hear snatches of conversations from the various soldiers, sailors and airmen now back on home ground. Boasts of how much drink would be taken, how many women would be shagged and how much good food would be eaten seemed to fuel the bulk of the excited discussions.

The Welfare Officer, Major Perry from 45 Commando, broke the silence between them by running through what would happen next. A car and driver were waiting to take them to the Royal Marines' Reserve barracks in London where there was a room in the Sergeants' Mess for Finn. Major Perry wasn't sure whether Finn would have wanted to go direct to the family home in Hersden, Canterbury but had made the decision to put Finn up in London until he was sure what he wanted to do. He was aware that Finn had his own place in Arbroath where he was stationed but thought that Finn would want to remain in the southeast until he had sorted out all the necessary arrangements. *Arrangements? Like booking a flight or a hotel? Arrangements? Was that how the military referred to burying your only living family?* Not trusting himself to speak, Finn merely nodded his assent.

Traffic from Brize Norton was almost static and Major Perry cursed and turned to Finn.

"Not sure how much of the news you were getting out in the sand Sergeant Douglas but this bloody cyber-attack is crippling everything at the moment. Internet, phones, airports, banks and of course, traffic. Don't think many of us truly appreciated how linked to the digital world our whole existence is."

Finn felt that some response was required although in truth, he would have been happier left alone with his memories of his mum and Katy, gorgeous little Katy and her cheeky smile.

"I heard a bit about it last week. What's actually happened?"

Grateful for the diversion, Major Perry explained the background to the current crisis. A series of cyber-attacks aimed at all levels of the nation's infrastructure that brought much of the country to a grinding halt. Internet and mobile networks were hit the hardest, banks and trading, all forms of transport and of course intelligence and security were suffering badly too. The Russians were being blamed but they of course were denying any involvement. Parliament and COBRA were meeting round the clock to deal with the fallout. There had been civil disturbances in many cities with runs on the banks as people tried to withdraw their cash, supermarkets being overrun as panicked citizens grabbed what they could before stocks became depleted. The inevitable looting and riots as control was lost. Things were a little better now apparently, more calm prevailed and a bit of the old blitz spirit was starting to show in the face of adversity.

"Except in traffic." The Major pointed out the window. "Traffic lights are down so a lot of that job is being done manually now, hence the snail's pace."

Finn nodded, taking in the words but returning immediately to his last memories of his mother and little sister. Katy was only eleven years old. Would always now, only ever be eleven years old. She shared his curly black hair and easy smile and always looked like she was ready to burst out laughing at any moment. She loved gymnastics, baking and some boy band called The South; Finn recalled with a stab of pain the joy she had shown when he surprised her with front row tickets for one of their concerts. Her squeal of delight and how she had thrown herself on to him, arms around his neck, shrieking her happiness to the best brother in the world.

Nick Perry glanced at the sergeant beside him and saw that he was off in a world of his own. *How the hell do you deal with something like this?* When he had received the call from the Commanding Officer that there was an imminent

33

compassionate situation, he had assumed that there had been a fatality in Libya and was mentally preparing for the repatriation procedure. He really couldn't say what was worse; informing a relative that their son had died while on active service or telling a marine that he had lost his close family while he was deployed. This was the first time in his capacity as the unit's Welfare Officer that he had dealt with the latter of the two and truth be told, he would rather never repeat the experience. He had carried out several Casualty Notifications to soldier's families and while unpleasant, he was confident with the process. This situation however placed him in unfamiliar territory and he felt awkward and unsure of his responses. He imagined what he would feel if something like this happened to Tilly and the boys and found his throat constricting and eyes watering at the mere thought of such a thing.

Finn dozed in and out of a fractured sleep where his memories mingled with dreams that became difficult to distinguish between. In some cases, he was travelling home on leave to see his mum and Katy and would awake, surprised at the presence of a driver and a Major with him in the car. Reality would then return and with it the fire of pain and sorrow within him. Now and then silent tears would roll down his face, mapping their way through his stubble before dropping off the end of his chin and darkening the camouflage pattern of his uniform.

The journey seemed interminable and Finn was not even aware of where they were until the vehicle came to a complete stop and an armed marine approached the car and checked the identity cards of the major and the driver. He made to get his own card out but the marine had already turned away and made a signal to the sentry box. A brief moment later the door opened and the driver entered a small open area where several other vehicles were parked. A Warrant Officer with a clipboard stood by an open door and raised his hand in greeting, walking towards the car. Finn grabbed his bergan and holdall from the boot of the car and made his way towards Major Perry who was writing on the Warrant Officer's clipboard. He looked up as Finn approached.

"Sergeant Douglas, this is Sergeant Major Layton, he's in charge here and your point of contact should you require anything during your stay."

The Sergeant Major put out his hand and spoke in a soft Welsh accent. "Sorry for your loss, Finn. Fucking terrible news mate, terrible."

Finn shook the hand and nodded, not trusting himself to speak, throat tight and eyes hot as he acknowledged the condolences. By unspoken agreement the pair then gave Finn a brisk brief on the routine for the next week or so while he would be staying in the barracks. He was given an accommodation key and the driver took this and Finn's belongings to the room while Finn remained and listened to the rest of his briefing. Major Perry would return in the morning to take Finn to the coroner's office where details of the bodies' release and subsequent funerals could be finalised. Thereafter they would go to the family home and Major Perry would guide Finn through the process of informing friends, family and neighbours as well as dealing with his mother's solicitor and any will that she had left. They would cover no more tonight as it was already very late and Finn was utterly exhausted. The Major would meet Finn in the Mess for breakfast at seven thirty and brief him again on the plans for the day and any other updates or changes. He shook Finn's hand and ordered him to go and grab some rest before he collapsed. Finn wished them both good night and made his way to his room.

Sergeant Major Jay Layton knew of Finn Douglas although he did not know him personally. They had both received their gallantry awards at the same investiture; both men awarded the Military Cross for separate actions in Afghanistan. Douglas had been a corporal back then and had stormed a Taliban position in Sangin that had pinned his section down, killing two of his lads. Jay recalled hearing Finn's citation and being impressed by the corporal's disregard for his own life while protecting those of his men. He turned to the Welfare Officer.

"How's he holding up?"

Nick Perry sighed. "About as you'd expect. Dealing with it in his own way. Quiet, withdrawn, stunned; choose your adjective."

Jay nodded and looked at Finn's retreating back. "What a fucking thing to deal with. We all expect to catch it up when we're knocking on doors in the shitholes of the world but this? Bang out of order." Nick Perry nodded his agreement and looked at his watch. "Right Sergeant Major, I'm going to write up today's report then get my fat one down for a few hours. See you at breakfast in the morning as well?"

"Yeah boss, I'll be in around seven so I'll catch you both then."

The Welfare Officer thanked the Sergeant Major for his help and made his way to his own room. As he walked, he reached for his mobile phone to check for any messages from Tilly before he remembered that the networks were still down. *Fucking Russians, no doubt we'll be at war with them as well soon enough.* Rubbing his tired eyes, he decided to leave the report until the next day. There wasn't a whole lot to put in it and it wasn't as if the Internet was up and running to allow him to e-mail it anyway. No, he decided, he would get some sleep and find a landline in the morning and ring Tilly and the boys. The thought of the call made him appreciate his wife and children all the more and how much Sergeant Douglas had lost. His heart went out to the lad, truly went out to him.

2

The days passed in a blur of meetings, condolences and platitudes. Coroners, funeral directors, solicitors, friends and work colleagues of his mum, their neighbours in Hersden. Major Perry dealt with the initial meetings and introductions and guided Finn through the bewildering process. The lack of any other living relatives made the situation somewhat easier as there were no other parties to consider other than Finn and what he wanted in terms of funeral arrangements. The will was also straightforward. Finn was the sole heir. As the house had been paid off many years before with the insurance money after his father's death, there was not even any worry of debt to be concerned with.

Finn found that he was becoming two different people; the stoic, capable Finn who dealt with the admin and details of the situation and Finn the wreck, the sobbing mess weeping into the stiff military sheets of a room in the Sergeants' Mess. At some point he became numbed to the whole process and seemed to operate on autopilot, being where he needed to be in body at least if not in mind. He had no appetite, coffee being adequate enough for his needs. Despite being exhausted he slept little, whatever snatches of rest he did get being broken. The boy remained an intermittent companion, usually appearing when Finn was alone, a silent sentinel in the shadows. Finn recognised on one level that something was very wrong with him, that the boy wasn't real. On another level however he felt that he deserved the boy's silent presence as a reminder and rebuke for his terrible action that day. In the mornings when he shaved, he could see the dark rings beneath his eyes, the network of red blood vessels prominent in his eyeballs.

When they went to the family home, Major Perry made the excuse of having to get back to the office for a few hours. Finn was grateful for the man's discretion and thoughtfulness. He wasn't sure that he wouldn't break down and preferred be alone and deal with it himself, rather than face the awkward sympathies of an onlooker. Finn wandered the house, eyes moist as he took in the contents of the empty home. His mother's awful 'snow angel' ornaments occupying the shelves, sills and cabinets of the living room. He smiled a little as he remembered he and Katy shopping for their mother's birthday and Christmas presents, seeking out the latest limited-edition ornament to supplement the collection, their laughter at the shared dislike of the twee collection. They would tease their mother good-naturedly about the terrible figurines and she would laugh in return and inform them that it was a question of taste and that it was so sad that her children had none.

The kitchen was spotless as always, his mum having been a house-proud woman. Some of Katy's pictures were pinned to the fridge door with magnets; selfies with various friends, a picture of the three of them together at the German Christmas market, several pictures of wolves. Katy loved, *had* loved, wolves, fascinated by the animals and everything about them. He recalled being on leave some years ago with her sitting on his knee, telling him how wolves were misunderstood and maligned by people and that they were amazing animals. Tears fell from his face as he made his way through the rest of the house, each object and item triggering a memory and underlining the fact that memories were now all that he had.

He sat on Katy's bed, holding Akela, her cuddly toy wolf in his hands. He had painted the room with her when she had announced that she was a little old for the pink princess look and required an update. Finn had taken her to choose paint and recalled her excitement and the fun they had re-decorating the room. He stood and took down a framed picture from where it took pride of place on the wall. It was he, Katy and their mother outside Buckingham Palace just after his investiture. He was in his blues, holding the boxed Military Cross in front of him with Katy between him and their mother, all smiling and proud. Katy had loved that day; the new dress, the hat, going to see the Queen. Finn loved the photograph. They had always been close as a family and their smiles of delight leapt from the image, highlighting this fact. He looked around the room, taking in the other photos, pictures, posters, the iPod dock, television, the pile of books.

He stood and placed the plush wolf down on the bed, smoothing the duvet where he had been sitting. Realising the futility of this he made a sound between a sob and a sigh and left his sister's room, making his way to his own. In comparison with Katy's, Finn's room was more subdued. He stood in the doorway and scanned the interior. The photos from various parts of the world, his passing out photograph with his troop in training, his boxing trophies and his framed citation for his Military Cross.

He hadn't been back home as much as he'd liked in recent years, the conflicts in Iraq, Afghanistan and Libya keeping him busy for the best part of every year. When he had managed to visit, they had always been wonderful, the love of a mother and sister making the journey one of anticipation rather than obligation. He'd last seen them around eight months previously, just before the final part of his pre-deployment training in Jordan. It had been a great week together and he'd spoiled Katy with the gift of a new digital camera to aid her newfound passion for photography. He'd also allayed his mother's fears about the forthcoming deployment. She had experienced his multiple tours of Iraq and Afghanistan but felt differently about the war in Libya. He could understand her misgivings; the war in Libya was receiving very little support with the general public exhausted and fatigued by the cost and duration of the previous conflicts. The mistaken targeting of a wedding party and a funeral where hundreds of innocent people were killed had been covered relentlessly by the media who were spinning a narrative of out of control soldiers on a killing spree with little regard for the lives of the innocent. Finn knew, of course that this was not the case. He had explained to his mother that intelligence was rarely black and white and that, inevitably, mistakes were made, but that it was important to remember that they were mistakes and not deliberate policy. He had hugged her as he told her that Libya was no different to Iraq or Afghanistan and that he had returned safely time and time again from both countries. She had brushed it off with a remark about worry being a mother's prerogative, no matter how tough and hard her boy was.

Finn made his way back to Katy's room and sat on her bed, head in hands. The thought that had been circling the fringes of his consciousness now came, unbidden and unwelcome to the front of his mind; *had they suffered?* The coroner had gone to great pains to assure Finn that they would not have known anything about the blast, would not have felt any pain. Finn had nodded his acceptance of this fact at the time however he had immediately thought of the friends and colleagues he had lost to wars over the years and the standard statement to their loved ones from the military; *they did not suffer.* Was this too, simply the policy of the coroner? A well-meaning gesture to give the grieving relatives what little comfort they could from such a horrific situation? He stood, eyes darting round the room for any distraction that would divert him from this train of thought. He picked up a brochure that was lying on the bedside cabinet, something Katy must have been reading recently.

It was a glossy publication about a wilderness area in Scotland where wolves had been reintroduced into the ecosystem some years ago. As he opened the brochure, Finn recalled his sister telling him about this area and how she wanted to go there with her camera and photograph the wolves. He saw that the wilderness area encompassed the bulk of an island chain in the Outer Hebrides of Scotland and that the wolves had been reintroduced to their habitat over seven years ago now. He read the booklet from cover to cover, initially grateful for the distraction but soon engrossed in the description of a pristine wilderness where these animals now lived and flourished. He jumped as the telephone shattered the silence of the house. Taking the brochure with him he returned to the living room and picked up the handset. Major Perry. The officer explained that he had concluded his work and would be around to pick up Finn within the hour. He apologised for the use of the landline but the mobile networks were still not working correctly. Finn agreed to the timing and hung up, the silence in the house complete once again after the intrusion of the call.

3

The funeral was hard. His mother and Katy had been well liked and the turnout of mourners was huge, much bigger than Finn had anticipated even though Major Perry had warned him that there would likely be a large attendance. Finn held it together for much of the service and the reception back at the family home but had taken refuge in his sister's room at one point to weep in private, not wanting to be seen by anyone. He could feel the change within him; the well-intentioned sympathy and condolences from people were starting to anger him. Until now, he would feel the onset of tears and sorrow but since the funeral an inexplicable cold rage was growing within him. He couldn't wait until everyone was gone and he could be alone again. He didn't want to upset anyone, well aware that his feelings of anger needed to be repressed, but he was finding it difficult to do so. He needed to concentrate. He began treating the day as a military task, something to push through, leaving the emotions for later. He found that this helped. Disassociating his actions from his feelings allowed him the luxury of accepting people's sympathy without reacting in a negative manner and causing offence. The day dragged on but in twos and threes, the mourners departed throughout the afternoon and just as night was falling the last person, a lady from his mother's former work place, said her goodbyes. As the door closed, Finn leaned against it with his forehead and breathed an audible sigh. He walked over to the drinks table and poured a large slug of Laphroaig into a glass. As he drank the smoky whisky, he looked at the room around him, taking in the randomly placed chairs and paper plates with food and cake remnants. He would clear it all up soon; first he wanted just to appreciate the quiet. He sat on one of the dining chairs and took another big drink, relishing the peaty burn in his throat. He felt empty now, devoid of any emotion. Major Perry wanted to meet him tomorrow and discuss Finn's options regarding getting back to work. He had made it clear that the marines would support Finn and assist him in securing whatever position he felt up to taking on. Equally, they were happy to grant an extended period of leave, should Finn feel unable to return to work so soon after his loss.

Until this point, Finn had not thought much about what he would do once he had buried his family but the issue was now forced upon him. He didn't know what he wanted. On one hand he knew getting back to work would give him something to focus on and the support of the lads would be invaluable in helping him come to terms with the situation. He did however feel exhausted. Exhausted and empty and with no appetite for decision-making. He decided to get drunk. Glancing at the table he saw that the Laphroaig was still three-quarters full, the fiery spirit not being to everyone's taste. *Good. That should be enough to be starting with.*

After some time, he began to doze off but woke with a start, sensing he was no longer alone. He smiled, picked up the glass from the side table and raised it in a mocking toast to the small figure in the shadows by the curtains. Finn no longer felt any fear when the boy appeared, and he gave a low, drunken chuckle as he lowered the glass and took another drink. He was almost at the point where he was talking to the boy, as he was practically the only constant person that remained in Finn's life. Finn found this thought hilarious and burst into loud laughter at the idea of a dead child's ghost being his only companion. The laughs slowed and evolved into sobs, his chest heaving and tears streaming down his face as he lowered himself onto the carpet and curled up in a ball.

When Finn woke, he wondered where he was for several moments. He groaned as he registered the stiffness in his limbs from his uncomfortable sleeping position. His mouth felt fuzzy from the whisky and he rose on unsteady legs and walked to the kitchen to get some water. The clock showed it was almost six thirty and that he had about an hour before the Major showed up. He tidied the living room and washed the remaining glasses and plates before he went upstairs for a shave and shower. He ironed a shirt and a pair of chinos and dressed, keeping an eye on the time as he did so. Packing the rest of his belongings in his grip he sat back down in the living room and waited for Major Perry's arrival. Finn still hadn't decided definitively what he wanted to do but believed that he wasn't ready to return to Libya just yet and the marines would probably be of the same mind-set. He thought about going back up to Four-Five Commando at Condor, where at least he had his own flat in Arbroath. The unit would be quiet with the bulk of the commando deployed on operations in Libya and it would provide him with a bit of time with which to come to a decision. He settled on this course of action and took a last look around the room before picking up his bag and walking out the front door.

4

Finn had been back at Condor for a week, reporting initially to Base Company's Sergeant Major, Ron Fellowes who gave Finn some basic admin tasks to fulfil on his behalf. Finn recognised that this was as much about keeping him occupied as anything else but again, was grateful for the distraction. Ron was good bloke, a cheery Yorkshire man with a booming voice and big grin. Finn had worked with Ron off and on over the years and had always got on well with him. He was now running Base Company; the marines responsible for the security of the unit while the rest of the commando were deployed. The makeup of the company seemed to fall into two categories: older, experienced guys and the younger marines straight from recruit training at Lympstone. The older guys probably volunteered to get a break from operations and have a bit of stability with the family. The young guys wouldn't have a choice, they would have been drafted to Four-Five straight from training and would remain with Base Company until the unit returned from Libya whereupon they would join their allocated companies and become part of the unit proper. Finn did notice however that almost all of these young men had placed their names on the list to be considered as BCRs:

Battle Casualty Replacements. These were marines who would be sent out to Libya to take the place of the dead or wounded within the commando. Finn didn't blame them and as a young man he would have done the same. The worst thing in the world a marine could imagine was missing out on going to war while all his mates and oppos went. A few of them had begun to ask him what it was like out in Libya, respectful and almost bashful in their approach. Finn knew Ron had probably briefed them not to bother him but the odd one or two would engage him in conversation during the working party tasks they found themselves conducting throughout the base.

Finn answered their enquiries truthfully, neither sensationalising the action nor downplaying it. With another six months of the year-long deployment left the young men were hopeful that they might be rotated out to relieve weary troops. Finn knew this would not be the case. The fighting in Libya was the fiercest that he had ever seen, insurgents backed and trained by Iranian Special Forces really bringing the fight to the coalition effort. The marines needed every experienced commando on the ground and there was no appetite for the replacement of seasoned fighters with raw soldiers. Nonetheless, he did not want to crush their morale so made non-committal statements that indicated anything was possible.

His days were fine up to a point. The basic tasks and illusion of activity helped keep his mind from retreating into the cave of grief that seemed to encompass him in the evenings. He found he could not sleep unless drunk and consequently was really putting away the bottles of Islay's finest. This helped him to cope with the unannounced visits from the boy, his drunken state seeming to accept the manifestations with humorous resignation.

Phys was also helpful; running and weights sessions giving him the opportunity to vent his anger and at least benefitting him by taking his mind off things for an hour or two each day. One of the things he most liked was to conduct a wandering patrol of the base at night, ostensibly checking the fences and grounds for signs of intruders and that all the key buildings were secured. The MoD Police usually took responsibility for these but Ron had insisted that marines also carry out these duties as part of their work routine since the camera system was not functioning properly due to the software being affected by the cyber-attacks. Finn enjoyed the solitude and the quiet of the evening, patrolling the perimeter fence in the cool night air, disturbed only by the occasional cackle on his radio from calls between the other members of the guard. Only on rare occasions would he catch a glimpse of the boy during these patrols, another reason he grabbed at the opportunity where possible.

His last task during these patrols was to check the unit armoury and magazine, ensuring the weapons and ammunition of the commando were secure. As only a sergeant and above could be responsible for this, the task fell to Finn to check the locations nightly. Every Friday he had to physically enter the buildings and check each weapon, grenade and bullet were present and correct. As the unit was deployed there was never any real variation in this and it was almost a box ticking exercise but Finn didn't mind. He still hadn't come to any conclusion about what he wanted to do in the long term although he was starting to think about his guys out in Libya and how they were getting on. A rare grin crossed his face as he recalled the characters in his troop; Big 'Bungy' Williams, a honey monster of man with a wicked sense of humour that made everyone laugh, 'Florence' Nightingale, two section's corporal and one of the best soldiers Finn knew, Bob 'Dinger' Bell, one section's phys-mad corporal and probably the fittest guy in the unit. Dinger was training for Special Forces selection and hoped to be loaded onto next summer's course. Finn felt a twinge of guilt that he had not made any attempt to find out how the guys were getting on and resolved to pop into the operations centre on camp and see if he could get a secure line through to Libya.

As he returned to the guardroom, he saw Ron and several of the guard standing outside the building beside the unloading bay. As they spotted his approach, he noted the younger men moving back inside and Ron walking towards him. Finn couldn't put his finger on it but something in the Sergeant Major's manner brought a small flutter of nerves to his stomach. Finn drew his pistol and unloaded it at the bay, checking the breech and barrel to ensure no round was lodged before he fired off the action and replaced the empty

51

weapon back in the holster. He looked at Ron who sighed and put his hand on Finn's shoulder.

"Finn, I just got a call from theatre mate and thought you'd want to know. Three of your lads caught it up and another two are VSI. I'm so fucking sorry mate; I can't believe this is happening after all you've already been through."

Finn nodded slowly taking on the words but feeling nothing but emptiness inside him. He cleared his throat.

"Who?"

The Sergeant Major took a small piece of paper from his pocket and read aloud.

"Corporal Davies, Marine Heywood and Marine Morris were killed and Marines Faulkner and McEwan are the injured." He replaced the paper and looked up again at Finn. "I'm so sorry mate, I can't even imagine what this must be like for you. Look, I've got Corporal Stevenson to step up and take over your duties, why don't you go home and take a few days off? I'll call you and let you know about funeral details and when the VSIs are in country."

Finn shook his head. "No. It's better I've got something to keep me occupied Ron. If I stay at home, I'll just drink myself into oblivion. The best thing you could do is let me just crack on with the work routine here, keep my mind off things for a bit."

Ron tilted his head to one side. "You sure mate? I get that being on your own is sometimes worse but equally, you'll need a bit of time to take all this on board. If you are set on staying though the *schooly* is coming in tomorrow and he's a TRIM counsellor if you want a word."

Finn knew that Ron meant well but the last thing he wanted was to spend an awkward half hour with the unit's Education Officer or '*schooly*' as he was known. The *schooly* was a Trauma Risk Management or TRIM counsellor, qualified to assess and manage individuals who were suffering from trauma related incidents. While useful to some, Finn had seen far too much war and dealt with whatever demons he had by himself, to feel any urge to use these services now. *And what of the boy?* What would a TRIM counsellor make of that? "No Ron, that's not really how I deal with stuff. I'm better getting through this my way. Look, can we grab a wet together and you fill me in on what happened?"

Ron nodded and indicated with his head. "Okay mate, let's head back down to the Mess and we'll have a toast to the lads with a Talisker or two and I'll tell you what I know."

Finn returned the pistol and ammunition to the guardroom where he was aware of the discreet glances the younger marines were regarding him with. He turned to the corporal seated behind the desk and informed him that he would be in the Sergeants' Mess should there be any problems. The corporal assured him that there would be nothing that he could not take care of himself and would see Finn in the morning. Ron was waiting outside and the two men walked down the long road in silence, each lost in their own thoughts.

5

It took over a day for the loss of his men to hit Finn. He had been looking at some old photos on his laptop when without warning his chest started heaving and he broke down in sobs. He'd known each of the guys really well; they'd worked together for over two years and had been part of Finn's tight-knit troop. Ron had told him that they'd been caught in a well-planned ambush and could not get any air support in time to extract. Finn wondered if he had been there whether or not the men would still have died. He did not know all the details of the operation the men were involved in but was feeling the guilt of not having been there to keep them safe. On one level he knew there was no such thing but he'd kept the remainder of his guys alive after that first attack, even when the odds had been stacked against them. He'd thought that he couldn't cry anymore, thought that the last of his tears had been shed for his mother and Katy, but here he was, once again weeping heavily, this time for lost friends and colleagues.

After a while he sat back on the sofa and looked at the ceiling. He was numb and hollow inside and unsure of everything. He'd lost his entire family and some of his best lads in the space of a month. For the time being he was still going in to work but he was going to have to come to a decision at some point on what he wanted to do. A part of him wanted an immediate return to Libya and retribution for the friends he had lost. Another part however, seemed to have had enough, saw only futility in that path. He realised that for the bulk of his adult life, he had been at war with one nation or another and that in reality, it had just been the same war interrupted only by the inconvenience of borders. He also came to the conclusion that everything was now worse than before. Iraq, Afghanistan, Libya, Algeria, Somalia, Syria; the world was aflame with conflict that seemed for Muslims to be a war against their religion and to the rest of the world a confused, ill-defined campaign against a vague terrorist threat. His mind fixated on this idea for some time, the futility of war, the waste of young lives, and the lack of positive effect. The maudlin mood took hold and he found himself drinking his whisky in a morose frame of mind, questioning everything he had ever believed in. Was he perhaps being punished for his part in these wars? Was God singling him out for the deaths he had been responsible for over the years? Was it karma? He turned to the small figure of the boy, a darker shape in the unlit corner of the room. *Well? What do you think? Is all this because I've killed people? Because I killed you? Why not just kill me then? I'm the one to blame here. I'm the killer.* Finn stared into the corner, but the silence remained.

He came to the gradual realisation that he had had enough. He didn't want to go back to war. He didn't want to go back to the marines. He just wanted to be alone. Somewhere quiet with no people, no conflict, and no issues. His mood lifted as the decisive element took hold. Yes, somewhere he could just be left alone, untroubled and unfettered. He stood and refilled his glass, brow furrowed in thought. He reached for his laptop again and noticed the small stack of papers that he had brought from the family home. His eyes were drawn to one in particular and he felt a sudden excitement grow within him. He now had a destination. It was perfect and he could not believe he hadn't thought of it sooner. His breathing quickened as his mind raced with the mental preparations for his plan. He smiled as he remembered that tomorrow was Friday. The timing could not have been any more perfect. Everything was pointing to this decision being driven by fate and guidance rather than opportunity and Finn raised his glass to his lips as he went through a checklist of everything he would need to achieve his plan. Tomorrow was Friday and he needed to be ready if his plan was to work. He looked back at the corner of the room to gauge the reaction of his silent companion but the boy was gone.

6

Sergeant Major Ron Fellowes had little time for the Military Police and all they represented. *Who the hell joined an institution like the military with the sole purpose of investigating and locking up their own kind?* To be fair, the oldest of the pair, the Warrant Officer, wasn't too bad, seemed to hold some sympathy for Finn and what he was going through. The younger one, the Sergeant, was to put it bluntly, a prick. The Warrant Officer cleared his throat and spoke.

"So, the first time you noticed the rifle and ammunition missing was on Friday? And you notified us on the Monday after your own internal enquiries were exhausted is that correct?"

Ron nodded and the policeman continued in his soft Geordie accent.

"And I see from the copies of the armoury and magazine logs that Sergeant Douglas last accounted for the weapons and ammunition when he was duty Sergeant the Friday before. When did you last have contact with Sergeant Douglas?"

Ron leaned forward. "The Friday afternoon when he was last on duty, Finn asked for the next week off to take care of some things and to go visit the injured lads from his troop. When we discovered the missing rifle and rounds, we tried to contact Finn but the mobiles were still down and he wasn't answering his landline. I sent a couple of the guard round to his flat but he wasn't there either. Eventually I got in touch with Selly Oak hospital and they told me Finn hadn't been down there either."

"Do you or any of your guys know where he might be heading with a 7.62 rifle and over a hundred rounds of ammunition?"

Ron shook his head. "None whatsoever, and I mean that sincerely. This isn't a case where we are covering up for one of our own. I'm genuinely worried for Finn as I haven't got a clue what the hell he is up to or where he is going."

The Sergeant spoke, his nasal Liverpool accent unable to conceal the sneer apparent. "Well, you'll excuse us Sir if we don't take that at face value. We're pretty used to people covering up for one of their own in a deluded notion of loyalty."

Sergeant Major Fellowes leaned across the desk and pointed at the younger policeman, finger vibrating with rage. "Listen here you little shit. When a Royal Marines Warrant Officer tells you he's speaking the truth, it's the truth. And if you ever question it again, I will leap across this desk and tear your fucking throat out. Do I make myself clear?"

The Sergeant flushed and was about to reply when the older policeman interjected. "Sergeant Major, no-one is doubting your integrity. Sergeant Callaghan here can sometimes get a little carried away; let's his suspicions get the better of him. I apologise for any offence caused."

Ron maintained his hostile stare for several seconds before turning his attention back to the Warrant Officer and nodded, satisfied with the apology. "Okay. What happens now?"

Warrant Officer Gary Finnegan sat back in the chair and took a sip of his coffee before replying. "I've set up a liaison with Police Scotland. As Sergeant Douglas lived in private accommodation, they are going to get a warrant to enter and search his flat and we'll see what that throws up in terms of evidence or clues to his whereabouts. We'll be with them when they do this, as we will have lead on the investigation so it may be that I might contact you for any confirmation of whatever we find. They have also got a description out across all constabularies and especially those with significant Muslim communities." Seeing the questioning look in the marine's eyes the policeman continued. "It's not out of the question that Sergeant Douglas is seeking revenge for the deaths of his friends and family and is engaged on some ill-conceived campaign to extract this."

"No, I never got that from him. He just didn't seem to be in that frame of mind."

"Be that as it may Ron, he's been AWOL for ten days with a weapon and ammunition and could be just about anywhere ready to do anything." The policeman stood and put his paperwork back into his briefcase. "I'll be in touch as soon as we get anything of interest. On a similar vein I'd appreciate it if you would do the same; keep me abreast of any developments, contact, fact or rumours that you come across. We desperately need a lead on this to keep the lad safe."

Ron stood and made his way around his desk offering his hand and shaking that of the policeman. "Thanks Gary, I'll let you know the moment I hear anything. I'll brief the CO this afternoon when he gets back from MoD. Let me see you out."

As he passed the Sergeant the younger man thrust out his hand towards him. Ron ignored the gesture and brushed past the policeman, causing him to stumble against his chair. As he picked up his own bag Sergeant Callaghan fought to conceal the fury he was feeling at the Sergeant Major's treatment of him. *Fucking marines! All the same, bloody arrogant prima donnas who think they are above the rule of law and those who enforce it. Well, we'll soon see when we get a hold of Sergeant bloody Douglas and lock him away for the rest of his proverbial.* Yes, and he was looking forward to personally delivering that information to the Sergeant Major who had just threatened then dismissed him without a care.

As they returned to the car Gary Finnegan turned to the Sergeant and placed a hand on his chest, stopping him in his tracks.

"Cal, you really need to learn a bit of sensitivity when dealing with people. You can't just accuse a Sergeant Major of being a liar based on a quick conversation. That man is more than willing to help. He's genuinely concerned for the safety of one of his lads."

"He fucking threatened me sir! You heard him; outright threatened to assault me! We should have had him on that, taken the wind out of his sails a bit. Fucking bootnecks! Think they're God's gift, they really do."

The Warrant Officer rubbed his hand over his tired eyes and regarded his subordinate. Callaghan wasn't a bad kid really, just inexperienced and a little over-zealous in the application of his job. There were quite a few within the Military Police like Callaghan; individuals who wielded the power of their cap badge too free and easy. "He got a bit hot under the collar because you offended him and called his integrity into question. It's hard for you to understand Sergeant Callaghan, but marines, paras and infanteers are all a very close-knit bunch; they've been fighting wars non-stop for fifteen years now. We walk in and instantly we are the outsiders; we always have been but it's worse than ever now. But we need them to trust us. We need them to feel confident that they can pick up the phone and call us with any information that will help us. But we can't do that if you are hell-bent on offending and alienating everyone we talk to. I don't need to remind you that Sergeant Douglas is roaming free in the UK with a sharpshooter's rifle and over a hundred rounds in his possession."

As he watched the Warrant Officer get in the car, Cal felt his cheeks burn with humiliation. His superior had just stuck up for the marines over him. *Bastard!* Still, he should have expected it. Warrant Officer Finnegan wasn't a real Military Policeman in the strictest sense of the word; he had transferred from the infantry some years ago after being wounded in Afghanistan. Hardly surprising then that his loyalties remained with the grunts and knuckle draggers.

7

Finn dragged the kayak up on to the shingle of the beach and looked for a suitable spot to conceal it. He spotted a mass of low-lying brush and slid the empty craft deep into the thick foliage, ensuring it was well above the high tide line. Shouldering the large bergan backpack he left the exposed beach, making his way into the small wooded area in front of him. He placed the pack carefully on the ground, ensuring the cased rifle remained upright and removed a water bottle, drinking deep from the vessel before returning it. Looking around him he felt a flicker of excitement at the prospect of what lay before him. He had found his place, his wilderness, his retreat from the world and the death and heartbreak it held. And all because of Katy. Beautiful, wonderful little Katy and her love of wolves. And here he was, in the Outer Hebrides on the very islands where Katy's wolves were roaming free. That night back at his flat when he had, by chance alighted on the pamphlet he had taken from Katy's room he had experienced an epiphany, the answer was so perfect: A de-populated wilderness of islands, mountains and sea with only the animals his sister had worshipped for companionship. He felt a connection to Katy here but also a sadness that she was not here to share in the wonder. He would have to tell her himself; describe all the wonderful things he experienced on the islands.

Once he had made his mind up, Finn had wasted no time in researching the details needed for his plan to work. First, he had read everything he could on the islands themselves. The main islands of North Uist, South Uist and Barra as well as the myriad smaller isles all returned to the wild nearly ten years ago. All the locals had been re-housed and provided with business grants and money to assist in their relocation to the main island of Harris. Apparently, the settlements had been so generous that very few had resisted. The benefactor was a multi-billionaire, Paul Taylor, who had a passion to see Scotland re-wilded with its entire former fauna and a healthier ecosystem restored. The islands' project was his on-going experiment and testament to his dream. Regular articles mentioned the first wolves he had introduced, their immediate effect on the deer population, their first litter and their continued success.

Taylor and his family resided in the estate at the very north of the island in Monach Hall, a stunning baronial property of dark sandstone, turrets, towers and crow-stepped gables. The only other human inhabitants on the islands were a few older crofters who had not wanted to relocate due to their familial ties to the land. Taylor employed these individuals to help in maintaining the roads and the hides, and to report on the movements of the wolves whenever they were seen. One road dissected the main islands with irregular hides at the side of the road from which paying guests could look out in comfort for sightings of the wolf pack. Finn was happy that he could stay well-hidden from any of these locations, the size of the islands and the cover afforded from the woods and forests meaning it would be very unlikely that he would be seen. Added to the fact that autumn was well and truly here and winter would soon follow, the few visitors who were currently coming would soon dwindle to nothing.

He had been careful to leave no trace of his intended destination and indeed had gone to great pains to leave a false trail that he hoped would lead those looking for him to the Brecon Beacons in Wales. He had left some photographs of his troop on their last visit there, a couple of years ago. It was also common knowledge that he loved the mountains and the Brecons were a regular haunt of his. He had taken several thousand pounds from his bank account, casually dropping in the fact that he needed a new car, a four-wheel drive. He'd then bought a one-way train ticket to Bristol, again hoping to lead his pursuers to the conclusion that he was headed to the Welsh mountains. Finn knew that they would be looking for him in earnest; you couldn't just steal a rifle and ammunition and walk away without consequence. He needed the rifle to see him through the winter. His snares and traps would be fine for smaller game and birds but to take down a deer and secure the protein he would need required a decent rifle. On his last Friday duty, he had taken the rifle, ensuring that he signed to say all the weapons were present; he hadn't wanted someone else to get the blame for the missing weapon. He'd then used the master keys to gain access to the adventure-training store where he had procured the kayak and other useful equipment. He had also gained access to Chris Butler's room in the mess and taken the keys to his big van, which had been parked at the bottom of camp. Chris had already had his R and R so wouldn't be back from theatre for another five months or so. By then, no doubt, the local police at Mallaig would have reported the presence of the van and been in contact with the DVLA. They would eventually conclude that Finn had taken the vehicle there but with such a wide area to cover he still felt confident that they would not identify his final destination.

It had taken Finn several days to make the crossing by kayak from the mainland, bivouacking on Skye before crossing the Little Minch and reaching the eastern coast of North Uist. He had been fortunate with the weather, dry and calm with a small groundswell rolling under him as he crossed the seaway. Making his way to the western side of the island he'd paddled south to an area he had noted on the map as being devoid of buildings and with ample tree cover to conceal his movements. And now he was here.

With the kayak and paddles concealed from view he shrugged on the heavy pack and rifle and made his way inland and into the woods. The damp, peaty smell filled his nostrils and an occasional birdcall accompanied him as he made his way through the forest. When he was researching the islands, he had picked this area for its inaccessibility and the rough, wooded terrain that covered the land. His aim was to make camp in one of the wooded ravines that ran off Ben Mhor; in an area where there was no real reason another person would have to travel through.

He entered a world of green. Lichens, ferns, mosses, leaves, needles and grasses punctuated only by the darker sentinels of the forest's tree trunks. He felt a sense of peace envelope him as he progressed through the arboreal landscape, his breathing and the distant sound of birdsong the only accompaniment to his journey. Checking his compass at regular intervals he maintained his easterly path towards the foot of the Ben. The terrain changed as he began to encounter small ravines and streams flowing between the raised ground. After several miles he could feel the incline of the ground increase and the tree cover grow denser. The sound of rushing water reached him and he knew from the map that a decent sized stream was somewhere to his front. Cresting the next area of high ground, he saw the stream in front of him, a dark, peat-stained burn with flashes of white where the water broke over the submerged rocks. He reached the bank and leaned his pack against a tree then made his way to the water's edge where he scooped up some of the frigid water and drank it. Smiling at the cold, clear taste, he took several more handfuls to quench his thirst. Sitting back on his haunches he surveyed the land around him and came to the conclusion that he would set up his camp nearby. There had been no sign of any human presence whatsoever on his journey so far and the terrain itself was not attractive for easy transit. Indeed, he had noted only a few light game trails between the trees. Retrieving his equipment, he crossed the stream and started to search in earnest for a suitable spot to make camp.

Finn could not shake the sensation that fate was lending him a helping hand. He cast his eyes over the derelict building again, this time making an assessment of the work he would have to do. An old stone building long abandoned and reclaimed by the wild, almost invisible among the trees. The four walls remained standing but the roof had fallen in a long time ago, any trace of the ancient joists rotted and repatriated to the earth. Looking around the area he could see no sign that the building had been visited for years. With a bit of hard work, the building would more than suit his needs, although he would have to replace the roof and make the dwelling watertight again. The chimney column, while obviously a mass of loose stones was not beyond repair and a fire could once again heat the cottage. It was more than he could have hoped for, finding such a building in the very area he had intended setting up camp. Glancing at the sky between the tree cover, Finn could see that night would not be long in falling and decided to set up a temporary camp where he would live while he worked on the repairs to the cottage. He moved off to one side of the building and took the tent from his pack and proceeded to set his shelter up beside one of the stone walls. Soon he had his tent erected and was inside, setting up his small cooker and pans for his evening meal; a boil in the bag Lancashire hot pot, courtesy of the Adventure Training store back at Four-Five Commando. As he busied himself with his preparations his mind ran over the materials he would require to return the cottage back to a habitable state, much of which were available to him within the forest. He did not need it to be anything luxurious, merely weatherproof and capable of keeping him warm during the winter months. His tent could achieve the same aim but he was now set on exploiting his good fortune and creating a semi-permanent home for himself in the wild.

As he placed the foil bag in the pan of boiling water he smiled and spoke softly to himself. *Thank you Katy, thank you so much. Your island is beautiful and I'm going to love living here. I've even found a small cottage that I'm going to fix up so that you don't have to worry about me being cold through the winter. Tell mum I love her sis. I love you both.*

8

Gary Finnegan looked at the map of the Brecon Beacons before him and studied the marker spots that covered it, indications of the areas that his teams had searched and cleared. Sergeant Douglas had been on the run for over a month now and the Military Police and even the regular police had not one lead to show for their efforts. The initial flurry of sightings that followed the media release of Douglas' picture proved to be the usual mix of mistaken identity and crank callers. Finnegan doubted that Douglas was here. Yes, all the evidence had led them to this spot but there was just no way someone could have remained undetected on these sparse-covered hillsides all this time without so much as a sighting.

Sergeant Callaghan walked into the room and stood beside his superior, following his lead and also staring at the map.

"What's your thoughts sir?"

Gary glanced at Cal and sighed, running his fingers through his hair then pointing at the map. "I don't think he's here Sergeant Callaghan, I just don't think he's here. No trace, no sightings, no reports from the rangers on any suspicious ground sign.... I just don't see it."

"But the evidence..."

Cal did not get a chance to finish as his superior turned on him.

"Evidence? A couple of photos, a train ticket and a few marines who remembered that Douglas likes it here? What was the one adjective that kept cropping up when we interviewed people about Douglas? Do you remember?"

The Sergeant opened his mouth but was once again denied the opportunity to speak as Sergeant Major Finnegan continued his tirade.

"Intelligent. Every single person we spoke to described him in glowing terms but the one word I kept hearing was intelligent. I don't think it's out of the realms of possibility that Sergeant Douglas deliberately left those photos and bought that train ticket to lead us on this wild goose chase we've been running for the last month."

Sergeant Callaghan shook his head. "Sorry sir, I disagree with you. He's a bloody bootneck for crying out loud, a knuckle dragger, not MI5! There's no way he had the foresight to lay down a false trail. He's here somewhere and we've just been unlucky not to have got him yet but we will; there's only a few places left that he could be hiding."

"You know Sergeant, that's your problem. You look at Sergeant Douglas and see a bone-headed Royal Marine gone AWOL with a gun. I see a very smart, decorated soldier with mental problems trying to sort his head out. A man who has been leading other men into battle for years against all manner of enemies. In short, an intelligent man trained and equipped to evade pursuers and survive for extended periods of time. So, you'll forgive me if I don't share your rather simplistic viewpoint."

Cal was losing his temper, could feel the blood rising in his cheeks. "All right then sir. If he's so smart and he's not here, then where the hell is he? By now someone, somewhere would have reported seeing him or at least some activity that might indicate where he is. He's not with any of his mates that we know of. He's not been seen at any of his favourite haunts, no ex-wife, no kids, no girlfriend; there's nowhere else he can be."

Gary Finnegan smiled and placed his hand on his colleague's shoulder. "Okay, okay, calm down Cal. You're right, we have nothing at all to go on except this lead and we need to follow it to the bitter end. I just think that a clever man with a stolen rifle and ammunition would be a little more careful about leaving a trail of breadcrumbs to the door of his hideout."

Cal nodded, mollified by the apology. "I get that sir; I truly do but I just think that you give Douglas too much credit. He was probably not even aware that he had left those photos out and hasn't bothered covering his tracks because he wasn't in a stable frame of mind."

"Fair enough Sergeant; we'll agree to disagree. In the meantime, carry on with the search and keep me updated with any progress. I've got a meeting with the CO this afternoon and he'll want my balls on a plate for the lack of progress on this one so if you're going to find Douglas here can you make it before 1500 hours?" Gary smiled as he left the room and made his way into the sweeping rain that soaked the ancient nissen huts of Sennybridge camp.

Cal Callaghan watched his superior leave with no attempt to disguise his contempt for the man. He sometimes felt that Finnegan actually liked Douglas and that this was clouding his judgement. Cal would find him and find him soon, here, in the Brecon Beacons where the evidence and not some stupid hunch, dictated the fugitive would be. Then Sergeant Major bloody Finnegan would see what real police work looked like and the Royal Marines would learn the lesson that no one was above the law.

9

As he sat warming his hands to the fire, Finn reflected that the weeks that he had taken to repair the cottage had all been worth the effort. The logs, mosses and bracken that he had used for the roof were further supported with lengths of plastic sheeting he had appropriated on one of his salvaging missions. He had been pleasantly surprised with how many items of use he had managed to locate in his nocturnal excursions searching abandoned crofts and settlements. His small dwelling, once a dilapidated shell was now weatherproof, insulated and camouflaged against all but intense scrutiny. He had built an additional lean-to at the side of the cottage as a work area and store where he dressed and prepared the game that he trapped or shot. Rabbits, hares, grouse, fish, pheasant and deer were the staple of his diet. He had also found various vegetables growing wild in abandoned plots, which he used to supplement his heavy protein-based intake. Hardy root vegetables in the form of turnips swedes, carrots and potatoes. Finn was pleased with his good fortune but cautious to leave no obvious sign of his presence.

One evening when he was scouting near Balivanich he had caught a slight movement from the corner of his eye and had taken cover in a deep clump of ferns to observe whatever had caught his attention. He had seen a man walking along an old road, fishing rods on his shoulder and a brace of large fish hanging from his hand. In the limited light Finn hadn't been able to make out specific details but by the man's posture and gait determined that he was old. Finn concluded that he was one of the crofters who had elected to stay on the island. Finn had waited for a long time before moving, ensuring that the man was well away from the area. As he'd made his way back inland, he noted a distant light coming from a building and figured this to be the old man's home. A reminder, if indeed he had needed one, that there were a few people moving around on the island.

Relaxing in an old car seat that he had placed against a wall of the cottage Finn ran through his nightly routine of bringing Katy up to speed with his daily activities. Eyes glazed, staring at the fire, his soft monologue filled the small room.

Winter's on the way Katy; there was a real nip in the air today and a wee dusting of frost on the Ben. Saw a killer whale off Hornish Point, breaching out of the sea. It was so beautiful you would have loved it. Still no sign of your wolves yet but I did find a deer carcass with lots of broken bones so they are definitely here! I can't wait to see them but I think they know I'm here and are giving me a wide berth. Winter's nearly here though and I'll be able to track them better as they'll be taking the deer that are leaving the high ground. Right, I'm knackered now so going to get some sleep, as I want to make an early start tomorrow. I miss you Katy and can't wait to see your wolves and tell you all about them. Night sis.

Finn rose and wiped the tears from his face, making his way outside into the cold night. His breath fogged in the frigid air and as he relieved himself in the ferns and looked up between the tree canopy to the sky above. The air was clear and the stars were bright against the black backdrop of night. Despite the sadness he always felt when he thought of his dead family and friends, Finn felt an innate sense of peace out here. Everything was reduced to a bare simplicity, the world of command, leadership and responsibility far removed from his island existence. The boy was also absent from Finn's new home. He had not seen any sign of his spectral companion since leaving the shores of Mallaig. Finn took this as another positive sign that he had been guided to this place all along.

Before heading back in to the warmth of his abode Finn checked to see that the smoke from his fire was still being dispersed through the various outlets he had designed in order to lessen the signature of the smoke within the woods. Pleased that everything was in order he shivered in the cold then hurried back inside, ready for sleep.

10

Paul Taylor watched the first snows of the island drift past the bay window of the morning room and settle as a pale dust on the dark earth outside Monach Hall. He had been expecting it for several days now, the roiling black clouds racing across the Atlantic heralding the onset of the cold. The ice in his glass clinked as he raised the drink to his mouth, the deep amber liquid catching the light through the cut crystal of the whisky glass. Sighing with contentment he looked around the room and smiled as he saw Jura, the older of the two deerhounds lift its head and regard him.

"It's okay lad, just enjoying a well-earned Ardbeg."

The door opened and he looked up as his wife walked in. Without preamble she nodded at him as she made her way to the sofa by the fire.

"Got one of those for me?"

Paul groaned theatrically as he prised himself from the comfort of the window seat.

"And we'll have a little less of the dramatics please Mr Taylor. You should be honoured to play host to your adoring wife!"

Paul laughed as he poured the drink. No ice. Fiona was one of those few women who enjoyed the burn of the Islay malts without dilution or addition.

"There you are my *adoring* wife. Cheers."

The pair sipped quietly for several moments, the room silent but for the occasional snap from the wood knots exploding in the fire. Fiona Taylor turned to the dogs lying sprawled on the large rug by the hearth.

"Look at those two. I'm sure they've forgotten they are meant to be a hardy country breed." With a wry smile she caught Paul's eye. "Must take it from their old man, eh?"

Paul pretended offence, spluttering his drink. "For your information, this old man has been up and down Beinn Mhor and Hecla today." He watched as his wife of twenty-three years chuckled quietly and sipped at her drink. She was as beautiful now in her forties as he had ever seen her. With her glossy black hair and tanned face that testified to a love of outdoors, she was bestowed with a natural beauty matched by her personality. Paul always felt blessed whenever he thought about their life together. Fiona remained the love of his life, his partner in absolutely every sense of the word. A good life full of love and happiness until...He felt his throat tighten a little as the memory threatened to engulf him with a sudden assault. Henry. Their handsome, clever, popular boy. Their only child. Their wonder.

Henry's death had nearly destroyed them. The ridiculous suddenness of the loss. Speaking on Skype with him one afternoon, a visit from the local constabulary the next. A young platoon commander in Helmand killed by a roadside bomb. *Surely there was some mistake? They had just been talking to him yesterday. The Ministry of Defence made these errors quite frequently didn't they? It couldn't be Henry, he was too...alive, too full of light and life; his death was impossible.* But it wasn't impossible. It was their boy, their darling boy. Barely twenty years old and torn to pieces by a rusty cooking pot stuffed with explosives and nuts and bolts. His life extinguished by the side of a dusty gravel road in an unpronounceable Afghan village. The agony had been a level of hell that neither of them had previously encountered. Then the numbness; the empty existence they muddled through day by day. The visits to Henry's room in the dead of night to sit on his bed, pick up his framed photos, stare at the smiling teen behind the glass and weep in silence. The well-meaning friends and their expressions of concern and advice. Tips to help them 'get over it'. They'd found that you didn't get over it; you only get through it, bit by painful bit. The memory still had the power to bring on the blackness but Paul found it lessened in both frequency and strength over time. Talking to Fiona, she had admitted similar feelings. On Sundays they walked to Henry's grave in the family plot beneath the big redwoods and stood arm in arm, reminding themselves of some of his mischievous antics. They would laugh, cry and say goodbye until the next week. Paul did not know what a shrink would make of their visits but it certainly seemed to help them in dealing with the rawness of their loss.

The last few months had been the closest to they'd felt to normality since Henry's death. A new litter of cubs from the Freya pack had caused great excitement when old Angus from Grogarry had rang them with the news of his sighting. It had taken Paul, Fiona and the rest of their estate team over a week to locate the new litter, the vast area and weather scuppering their efforts at every turn. They were rewarded in the end as from within a temporary hide overlooking a loch near the old settlement of Carnish, Freya, the female manifested as a wraith from the mist-shrouded forest. The wary wolf had observed the shores of the small loch for a long time before advancing from the shelter of the treeline followed by Odin, the large male and a stumbling procession of small dark lumps: the cubs, six in all. Paul recalled Fiona reaching blindly for his hand as they stared through the binoculars at the newest additions to the islands' wolf population. He had taken his wife's hand and been overcome with emotion. Glancing at her he had seen rivulets of tears rolling unchecked down her cheeks and falling to the insulated mats they sat upon. New life in a time of sadness.

He was interrupted from his reverie by his wife's question.

"Did you get any internet access today?"

"No darling, not a jot. Guess this bloody cyber-attack thing is still cocking things up." He chuckled as he re-filled their glasses. "Still, the postal system is busier than it has been in years; never had so much mail!"

"Yes, I know what you mean. We've always been a bit behind the curve out here in terms of connectivity but this lack of mobile, internet and everything else seems to have slowed everyone down a bit. Not bad thing in some cases."

Fiona accepted the drink from her husband and took a sip, lifting her head and indicating the world beyond the window. "How's the snow looking? Thought if it settles, we could get the cross-country skis out tomorrow and blow out the cobwebs. That is if you're not feeling too old?"

Paul grinned at the barb. "No, I think I'll be fine. Sounds like a great idea. It looks like it's heavy now but it is a fast-moving front so we could be blessed by clear conditions tomorrow. I need to be back by the afternoon though, I have a call coming from that wildlife journalist from *The Times*."

"Oh, I forgot about him. When is he looking at visiting?"

"Next week if all goes well. He's going to fly into Stornoway and drive down by car. I've told him if the roads are bad, we'll get him choppered down."

Fiona nodded. "Yes, good idea. We usually get a good old arctic blast for a few weeks around this time. I remember him I think from last year. Rory, isn't it?"

"Yes, that's him. Rory Starkey. Very onside with the whole project; was a big defender of us in the early days."

"Good. He'll be excited about the new arrivals then. And of course, he'll be the first journalist to see them."

Paul nodded and cleared his throat. "Okay, enough shop talk, let's move on to something more pressing. What are you cooking for dinner?" He barely avoided the heavy cushion as it was launched across the room.

11

Sergeant Major Finnegan fought to keep the excitement from his voice.

"How long has it been there? Okay, your best estimate then?" He was silent for some time, concentrating on the voice at the other end of the telephone, scribbling frantic notes in his small notebook.

"Brilliant Sergeant. Thank you so much for your help and I'll be in touch with anything we turn up at our end. Thanks again." As he replaced the phone back in its base, he allowed his repressed excitement its freedom and slapped the desk with a huge smile on his face as he strode to the map of Scotland on the wall. A Sergeant at Four-Five Commando's base in Arbroath had called to inform him that another marine's vehicle had been reported abandoned in Mallaig, in the western highlands. According to the local Bobbies up there, the vehicle had been there for some months. The marines had investigated it at their end and found that it had been stolen from the base at some undetermined point in time. Remembering their directive to report anything suspect or strange that they encountered, the Sergeant had rung the Military Police with the news, apologising for bothering them with such a trivial matter.

But Gary Finnegan knew the matter wasn't trivial. It was Douglas. He could feel it.

Looking at the map, he could see Mallaig was a small port on the north west coast of Scotland. *What the hell would Douglas be doing up there?* By choosing a port, surely that indicated that he travelled further afield. The map showed ferry transit lines from Mallaig to Skye. Skye? Would Douglas have gone to ground there? Gary's mind raced as he explored all the possibilities open to Douglas. The most obvious one was that the lad knew someone there, or at least had a connection with the island. He wrote his thoughts and theories as they came to him and added lines of enquiry he intended to pursue against each one. Ferry operators, security recordings from the boats, check out Douglas' friends and colleagues who had links with the island. His list expanded over the page and he paused as he thought how best to proceed. First, put an end to that bloody wild goose chase in Wales. It had been scaled down over the last month, much to Sergeant Callaghan's disgust, but was still a drain on what limited manpower they had at their disposal. Even the regular police had lost interest in Douglas, more pressing problems to address. To that end, Gary found himself in the unique position of leading the investigation by default. Usually the police would lead on an armed individual roaming the country but they had enough on their plate dealing with the recent spate of bombings around the country. The cyber-attacks had crippled much of the interconnectivity within the emergency services and consequently everything was much harder for them on all fronts.

He would need hard evidence that Douglas had taken that vehicle. His Commanding Officer was struggling to cover all his responsibilities and would demand nothing less than incontrovertible proof before he signed off on a new line of enquiry. He made a note to call upon the local police in the Mallaig area and gain as much information as he could about the likely options open to Douglas. First though, he wanted to get back up to Arbroath and investigate exactly when this vehicle had been taken, and why. It was a pretty big van and with a striking colour scheme that was far from discreet. Why would Douglas take something like this when he could have used his own vehicle and hidden it somewhere less conspicuous? He would know that the police would find this van at some point and link it to him. Was it just convenient at the time? Easy access to the keys? The military policeman thought Finn too smart for this. No, Douglas had a reason for taking this vehicle and he needed to find out what it was. The lad had been on the run for over two months with not a whisper of a credible sighting to steer the investigation but Gary could feel that this was it, the first solid lead they had on Douglas' whereabouts. Excitement still running through him he gathered his notes and headed out of the office for home where he intended packing quickly and making his way to Scotland that very night.

12

Despite the heat from the small radiator near the helm, André Voster remained cold. He had his hands jammed in his pockets and chin thrust down onto his chest to conserve his body heat. Beside him, the captain of the boat and Voster's two accomplices Jamie and Sandy, seemed not to feel the chill, light sweaters being their only barrier to the cold. Trying to keep his mind from his discomfort, André stared out past the wheelhouse into the night beyond. There was nothing really to see, bar the odd glimpse of white as the wind whipped the crests of the rolling waves.

André hated Scotland; had done since within an hour of landing at Glasgow airport. *Incredible!* Literally an hour after arriving he had checked into his hotel, gone to the bar for a drink and found himself in a fight with a drunk local mouthing off about apartheid. To be fair it had been a short-lived and one-sided event but André had been more worried about drawing attention to himself. That was why he had only struck the idiot once. In another place and time André would have destroyed the man, prolonging his suffering, breaking his bones and splitting his skin. But this was not that time. This was an easy job with a huge payment and he had no intention of allowing a bar squabble with a fat drunken oaf to fuck it up. He had moved to a different hotel the next day as a precaution and kept a low profile until meeting with the two local guys he had signed up to assist him with the job.

Looking at them now, André knew he could have done better, but time was an issue on this job and consequently he had been robbed of the luxury of choice. He had met both men in different times and places in the past. Sandy, the larger of the two, André had worked with in Nigeria hunting down the kidnapped schoolgirls in the jungle. Sandy had been an advisor to a Nigerian special forces squad, working, like André for Eeben Barlow's STTEP; the infamous South African mercenary firm. Although Sandy was Scottish, he had South African citizenship and had been a member of Koevoet, the special paramilitary unit, before hitting the mercenary circuit. The other Scottish member of his team was Jamie Morris and again, André had worked with Jamie back in the days when they roamed the armpits of the world with EO: Executive Outcomes, Eeben Barlow's first private army of South African mercenaries. André did not have any particular fondness for either man but he had needed local guys he could trust to set up the logistics of the operation. Sandy and Jamie, like most men in their shadow world, had numerous criminal connections that André would need access to in order to pull the job off. Jamie's particular skill was in tracking, man or beast, in any terrain or environment. Jamie was one of the few non-South Africans to have been retained on EO's payroll. And tracking would make or break this job. It had been Jamie's suggestion that winter would be the best time for the operation due to the tracking being much easier during that season.

To take his mind off the cold, André pulled out his iPad and clicked on the folder with the collated information he had at his disposal. He opened up the copy he had made of Monach Hall's last update on the wolf packs and refreshed himself with the details once again. With the Internet down most of the time, André had been relegated to taking snapshots of newspaper articles and storing them on his device. The last update he had was from late summer when the news that the Freya pack would soon be joined by a new litter of cubs, expected imminently. Monach Hall was clever not to divulge any details on the whereabouts of the den or the exact date but that wouldn't be a problem. That's why Jamie was here.

Looking up for a moment, André caught his reflection in the glass of the wheelhouse, a rugged face cast in the blue light from the computer he was holding.

"When do we get there?"

The captain, an older, taciturn man with disgusting breath and terrible body odour replied in a hard-Glaswegian accent that André had to almost interpret before he could understand the statement.

"Half to three-quarters of an hour."

Looking at his watch, André was pleased. This would still give them a few hours of darkness with which to make their way inland and establish the first of their camps. He nodded at the captain. "That's good, right on time. Jamie, Sandy, with me. Let's check the equipment for the last time before we deploy. I don't want any surprises." As he made his way out of the wheelhouse he glanced back and caught Jamie rolling his eyes at Sandy, clearly feeling another check was excessive. *Lazy bastard!* If André had learned one thing in over thirty-five years of operations, it was that you always did your final checks prior to deploying. There was no time to deal with Jamie's transgression at the moment but André had no intention of letting it go. Lack of respect had to be dealt with hard measures, serving as both punishment and deterrence. Another lesson learned from decades of fighting.

The cabin felt claustrophobic with the three men squeezed against the walls as they conducted the final checks of the equipment. André handed out the satellite telephones and radios, ensuring each was examined for power levels and a brief comms check given to provide proof of serviceability. The tranquiliser guns, gas cartridges and darts were also given a thorough going over before being returned to their cases. The small cages that the cubs would be placed into were scrutinised to make sure that there was no weakness in them that the little wolves could utilise to escape. The client was paying a small fortune for these four beasts and André had no intention of messing that up. There was also the hint that, should this operation go well, the client might engage André's services for other, similar operations.

When the job had first been put to him, André had initially been bemused. The capture of four wolf cubs for a wealthy oligarch had certainly not been what he was expecting when the call had come through for a discreet meeting with his broker. André's broker, Dieter, had never let him down, always providing him with solid, well-paid work for established clients. This, however, was a departure from the norm. Dieter had informed him that an oligarch currently living in Europe had made enquiries about how to get hold of wolf cubs for his private estate. Money was no object but the animals had to come from the wild, so stealing from zoos or wildlife parks was out of the question. As the oligarch wanted full disclosure on the provenance of the beasts, this was an important condition. It had been Dieter who identified the wolf packs of the Outer Hebrides as being a strong possibility due to the on-going cyber-attack tying up the forces of law and order for the near future. André had agreed with this assessment; his initial thoughts of central Europe or North America and the inherent logistical headaches they presented now discarded. In the following weeks and months, he had researched every aspect of the operation and what he would need to achieve it. He'd relayed his findings to Dieter and specifics were discussed in terms of money and timings. The client was pleased with the plan and informed Dieter that André and his team needed only to get the animals to Glasgow; his own people would take care of things from that point. André too, was happy with the plan and the operation, certainly one of the easiest tasks he could remember taking on. He knew better than to ask who the client was, happy with Dieter's guarantee that it was a good job for a reputable client.

Jamie and Sandy had jumped at the offer, like André, seeing it as one of the least arduous jobs they had ever been given. Once complete, André had outlined the plan and what would be required to achieve it. Map recces, wolf behaviour traits, training on the tranq equipment and sourcing a suitable boat and a captain who valued money over details.

And now here they were, minutes from the second phase of their operation: the insertion. The three men made their way on to the deck and took the covers from the rigid inflatable boat they would make the next leg of the journey in. They formed a human chain and passed the recently inspected equipment from the cabin and into the smaller boat where it was loaded and secured. André worked fast to help stave off the cold wind that whipped along the deck of the trawler and over the bow of the inflatable. An indecipherable yell from the captain was followed by a change of direction, the trawler wallowing now in the cross seas as it made its way landward. André looked up to see Jamie and Sandy give him the thumbs up, indicating all the equipment was now loaded. André jumped out of the boat and opened his pack, pulling out a down-filled jacket and putting it on without haste, desperate for the heat. *Bloody Scotland!* No good for a man who had spent most of his adult life in the heat of other continents. The last equipment checks he conducted himself. The weapons; a rifle and a pistol. The pistol was his own, a Glock 19, light, reliable and familiar and he loaded the gun then holstered it and the two spare magazines on the pouches on his belt. The rifle, a Diemaco C8, was a team weapon; brought along just in case they needed a little firepower to assist in their extraction should things go wrong. André didn't expect anything to go wrong but again, experience had taught him that while you couldn't predict the future, you could be ready for it. He loaded a magazine on to the weapon then passed it and a webbing belt of pouches to Jamie who donned the belt and slung the carbine over his back, tightening the sling a little. He shook his hips and nodded, happy that the spare magazines in the pouches were not smashing against each other and making a noise.

The captain yelled again from the wheelhouse. Perplexed, André turned to Sandy for an interpretation.

"Five minutes."

The men began releasing the straps that secured the smaller boat to the trawler and had just finished when their progress slowed to a halt. The captain approached them and assisted in the lowering of the inflatable boat. When the smaller boat reached the water, André turned to the captain and shook his hand. "Thank you captain, good job. Every day at twelve and six I'll call with an update for you on the sat-phone so make sure it's with you at all times. Equally, if we need an emergency evac I'll brief you on where and when I need you. Got that?"

The captain nodded and uttered something that again, André couldn't decipher but sounded vaguely like a form of assent. André recoiled as the man's breath wafted on the breeze and into his face. Wasting no more time the rangy South African climbed over the side and down the rope ladder into the waiting boat below. He sat down and looked back up at the trawler, giving the captain thumbs up. The captain grinned down at André, a row of yellow, rotted teeth in full view. André shivered as he turned his attention to his own crew. Jamie started the engine, a small outboard that kicked up a cloud of fumes before settling into a regular idle. As André watched, he saw the man look down at his compass and then look up again to catch André's eye. André turned his head and saw Sandy at the bow, laying down against the crates facing over the front of the boat, rifle at the ready. André nodded to Jamie and steadied himself as the throttle was increased, the small boat gaining speed and skipping over the waves. Glad to be off the trawler André glanced back and watched the diminishing figure of the captain on the deck and shuddered with disgust at the memory of the man's awful personal hygiene. Who knew, when this was all over, he might just give the captain a little bonus for his work. A tube of Colgate and a can of deodorant seemed about right.

13

The cold hit the old man the moment he threw back the blankets. Shivering he sat up in the bed, lowered his legs to the floor and shuffled his feet into his slippers. He stood with a little difficulty, stiff from lying down, old age and its curse of degeneration apparent. Eva, the collie looked up from her basket as he passed.

"No, no lass, not time to get up yet, just need to see to maself that's all." Turning the toilet light on, Angus Maclean caught sight of his reflection in the mirror as he passed, the grey hair and white beard framing his tanned, wrinkled face. He was getting old. Really old. As he finished his ablutions he thought about his age for a moment. Eighty years old, close enough to eighty-one to be truthful. Still, wasn't in too bad a shape for his age all things considered. Could still check his creels, till the vegetable patch, dress a deer, lift a salmon or two. But it was getting harder with each passing year. Still, God hadn't made man to live forever and he was well past his allocated three score and ten. As he turned the bathroom light off and shuffled back to the bedroom, a noise alerted him. Eva was stood in the middle of the room, hackles up, growling deep and staring towards the door.

"What's up lass? What do you hear? Is it the wolves?" The dog gave him a brief glance before returning her attention back to whatever it was she could hear. Angus listened but could hear nothing other than the sharp whistle of the wind as it played against the edges of the building. It would be the wolves that the animal was hearing. There was nothing else that it could be, their only neighbour being over four miles away. Angus chuckled and gave the dog's coat a pat on the way to his bed. "Come on you, leave the beasts be." The dog turned at the old man's voice but to his surprise did not return to her bed but lowered herself to the floor, attention still focused on the door and the soft growl in her throat continuing. Angus pulled the covers up and shook his head before turning out the sidelight and trying to get back to sleep. The dog would soon calm down, the wolves were never in the area long enough to be anything more than a novelty, something new and exciting for Eva to explore. Drifting off to sleep the old man thought that he would take a walk around the area tomorrow, look for any sign of the wolves in the remnants of the last snowfall.

14

Finn was almost invisible against the backdrop of the snow-covered mountain. His white Arctic outerwear and face mask camouflaging his form and presence. The view from the top was spectacular in the crisp, clear winter air. He had begun his ascent of Beinn Mhor before sunrise, wanting to be above the lower, more exposed slopes before the day had broken the horizon. He had hit the narrow ridge just as the sun appeared in the east, its golden glow warming the sea of the Little Minch and silhouetting the black peaks of the Cuillins of Skye. Resting against a rock on the lee side of the peak he looked north to the top of Hecla, a slightly lower hill than Beinn Mhor.

Finn was warm and comfortable, having put on some layers once he had completed his climb. This was the first time he had climbed the mountain and he regretted not having done it sooner. The views were astonishing: Skye to the east, Benbecula then Harris and Lewis to the north, Barra to the south, and to the west the wild Atlantic. He picked up the rifle, now covered with random pieces of white tape to match his own winter camouflage and used the telescopic sight to sweep the land below him. Small game, mountain hares and birds were the first signs of life that he picked up through the sight. He also noticed wisps of smoke coming from the chimneys of two separate cottages. The dwellings were miles apart but he was glad that he had seen where people were still living. He remembered from his research that they were older individuals who had not wanted to move because of strong ties to the land and that they assisted Monach Hall with reports of the wolves' movements around the islands. Still, they were no real threat to Finn or his forest home but it was good to know exactly where these people lived.

As he swept the sight across the land to the north he paused as movement attracted his attention. On the wooded, western flank of Hecla a small herd of deer were making their way off the hill, seeking grazing in the valley below. There were around a dozen animals with a mix of stags, hinds and young. Finn considered making his way down and taking one of the beasts for his own but decided that he didn't need the meat, his cold larder still replete with venison left from his previous kill as well as hare and ptarmigan.

A movement above the herd caught his eye for a brief moment but was gone an instant later. His heart quickened as he recalled the fleeting details of the sighting; a grey, pale shape highlighted against the dark of the forest behind it. Finn scanned the treeline, following its edge as it hugged the contours of the hill. There it was again! This time he could see clearly what he was looking at and held his breath. A wolf. A beautiful, solitary wolf loping through the cover of the forest. Finn released the breath he had been holding and followed the animal's progress through his scope. The wolf moved in a smooth, fluid motion through the forest, flitting in and out of view as it passed behind trees and shrubs. He let out an involuntary gasp as he made out a series of other ghostly forms shadowing the animal through the dark of the woodland interior: A wolf pack. These new additions came into focus as the treeline thinned near the foot of the hill and Finn could see their intention clearly for the first time. They were hunting the deer.

Alternating his attention between the herd and its stealthy pursuers, he looked to see if the deer were alert to the predators. The sedate pace of the herd's descent and their relaxed posture informed him that the wolves remained undetected. Even as Finn watched he saw the pack divide into two groups, with one edging slowly to the forest's edge and the other continuing their silent journey down through the trees and beyond Finn's limit of vision. He was fascinated by what he was witnessing. The wolves' actions had a military precision and effectiveness that he related to and he could foresee what they were trying to achieve. Without warning the first group exploded from the treeline and in an instant the deer were in full flight down the hillside, the whites of their terrified eyes apparent through the rifle's optical sight. The pursuing wolves were closing the distance with long bounds, their lithe bodies stretching to full length as they hurled themselves down the slope after their prey. Suddenly the second group of wolves burst from the depths of the forest and attacked the flank of the herd. The panicked deer veered away from the new threat and the sounds of their distress carried to Finn on his eyrie above the conflict below. Finn watched in awe as the wolves' cunning became evident. The deer, reacting to the sudden threat to their flank, had turned away from the attackers but in doing so had committed themselves to a steep, rocky slope which was now impeding their progress and separating members of the herd from the main body. The first wolf-group maintained their downhill momentum and fell upon the herd's stragglers taking down two hinds that had been unable to stay with the rest of the animals. The deer were brought to the ground in a succession of assaults by several of the wolves, each one clamping on to a leg, flank or neck until the beast was prone. The other wolves continued to chase the herd over the rise but halted the pursuit once it was apparent that the deer had gained too significant a lead on the predators. They watched the departing herd disappear over another rise then they turned around and trotted back down the hill, joining their companions as they feasted on the fresh kills.

Finn was ecstatic; he couldn't wait to tell Katy about this tonight! He felt a sense of privilege at having witnessed such an incredible event. He observed the pack for some time, noting how they all fed together but that there was a clear hierarchy that dictated who got the best of the beast. After a while he registered that his legs were cold and he really should be moving. Smiling at his good fortune he picked up his pack and rifle and began to make his way off the summit, taking care as he negotiated the ice-covered rocks. Glancing back at the animals in the distance he felt the warmth of the sun on his back and again, a sense of peace and belonging in this wild place.

15

The lad could have gone anywhere from Mallaig. The fact that he loved and was at home in the mountains made the matter more difficult for Gary Finnegan. After studying the ferries' camera footage for the past couple of months and interviewing the private boat owners who could have taken Douglas to Skye, the military policeman was reaching another dead end in his investigation. The lad could even have gone to ground in the Knoydart peninsula, an isolated rugged region with few residents, no roads to speak of and a network of forests and lochs that would provide Douglas with all he needed to survive.

The local bobby, a mountaineer himself, thought this unlikely. As he pointed out to Gary, if you were going to go to ground in Knoydart, you wouldn't dump your car in Mallaig unless you had specific reason to. The boat to Doune wasn't running for tourists and any fugitive would have to steal a boat to make their own way there, bringing immediate attention to themselves. It would make more sense to conceal the vehicle off the A82 or A87 and make your way into the area from there.

Gary knew that Douglas' choice of vehicle was the key to figuring out where he had gone. There was some reason that Douglas had needed that particular vehicle and Gary was close to finding out why. He was awaiting a call from the marines at Arbroath regarding when the vehicle had left the base and if anything had been reported missing around the same time.

The Welsh search had now been called off, much to the chagrin of Sergeant Callaghan. He did not buy into the theory that Douglas was in the north west of Scotland, believing instead that the marine had an accomplice who had taken the car to Mallaig as a smokescreen to confuse the search. Gary was starting to tire at Callaghan's dogmatic insistence that only his own avenue of investigation could be the right one. If he hadn't needed the manpower so badly, he would have thrown Callaghan off the case by now.

He jumped as the telephone rang beside him. The local policeman answered in his soft brogue before offering the handset to him without a word. Gary stood and took his notebook out, taking the lid off the pen with his teeth and dropping it on the counter. He felt the excitement course through him as Sergeant Major Ron Fellowes of Four-Five Commando confirmed exactly what Gary had suspected all along. The call lasted several minutes during which time the military policeman was mainly silent, save for the odd grunt of assent or request for clarification. After some time, he thanked the marine on the other end, hung up and looked over his notes. He was right. Douglas had taken the vehicle not because it was available but because he had needed its size, or more importantly, what it could carry. Nodding to the bobby he made his way outside into the winter sunshine, taking a deep breath of the cold air and tasting the tang of the sea upon his tongue. The marines had conducted an inventory of all the locations on camp that Douglas would have had access to and in doing so had identified missing items that they could not account for. A sea kayak, bergan backpack, snowshoes, cross-country skis, camping stove and fuel, survival axe and saw, four season sleeping bag, one-man arctic shelter, crampons, cam-whites and a list of other, smaller articles. Douglas had equipped himself in as thorough a manner as Gary would have expected and could live out in the wild for months without the need to expose himself. Of major importance was the sea kayak; Douglas had his own boat. He could be anywhere along this coast and its islands and it was no surprise now that none of the ferry operators or boat crews had seen hide nor hair of the lad. But where the hell was he going? Knoydart? Skye? Rum? Eigg?

Rather than point him in the right direction this latest information seemed merely to open up a host of other possibilities. Cursing quietly Gary made his way to the warmth of a coffee shop he had noted earlier. He needed to calm down a little and think this new information through. There was something he had missed or wasn't connecting yet. Something he had overlooked. The fact that there were no sightings of Douglas, no reports of unusual gunfire in remote areas, no farmers or mountaineers reporting unusual activity, was strange in itself. It was months now, well into winter and still no sign of the lad. Gary knew that this fact alone was important but he just couldn't put his finger on what precisely it was.

As he took off his coat and sat in the large leather chair by the fire, he reflected that the best hope they had of getting the lad was that of a sighting report from the general public. In his experience this was usually what tipped the balance in these long, drawn-out cases. Catching the waitress's eye Gary Finnegan decided to put Finn Douglas from his mind for the time being and enjoy the cosy fire with a hot coffee and scone while enjoying the sea views. Something would turn up. It always did.

16

Something wasn't right. Angus could feel it but couldn't quite put his finger on the cause. Eva was not herself either, the usually obedient collie requiring several commands to bring her back to the old man's side. At first Angus had thought the wolves were nearby, but he had seen Eva's behaviour when the wolves had been in the area before and she was nothing like this. The old collie was unsettled and ill at ease with her surroundings. The day found the pair among the old forest near Howmore, Angus looking for any signs of the wolves to report back to Monach Hall and Eva well, Eva seemed to be suspicious of everything at the moment.

The dog trotted forward into some ferns until only her rump was visible. Angus called on her twice but her attention was focussed on something in the brush. Tutting softly the old man deviated from the game trail he had been following and went to see what had taken his companion's attention. The dog looked up as its master approached and moved to one side leaving Angus with a clear view of the area. It was a hare carcass that the dog had found. The old man chuckled and was turning back to the path when something about the animal remains caught his eye. He bent down and picked the animal up, his white eyebrows raised in surprise at what he saw. The animal had been caught in a snare, evident from the raw wound that was prominent on the foreleg. In addition to that it had been cleaned and dressed by someone accustomed to such work and with a good, sharp knife. Turning the carcass around in his hand, the old man examined it for several minutes before lowering it back into the ferns. He brushed his hand on his trousers as he and the dog returned to the trail. Casting a quick glance back to the hare, his brow furrowed in deep thought, Angus wondered who could have done this. The reserve was completely off limits to people other than himself, David Neill down at Dalburgh and the Taylors. The estate team responsible for the reserve would never dream of laying traps and snares as any one of the wolves or their cubs could be lost to such implements.

Lost in his thoughts, the old man nearly missed the boot print as he strode along the trail. Crouching down, he examined the clear imprint of a sturdy boot cast in the rich, peaty loam. It was fresh, the old man deduced, as it had degraded very little from whenever it had been left there. Standing again, he looked around the forest with more scrutiny. *Who had been through here? And why?* As he looked beyond the print the hair on the back of his neck rose as he could see that the boot print on the track was a mistake. His experienced ghillie's eye could see that whoever had passed this way had taken great care to leave no sign on the track. To the side of the track however, there were indentations in the clumps of grass and moss that bordered the game trail. To the untrained eye these signs were barely visible, to Angus however they were as clear as day. He gave the dog a soft command and she returned to his side as the old man followed the discreet tracks that hugged the game trail through the woods.

He managed to identify the tracks all the way through the woods although on occasion he had needed to cast an eye around, as the harder ground was more difficult in locating the trail. Angus could still not figure out what the person was doing. There were no poachers here, hadn't been for over fifteen years. There was no hunting, fishing or shooting either. His suspicions were growing that whoever this was, they had no right to be on the islands, hence their caution as they transited the woods. Angus continued with his tracking of the stranger, stopping every now and then to pick up the trail from the point where it petered out. He knew that the forest thinned significantly in a few hundred yards and he would find himself on the old tarmac road looking up towards Hecla.

He watched as Eva darted around the game trail busy identifying and reading the scents and scat of the various woodland creatures. Up ahead Angus saw an increase in the light breaking through the tree cover and knew that he was getting close to the road. The ground was harder now and he was finding it difficult to pick up the trail. He paused for a moment then taking out his folding knife, cut a thin branch from an alder. He walked back several yards to the spot where he had last seen prominent signs of passage through the grass. Once there the old man went down on one knee and laid the stick on the ground. He placed one end of the stick against the centre of an impression and lined the stick up with the next indentation so that it ran through the dip in the foliage. He then cut the stick to size and checked it against the next series of tracks. Armed now with a stick that was cut to the length of the individual's gait, Angus struck out once again. Whenever he lost the trail on the hard ground, the old man placed the stick on the last print that he had seen. Leaving the end of the stick in the centre of this track he then slowly moved the stick in an arc until the free end fell upon the next footprint. It was an old trick he had learned from the Iban tribesmen in Borneo during his national service days and it had always served him well.

Getting to the road took more time than he had bargained for due to the difficulty in picking up the track over the rockier ground but the old man was pleased with his efforts. He might be old but there were some skills that never left you. Just as he reached the roadside Eva darted past him and crossed the weed-strewn tarmac, disappearing into the thick grass and brush on the other side. Angus cursed quietly and opened out his stride, calling on the old collie to return. By the time he reached the road he had given up looking for the tracks, angry now that the dog was ignoring him completely. She was never like this, not in all the years they had together. *What in God's name was wrong with the animal? The wolves? Was that what this was about?* Muttering to himself the old man crossed the road and pushed his way into the thick brush on the other side.

17

The dog caught Jamie completely by surprise. One minute he had been alone, checking on the battery power of the sat-phone, the next a black and white head appeared from the bushes, mere yards from his position. After the initial shock of surprise and relief that it wasn't a wolf, the true nature of his predicament became apparent; that wherever there was a dog, not far behind was its owner. Looking around him in panic, Jamie scrambled over to the cages and thrust them deeper into the bushes and well out of sight to the casual observer. There was nothing else in view other than his backpack and the rifle beside it, resting against a tree trunk just out of reach. As he was moving towards the weapon, he heard the bushes move behind him and the unmistakeable sound of a human footfall. For a split second he froze, undecided, the bruises on his cheek a reminder of André's intolerance for error. Turning to face the sound, he came face to face with the dog as it raced out of the ferns and bared its teeth at him. In one smooth movement Jamie sprang forward, grabbing the collie by its fur while drawing the fighting-knife from his boot. The dog opened its jaws in surprise and fear but the yelp was stopped by the thrust and cut of the blade in the animal's throat. Slinging the carcass behind him, Jamie stood and faced the bushes just as a man pushed his way into the small clearing.

Angus stopped at the sight of the man before him. He made a small exclamation of surprise and was just about to ask him who he was when he caught sight of the black and white fur behind the stranger.

"Eva. EVA!" He could see immediately that there was something wrong with his companion and he brushed the man aside as he stumbled over to the prone animal. Behind him, Jamie took several steps in the direction that the old man had come and studied the area, making sure that the old guy was on his own.

Angus howled and dropped to his knees staring in disbelief and shock at the horrific sight before him. The gash of the torn throat was exposed and blood continued to flow from the wound in a steady stream, covering the green grass around the dead dog. The old man sobbed as he reached a shaking hand and laid it on his friend's flank, warm but still and unmoving beneath him. He turned to ask the man what had happened and saw immediately that he was in trouble. The stranger was stood, relaxed but alert, arms by his side and with the dripping blade of a knife protruding from a fist. Angus rose with some difficulty, weakened by the shock of the situation. He pointed to Eva's corpse with a shaking finger. "You...you did that?"

The stranger said nothing, his eyes glancing briefly at the animal before returning to the old man. Angus saw only cruelty and a cold detachment in the stranger's eyes. There was an inherent badness in the man that radiated from him in waves. The old man had seen this in others over the years; thugs and criminals with no conscience or regard for human life. Angus knew what was coming but any fear in him was now displaced by the hot rage he felt well up from within. The man was a lot younger than Angus and was armed with a knife that he had shown he could use. But the old man was beyond reason. Angus yelled and ran at the stranger, his old body betraying the ambition he nurtured. Jamie Morris smiled as he nimbly sidestepped the feeble attack and smashed the pommel of the knife into the old fool's head. As the old man crashed to the ground, Jamie took a moment to look around him once again; ensuring no one had witnessed the exchange. Satisfied they remained alone he bent down, grabbed the old man by the shoulders of his jacket and dragged him into the clearing beside the carcass of the dog.

Angus moaned as he was dumped onto the grass. He felt nauseous and dizzy and couldn't see out of his right eye due to the blood streaming down his face. He was hauled to his knees and left in that position, head bowed and breathing in ragged bursts. Looking up he opened his good eye and took in the man before him. The stranger pointed the knife at Angus and spoke for the first time.

"Who the fuck are you old man, and why were you following me?"

Angus noted the strong Glaswegian accent and calmness in the man's voice, again, not a good sign that this was going to end well for the old man.

"I live here and I saw your tracks in the woods today so followed them. Who are you and why did you kill my Eva?"

The stranger smiled. "You and your dog are too fucking nosey for your own good. Can't have every Tom, Dick and Harry poking around our business now, can we?"

Our, Angus noted. So, the man wasn't alone. "So, what is your business? There's nothing here to steal, the poaching's just as good on the mainland. You didn't come here just to murder old men and their dogs?"

Jamie raised his eyebrows in surprise. The old bastard had balls, you had to give him that. He recognised he was going to die here with his dog but wasn't backing down an inch. *Credit where credit's due and all that.* He looked at his watch and saw that he needed to be moving soon if he was going to make the rendezvous point before dark. "Sorry old man, this has been fun and I'd love to stay and chat but I've somewhere I need to be." Without warning he reached out and grabbed a handful of Angus' hair, yanking the old man's head upwards and back, exposing the throat. In his other hand, a deft spin of the knife turned the weapon around and ready for the cut.

Angus opened his good eye, refusing the power of the terror that sought to engulf him. He would not give this barbaric thug the satisfaction of seeing his fear. He watched as the blade was lowered to his throat and pushed his chin up in a final act of defiance. Suddenly his vision was filled by a wraith, a spectral figure moving in front of him. There were several noises and the old man felt his hair released and a heavy crash behind him. He toppled forward and arrested his fall by thrusting out his hands. Looking behind him, he saw the prone figure of his captor among the ferns and grass. As he studied the unconscious thug and tried to come to terms with what had happened, he felt a hand under his armpit pushing him up and helping him to his feet. Turning back, his breath caught in his throat and he staggered backwards a step as he took in the strange white figure in front of him. The figure peeled back a white hood and removed the mask that had covered his face. A dark-haired young man now met Angus' eyes. Angus could see that he was wearing some kind of winter camouflage suit and facemask and was carrying a pretty impressive rifle. The young man spoke.

"I'm sorry I didn't get here quick enough to save your dog."

Angus was surprised to hear the English accent but nodded at the sentiment. The young man approached him and studied the wound on the old man's head.

"I think you should let me sort that out for you. It's a pretty deep cut and won't heal on its own."

Angus nodded in agreement, a wave of exhaustion now overwhelming him. He turned back to the prone figure and spat in its direction. "He dead?"

The younger man shook his head and gave a sad sigh. "No. I broke his leg and knocked him out cold with the rifle butt. He'll be in a bad way for a while once he wakes up."

"You should just have killed him. Wouldn't be many would miss that piece of work. He would have killed me if you hadn't arrived."

"No. I know what he is but I've had enough of killing. More than enough."

Angus allowed himself to be propped up against a tree. The young man retrieved a large pack from the bushes outside the clearing and hauled it over, opening a side pocket and removing a smaller pouch. Angus leaned back and closed his eyes, tiredness seeping in now that the adrenalin had left the old man. He inhaled a sharp antiseptic smell and opened his eye to see the young man reaching forward with a white tissue.

"Sterile wipes," he explained, dabbing at the gash and clearing the area around it. "Will sting a bit but will help stop any infection. I should warn you that the stitches will hurt like hell but nothing I can do about that."

Angus nodded to show he understood. "What are you lad? Army or something? What are you doing here?"

"No. I'm nothing. Just someone who wants to be left in peace. That's why I came here in the first place."

Angus reflected on the statement as he watched the young man preparing the needle and suture thread with quick, confident movements. "You know, that creature there isn't alone, there are others with him. My point being, you might find it hard to keep that peace you are so keen on."

Angus met the man's eyes and noted the sad softness in them. *Who was this lad, and what was he doing here?* Angus owed the lad his life but knew that whoever this thug was that was lying behind them, his associates wouldn't take kindly to one of their own being treated that way. The young man smiled apologetically as he raised the needle.

"I'll tell you once again; this is going to hurt like a bastard. Still, better than a cut throat any day."

"Well, seeing as you've saved my life and about to sew up my head, I suppose I should introduce myself. I'm Angus, Angus McLeish of Grogarry."

"Well, Angus McLeish of Grogarry, I'm Finn, Finn Douglas of nowhere in particular. Now, if I were you, I'd take a deep breath and grit your teeth. This is going to sting.

As the needle bit and the sutures pulled the torn flesh together, Angus's eyes widened as he felt the pain. The young man certainly hadn't been lying.

18

Hanging up the telephone in the drawing room, Paul Taylor turned to his wife who was waiting with undisguised curiosity, having heard one side of the conversation.

"Well, not sure where to start darling but that was old Angus from Grogarry. He stumbled upon some armed poacher or something and they killed his dog and beat him pretty bad."

Fiona Taylor rose from the chair and placed her hand on her husband's arm. "Good Lord! Is Angus all right?"

"Yes, he's okay. Apparently, some young man saved his life by knocking the poacher out."

"What young man?"

"I have absolutely no idea. Angus just said that a young man called Finn appeared out of the woods and saved him just as the poacher was about to cut his throat."

Fiona raised her hand to her mouth, eyes wide. "The poacher was about to cut Angus' throat?"

"Yes. The old man says he owes his life to the young chap, whoever he is. Oh, and apparently there are more of them. Poachers I mean."

"What do they want Paul? Surely, it's easier pickings for them on the mainland? We haven't had poachers here for over fifteen years. And just who on earth is this Finn character? What is he doing on the island?"

Paul Taylor's brow was furrowed in concentration as he shook his head slowly. "I have no idea darling but I'm going to get on to Inspector Buchan up in Stornoway and ask him to send someone down. This is a job for the police now."

A polite cough interrupted their conversation and Fiona Taylor turned and smiled apologetically to their guest. "Rory, I am so sorry. Didn't mean to exclude you but we're not all that accustomed to dealing with thugs and criminals up here."

Rory Starkey nodded and sat on the window seat as he addressed the owners of Monach Hall. "What's going on?"

Paul Taylor briefed the reporter on all the information that he had been given, concluding that they wouldn't know the whole story until the police had spoken to Angus.

"It seems unusual for a poacher to be so violent towards a person when they could probably have made good their escape. What are they doing that's so important they are willing to kill an old man to cover it up?"

Paul looked at his wife who shared his puzzlement. "I couldn't say Rory. I really couldn't say. This is like nothing I've ever had to deal with before."

The journalist remained thoughtful for several moments, stroking his greying beard. "And you have no idea who this Finn fellow is?"

"None whatsoever. Lucky he was there though. Angus says he patched him up and got him back to Grogarry then took off after that, just before the old man rang us."

"Would you mind if I tag along when you and the police go to talk to the old man? Can't help my reporter's nose for a story I'm afraid."

"Well....if the police have no objections, I'm quite happy. We would have been heading down that way anyway to start tracking the packs for your article. Let me get on with informing the police and I'll let you know when we're leaving."

As Paul and his wife made their way to the office, Rory Starkey remained deep in thought. There was something nagging at the back of his mind that he just couldn't put his finger on. Something about the information that gave a little spark of recognition, something he had heard before. He took the small notebook from his pocket and jotted down all the details of the conversation. He underlined the name Finn and put a question mark next to it. Although he was the current wildlife correspondent for *The Times*, he had a good journalist's instinct for a story and something told him that there was more to this than a case of poachers looking to lift a few deer from the islands. And he intended to find out what it was.

19

André Voster dropped the last of the gear into the cover of their makeshift shelter. "Where's the fucking rifle Jamie?"

Jamie looked up from his position on the floor of the small cave. He swallowed with difficulty, a combination of dehydration and the fear he felt as André's cold fury radiated across the shelter.

"He...he must have taken it after he knocked me out André."

André crossed the space between them and knelt by the seated man's side. Jamie was not in good shape. His eyes showed the semi-focussed effects of concussion, his scalp was crusted with dried blood and even though they had splinted the leg, it was a bad break. Sandy had advised against morphine due to Jamie's head injury but they had to give him it in the end, as he couldn't take the pain of the splint without screaming in agony.

When the call had come on the sat-phone André had been livid. Jamie was already two hours late for the rendezvous and both André and Sandy were convinced the idiot had fucked something up. And they were right. Jamie had been difficult to understand over the phone and it wasn't until he mentioned that an old man and someone else had left him for dead that André calmed down. As best he could, he interrogated Jamie, directed him to use the GPS facility on the sat-phone and read out the coordinates. It had taken the best part of an hour to find him and a further hour in darkness to get him back to their cave. They had retrieved all of the equipment that Jamie had been carrying. All except the C8. The bloody rifle. *How the hell had the moron managed to lose that?* This bothered André a great deal. Anything else that an investigating police officer might find could be attributed to regular poachers but the C8 was a different matter altogether. Even an inexperienced investigator would recognise that it was an unusual and serious weapon for a mere poacher to be carrying. There was also the possibility that it could be traced. André had tasked Jamie and Sandy to secure the weapons they needed for the operation but to ensure that they were clean and untraceable, to which Jamie had assured him was the case. Looking at the sweating moron sat beside him now, André knew that he couldn't have any confidence in this fact.

"I'll ask again. Where is the fucking rifle Jamie?"

"I don't know André, I told you all I remember. One second I was putting the knife to the old bastard's throat the next...Well...that thing came at me. Then I came to hours later when I called you."

André sighed and gripped the other man's chin hard. "Think, you fucking idiot. Think hard. Did they say anything to each other? Did they mention where they were going?"

"No! I told you, one second everything was under control, the next I was out and that was it until I called you." Jamie spat to his side and moaned as the small movement of his head brought a return of the nausea.

The South African stood and leaned against the wall of the cave, eyes hooded in the shadows of what little light the small lantern provided. The loss of the rifle worried him. It would bring a lot of attention to the islands; attention he could well do without. The assault on the old man would also bring down a lot of heat. André figured that this was as close to a serious crime as these islands ever saw. Added to these issues was the fact that his tracker was out of the game. Jamie couldn't walk, let alone track. What an absolute fuck-up. A noise from Jamie drew his attention back to the injured man.

"I think the guy who clocked me had a rifle."

André narrowed his eyes and stepped forward. "You think?"

"Yes. I'm pretty sure he did now I think about it. He smashed my leg first then I saw something heavy and dark coming for my head."

"And it couldn't have been the C8 he was using against you?"

"No, that had a sling on it and I would have seen that when he was attacking me."

André nodded and folded his arms. So, this mystery attacker was armed as well. Now with not just his own weapon but also their C8. Who the hell was this guy? And why didn't he take Jamie to the local authorities or at least tie him up until they arrived? It could only mean that he didn't want to have anything to do with the police either. Which made him more interesting. *What was he, a poacher? Someone else after the wolf cubs?* After several minutes' silence André came to a conclusion. He and Sandy would carry on hunting for the cubs. Neither man had Jamie's skills or experience but they did have a basic understanding and working knowledge of how to do it. They would also look out for any signs of the mystery man who had taken Jamie out of the operation and stolen their C8. André would make sure that this was the last time the stranger carried out the Good Samaritan routine.

Rubbing his hands in the cold, André was happy with his plan. He and Sandy would step things up, push hard to find the cubs. He stooped and reached into his backpack, pulling out his own sat-phone. As he left the shelter he turned to Jamie. "Right, I've got a plan to get on with the job and look out for that bastard that suckered you. First thing's first though I'm going to call the captain and get you medevac'd tomorrow morning." He shushed Jamie's protest and continued. "Sorry bru, you're out. Tough luck but that's the way it goes. Let me get hold of the captain and get a timing squared away for tomorrow then we'll discuss your pay and settlement figure. I'll be back in ten."

André strode through the dark forest, climbing the rocky rise above their temporary shelter. He leaned against a tree trunk and looked down the rolling sweep of woodland to the sea in the bay below, a white stripe of moonlight reflecting from the lines of rolling breakers. He did not call the revolting captain, never had any intention of doing so. He just needed Jamie to believe this was the case. Tomorrow morning, he and Sandy would carry Jamie down to the bay, uncover their boat and he would then send Sandy back to the shelter while he took Jamie out to rendezvous with the larger vessel.

Except there would be no rendezvous with any vessel. André was going to take Jamie out to sea, kill him, and throw his weighted corpse into the frigid waters. Was only fair considering how badly the idiot had jeopardised the whole operation.

20

It was absolutely freezing up here. Even the short walk from the aircraft to the terminal had made their eyes water in the biting, arctic winds. Gary Finnegan was never so grateful to enter an airport in his life, the comfortable warmth of the heated facility in direct contrast to the weather outside. He turned and smiled at Sergeant Callaghan who was regaining some of his colour after the severe turbulence of their flight. The pair followed the small crowd and the signs to the baggage reclaim and Gary spotted the uniformed figure waiting by the entrance doorway. As he approached, he stuck out his hand and smiled.

"Hi, Gary Finnegan, Royal Military Police. You must be… *Mahari*?"

The police officer laughed, shaking her head as she corrected him. "No, Mr Finnegan, it's pronounced *Vari*. In the Gaelic the letters Mh together are said as a 'V' so my name is like the Gaelic equivalent of Mary or Marie, just pronounced differently. Sergeant Mhairi Stewart, Police Scotland, Highlands and Islands Division."

Warrant Officer Finnegan apologised and introduced his subordinate. "And this is my assistant investigator Sergeant

Callaghan." The Sergeant shook hands with the police officer and stuttered over a pleasantry. Gary raised an eyebrow as he observed the younger man's discomfort. *So, Sergeant Callaghan is a little awkward around the ladies?* That was something Gary had not expected, having thought him to be over-confident if anything. In fairness, he had only ever seen Callaghan interact with the female members of their team, which was a completely different dynamic. Gary also noted that Mhairi was quite an attractive young woman and no doubt this was not helping Callaghan's composure. Before he could jump in and rescue his subordinate, Mhairi turned back to him.

"Okay, now we've done the introductions I'll give you a wee brief on what's happening next. We will be heading down to Monach Hall tonight and then Mr and Mrs Taylor will accompany us down to meet with the old man who was assaulted tomorrow morning. I'd appreciate it if only one of you was present with me for the questioning as I don't want to overwhelm old Angus."

"Yes, completely understand that Mhairi and I'll be with you during the interview while Sergeant Callaghan talks to the Taylors about possible locations where our boy could have gone to ground."

Sergeant Mhairi Stewart turned to address the Sergeant. "Well, you'll have your work cut out for you there. The country down there is wilderness; rivers, lochs, forests, mountains and pretty much unpopulated. From what I've read about your man, he has the training and the experience to stay hidden for quite some time.'

Sergeant Callaghan could not disguise the contempt in his voice as he replied. "Well, what he *could* do is pretty much academic at this point seeing as he didn't stay hidden. He's ours now. Speaking of which, are you all the support we've got? I was expecting such a serious lead to be taken on by a bit more support than this."

The police officer raised an eyebrow at the younger army man and gave him a wry smile as she turned to resume their walk. "I was just thinking the exact same thing."

Gary Finnegan shook his head and glared at Callaghan, tempted to clout the younger man for his unerring ability to offend and upset people, particularly those that they would rely on for assisting the investigation. Sighing, he followed the policewoman through the doors to the crowded carousel where he saw that their flight's baggage was already rotating on the large black belts.

Monach Hall was stunning, and pretty much everything that Gary had imagined a stately pile to be. On their arrival they had been met by the Taylors who had shown them their rooms and invited them for drinks downstairs. Gary's room was very comfortable; it even had its own en-suite, which he had not expected. The decor was in keeping with the status of the house; random Victoriana, ceramic water pitchers, prints of Highland hunts, rustic furniture. He soon unpacked his belongings, leaving his outdoor clothes on a chair in anticipation of the next morning's trip. He took a quick look at himself in the mirror then left the room and walked along the carpeted corridor back towards the staircase. He paused at the top of the stairs to examine something that had caught his eye on the way up. It was a leopard encased in a large glass box, the glazed eyes being the only indication that the beast was not alive. A brass plaque at the base of the display informed him that one Colonel Sebastian Farrar-Taylor, Second Battalion; The Royal Scots had killed the cat in India in 1840. The sound of someone approaching distracted him and Gary looked up to see his host, Paul Taylor making his way to the staircase.

"Ah, I see you've found an artefact from our less-enlightened ancestors." Paul stopped beside the military policeman and joined him in studying the immortalised predator. "How things change. Several generations ago my family roamed the globe killing anything they could mount on a wall and now here we are, protecting and nurturing the remaining wildlife we have."

Gary smiled and patted the side of the glass case. "Well, I'm pretty sure I know which side of the fence Leo the leopard would be sitting on"

Paul Taylor laughed and both men continued to descend the staircase where Gary was directed to the drawing room. On entering he saw that he was the last to arrive, Mhairi, Callaghan, Fiona Taylor and another man he hadn't met congregated near the fire.

"What will you have Gary? I'm an Islay man myself but I'm sure we could find you something a bit less pungent if that's your poison!"

"Not at all Mr Taylor, a nice Islay would be fine, no ice or water please."

Nodding with approval, his host busied himself with the drinks and Gary wandered across the room to join the others, met halfway by an inquisitive beast of a dog who approached him, tail wagging.

"Oh, don't mind Jura Mr Finnegan, he's soft as butter and an absolute pest for affection." Fiona Taylor ordered the dog to return to its bed and the animal trotted off with a small sigh of disgruntlement that had the group laughing. Fiona Taylor shook her head in mock displeasure. "Honestly, I swear sometimes they are worse than children!"

Gary nodded to Mhairi and Callaghan and was introduced to the stranger by Mrs Taylor.

"Gary Finnegan, this is Rory Starkey, wildlife correspondent for The Times. Rory has been a big champion of our little venture up here from the beginning and we count ourselves lucky to have him in our corner."

As the men shook hands Gary could see that the journalist was an outdoor man. The tanned, wrinkled face evidence of a life spent facing the elements. Paul Taylor brought Gary his drink over and then joined his wife and the others while Gary found himself being addressed by the reporter.

"Tell me Mr Finnegan, what do you think Douglas is doing on these islands? Wouldn't have thought this would be anyone's first choice of destination if they were on the run."

"Please, just call me Gary, no need for formalities. As for Douglas, I'm not sure but there must be some personal pull here that we haven't identified yet. As you say, this is not what I would consider a likely spot to go to ground."

The journalist nodded and took a sip from his gin and tonic before speaking again. "That makes sense. But what is he actually *doing*? Simply evading capture? Returning to the wild himself? And why the gun?"

"My own personal opinion is that the lad is broken. He's lost his whole family and a few of his friends in the space of a month. He's also been fighting for the past fifteen years and has probably seen the worst of war. As I say, it's only my personal opinion but I think the lad just snapped and wants to be as far away from the world as he can."

"And the rifle? I understand it's a 7.62 Sharpshooter?"

Gary nodded. "You've done your homework Mr Starkey. Yes, that's exactly what it is."

"And do you believe that he's capable of using this on someone? And please, it's Rory"

"Rory, I emphasise again that this is only my personal opinion but I believe he chose that rifle deliberately. He had an armoury of weapons at his disposal but took this one. I think he knew he was coming here all along and that the rifle is for taking down the deer to feed himself."

"That would make sense. He'd want to put the animal down with one shot; couldn't risk the exposure of chasing a wounded beast across the hills. How do you intend to go about finding him?"

"First of all, Rory, you cannot report any of the search details. Even if you try, the Ministry of Defence will hit you with a DA notice and stop the article going to press."

The journalist raised his hand. "Please Gary, I'm not a tabloid hack sniffing a scandal. I have no intention of writing up anything that would remotely endanger either your search or the people involved. I'm here to cover the progress of the new cubs to the Freya pack and update our readers on the success of the reintroduction of wolves to the United Kingdom. But there's no denying it, the Douglas story is quite fascinating."

Gary believed the journalist. The man had an air of gravitas that seemed to support his assertions. "I know Rory, I know. But the pressure here is quite considerable. Because the cyber-attack has crippled a lot of the communication infrastructure all over the country the police are beyond overstretched trying to cope with it. As you'll well know the riots and looting in the cities are being policed by army reservists. This search here should have around fifty people, dogs, and helicopters with thermal imaging cameras and a handful of boats. What have we got? Two military policemen and a Sergeant from the local constabulary. If, however, I get proof positive that Douglas is here, the MoD will send whatever spare troops they can find to sweep the island and bring him to justice."

There was a pause in the conversation as both men drank, the journalist finally breaking the silence.

"Point is; do you think he'll allow himself to be brought to justice?"

The military policeman sighed. "I really hope it won't come to that. If I can find him here, I think I can talk the lad down, bring him back with us and not run to ground like a rabid fox. Truth is even if we get sight of the boy, neither me or Sergeant Callaghan are as skilled as Douglas in survival and cutting around the wilderness."

Rory Starkey smiled and gestured with his head in the direction of the others. "Ah. I see you haven't asked our regular police sergeant what skills she brings to the party. Think you might be surprised and impressed in equal measure. Top up?"

Nodding his assent, Gary handed his glass to the reporter and joined the others in time to hear Fiona Taylor talking to Mhairi about the wolf cubs they were travelling south to locate. Gary allowed her to finish before he addressed the policewoman.

"I hear from a little bird that you might have some very useful skills or experience that will help us on this search?"

Mhairi Stewart grinned and nodded towards the reporter. "I see someone has been keeping you informed. Okay, I've got quite a bit of mountain experience and I know the land well down where Douglas was seen."

Paul Taylor interrupted the discussion. "I think the Sergeant is hiding her light under a bushel Mr Finnegan. Mhairi here was a qualified mountain guide before she joined the police. Climbed and hiked all over the world!"

Mhairi blushed at the public praise. "Yes, as Mr Taylor says, I was a mountain guide and I cut my teeth on the faces of the very mountains and hills that Douglas is roaming around. I will be able to help narrow down the possibilities of where he can and can't be and also how we might get to him and see if we can talk him down."

Blunt as ever, Sergeant Callaghan cut in. "Well, I can tell you now, there'll be no talking down. Douglas is an armed fugitive, a danger and a menace to the general public. If or when he is seen, we will report that sighting and request armed support to initiate the arrest."

Gary cleared his throat and made eye contact with the younger man. "That will be my call to make Sergeant Callaghan and if I have the opportunity to talk the lad out of this mess, I'll be taking it. At this point everything is conjecture; we will know more tomorrow when we speak to the witness. So, until then I suggest we keep an open mind about the possibilities that are open to us and not rule anything out."

The awkward silence confirmed that everyone present had recognised the statement for what it was: a rebuke. Cal felt his cheeks flush as the anger rose in him once again. He turned his face towards the fire and took a drink of his beer. The conversation behind him resumed, the more neutral

133

topic of the effects of the cyber-attack now the focus of the discussion. The young military policeman brooded at his superior's chastisement. *And in front of the policewoman as well!* She was a bit of a looker as far as Callaghan was concerned although she seemed to share old man Finnegan's soft approach to the investigation. *Probably why she was based up here at the edge of the world; basic work for a basic plod.* Still, he wouldn't kick her out of bed for farting. *Fucking Douglas!* Callaghan knew this case was consuming him, always in his thoughts and even his dreams. He knew a lot of it stemmed from his hatred of marines, or bootnecks as they were usually referred to.

When he was a young Lance Corporal, Cal had fancied one of the girls from SIB, the military police's Special Investigation Branch. She was only an admin clerk but very pretty and seemed to have a good sense of humour. He was shy around girls but used each and every opportunity to speak to her and get to know her better. He had been ready to ask her out anyway when he was invited to a social evening with the office staff. He had seen it as perfect timing, Diana would be there and he could exploit the occasion to get her on her own then ask her out. As luck would have it there was a small group of Royal Marines in the pub, tanned and fit from whatever tour of duty they had recently returned from. Cal had seen the immediate interest from the girls as they squeezed past the bar and the group of marines.

As the night progressed, he'd found it difficult to get any time alone with Diana as she remained within a group of the girls and he couldn't think of a way to approach her that would look natural. Then it happened. One of the marines returning from the toilet stopped and spoke to the girls and had them laughing within minutes. Cal had been furious at the sheer arrogance of the marine. To add insult to injury he had watched as the marine called over his friends and introduced them to the girls. Throughout the night Cal had seethed and drank hard, seeking solace in the numbing effect of the alcohol. He had watched as the barriers between the marines and the girls had dropped with arms around waists and heads leaning on shoulders. The little group had been getting louder as they became drunk and the marines' stories more outrageous. Cal's teeth had been on edge as he'd watched Diana howling with laughter, her hand on the muscled arm of the marine telling the funny tale. Without warning one of the marines had dropped his trousers and shown his buttocks to the group, showing them a tattoo of some description. The group had been roaring with laughter at whatever the tattoo signified.

But Cal hadn't laughed. Lance Corporal Callaghan of the Royal Military Police had marched over to the group, barged into the middle of them and produced his warrant card. He had delivered his rank, name and position in a loud, confident voice and demanded to see the identity card of the marine who had just exposed himself to members of the public. There had been a shocked silence until one of the marines had shoved him hard in the chest and told him to fuck off. Incensed with rage, Cal had pushed his way back into the group and informed the marine that he was under arrest for assault. Cal had woken up in the early hours of the morning in the barracks' medical centre with a broken jaw. For the next few days he had attempted to gather evidence on the marine who had assaulted him but had been met by a wall of silence from his colleagues. None of them had seen anything. The pub did not have cameras installed. Other than his aching jaw, there was nothing to indicate that anything had happened. In a fury he had confronted Diana in the car park one afternoon as she was heading out of the base. At first, she had stuck to her story of not seeing anything but then had lost her temper, letting fly at him with a tirade of abuse. The names had been nothing he had not been called before: jobs-worth, war-dodger, back-stabber, fake policeman. But the venom in which they had been delivered and the fact they had come from a girl he had really liked had been what hurt.

Around six months after his assault he had been walking down Colchester high street when he had noticed a familiar face; Diana. As some time had passed between the incident and he had not seen her for a couple of months, he had started to cross the road to speak to her. He stopped short when he saw the tall athletic figure approach then hug and kiss her. The marine. The same one who had pushed him then knocked him out in front of his friends and colleagues. He and Diana were obviously a couple. Cal remembered the feeling of helplessness that had assailed him that afternoon. There was simply nothing that he could do but watch them walk away, arms around each other and laughing as they made their way through the crowded street. Over the years he had come to nurture his hatred of marines. Their arrogance, elitism, lack of respect for law and order. He truly hated them. That was why bringing Sergeant Finn Douglas to a court-martial was becoming an obsession for the military policeman, to show the marines that no one is above the law.

Rory Starkey, Gary Finnegan and Mhairi had found unlikely common ground in that they had all, at some point in their lives, been in the mountains of the Hindu Kush; Rory covering snow leopards, Mhairi ascending virgin peaks and Gary fighting the Taliban. The Taylor's contributed to the discussion with tales of their ancestors rubbing shoulders with Kipling in the very same part of the world. The conversation continued to meander through general topics of interest, becoming more humorous as the drink flowed. Mhairi noted however that the younger military policeman remained isolated from the group, sipping his beer and staring into the fire. Feeling sorry for him she excused herself and joined him by the fire nudging him out of his reverie.

"Why so serious Sergeant? It's not the end of the world yet as far as I'm aware!"

Cal turned to the woman and smiled back. "Sorry, just get a bit upset when people don't see Douglas for what he is."

"And what is he Sergeant Callaghan?"

"Well...it's obvious isn't it? He's an armed individual who is AWOL from his duties and needs to be treated as such."

Mhairi circled the rim of her glass with her finger, looking down at the deep red of her merlot. "Yes, that's true. But don't you think he's been through a lot? That maybe he's just going through a bad patch and needs help rather than incarceration?"

"No, I do not! He's a criminal who has committed several crimes and is evading the efforts of the authorities to bring him to justice. He's not some bloody folk hero. Next you'll be writing songs about him like your bloody Robert the Bruce and William Wallace!"

Mhairi felt the anger rise to her face at the young man's patronising attitude but she fought it back and tried to lift the mood a little. "No, I obviously don't think that, nobody does. But you have to admit, he is a bit of a handsome devil!" She punctuated the last sentence with a wink and a gentle nudge of the man's arm, hoping for a smile or at least a release of the tension.

To her horror the military policeman thrust his face into hers and hissed.

"Handsome, is he? We'll see how handsome he is when I've got trained trackers and marksmen hunting him down. Why am I the only one who sees this guy for what he is? A bloody criminal dodging his responsibilities to return to war! A criminal. End of story"

Cal paused for breath and drew back a little, surprised to find himself in the policewoman's personal space. He looked around and realised that he must have raised his voice as the room was silent and all eyes were upon him. He thumped his glass down on a table and strode towards the door. "It's getting late so I'll say goodnight and see you all for breakfast." No one replied to him and he stomped up the staircase towards his room, their silence a ringing endorsement of his isolation in this investigation.

Sitting on the end of his bed he opened his bag to get his wash kit. Putting it to one side he pulled out the Sig Sauer P229 pistol and stood up as he checked the weapon remained unloaded. He picked a spot on the wall and punched the weapon out seeing not the faded fleur-de-lys of a wallpaper pattern but the face of the fugitive Finn Douglas. He imagined the shock and surprise on Douglas' face and pulled the trigger. The dry click of the hammer striking the pin was loud in the stillness of the room and Cal lowered the weapon, his fantasy consigned to memory. This was how Sergeant Finn Douglas Royal Marines should be brought to justice and this was how he would be if Cal got his chance. Smiling, he returned the weapon to his bag and hummed a quiet tune as he went about his ablutions.

21

Finn rubbed his stomach and moaned with contentment at his feeling of being full. The potatoes and carrots old Angus had given him had been the perfect supplement to his venison stew. He relaxed back in his car-seat chair and drank some of the coffee the old man had insisted he take. Quite a sharp cookie for an old fella, Finn reflected. He had seen that Finn could obviously take care of himself but had identified he would be appreciative of some small luxuries; potatoes, carrots, turnip, coffee, sugar, oatmeal, honey and a bottle of some home-made hooch that made Finn's eyes water.

Finn had insisted on helping Angus back to his croft. He had wrapped the dead dog in the unconscious man's groundsheet and carried it back for the old man. When they arrived at the croft Finn had asked for a shovel and the old man procured one from a whitewashed stone shed. A raise of the eyebrows had been all that Finn needed to do before Angus pointed to a small grassy area beside a bench. The old man had gone into the croft as Finn had carried out the burial of his animal, returning only once the dog was at rest beneath the dark, peaty earth. Angus had passed Finn the pillowcase bulging with misshapen lumps and had told him that it was some simple foodstuffs to help him out.

The old man had started to say that he would not tell anyone about what had happened but Finn had cut him short. He had impressed upon Angus that it was essential the old man called the authorities and let them know what had occurred. They needed to be aware that there were armed criminals on the islands who were prepared to kill to carry out their activities. The old man had eventually agreed to this but wanted Finn to stay with him, to give himself up when the police came. He reasoned that no matter what Finn had done, surely his actions this day would go well for him? He had appreciated the old man's sentiment but let him know he could not go back, that there was nothing for him back there. Angus had relented and began discussing elaborate measures to mask Finn's location. Finn had pointed out that if the Police arrived with dogs they would pick up on his trail and see that the old man had been lying. Finn had convinced Angus to tell the entire truth to whoever turned up, regardless of who they were or what they brought with them. Ensuring that he had been understood and that the old man was steady on his feet, Finn had said his goodbyes and left, heading north to lay a false trail before breaking east and south again, back to the wooded slopes of his home.

He paused for a break in the shadow of Ben Tarbert and looked through the rifle's telescopic sight at Angus' croft. There was some smoke drifting from the chimney and he watched, curious as the old man pushed an empty rowboat out into the bay. Finn chuckled to himself, guessing that it was some ploy by Angus to mask Finn's movements. He thought about the man who had attacked Angus and killed his dog. Finn had been watching the old man for some time, having descended from the higher ground after watching the wolves hunting. He had been curious as to what Angus was doing but soon identified that he was tracking something. It was then Finn had noticed a second man, alone and concealed on the other side of the abandoned road. As Finn studied this man and the area around him, he had spotted the carbine. He had known instinctively that something was amiss, the weapon completely wrong for anything other than killing. Finn had also seen that the old man and the other were not together and that the old man was following the other man's trail.

He had scrambled as fast as he could through the saplings and bushes while attempting to make as little noise as possible. Finn knew that when the old man reached the end of the trail things were not going to end well for him. When he reached the periphery of the clearing, Finn was just dropping off his pack as the stranger killed the dog. Swift and efficient, the man was no stranger to killing. Finn had used the distraction of the old man's arrival to cover the open ground before the stranger could react. He'd made it just before the old man's throat was cut and dispatched the stranger by smashing the rifle butt into his knee then the side of his head. Finn hadn't killed him but the stranger would be out of action for some time to come. He had also taken the carbine, which now lay propped against the stone wall of the cottage, the malevolent black sheen reflecting a soft orange from the glow of the fire.

Finn took the dishes outside and washed them in the lean-to, leaving them on the side of the wood bunker. The night was crystal clear again and cold. A hard frost would cover the earth by morning. As he turned to enter the cottage a sound interrupted his thoughts and the hairs on his arms and the back of his neck rose in response. The howl was clear and plaintive in the still of the evening, long and loud then tapering off into a gradual dissipation until silence was restored. Finn hadn't been aware that he was holding his breath until the howl had stopped and he exhaled. He turned to face the dark forest and wondered how far away the animals were. Another howl split the quiet, this time from further to the south. A chorus of several others joined it. The wolves communicated in this way for the best part of an hour, the gaps between each chorus getting longer and fainter until they ceased completely.

Finn was freezing but buoyed with excitement. He spoke, his breaths small white clouds against the black of the night.

Did you hear that Katy? They're here. Your wolves are here. I think that was two different packs, what do you reckon? The Freya pack and the Spean pack isn't it? What do you think they were saying? That was so amazing Katy. Your wolves, howling in the night,

143

just like wolves must have done hundreds of years ago all over Britain. You were right sis; this is the most amazing place in the world. Thank you for showing it to me. Okay, I'm freezing out here so I'm going to go in and get some sleep. I'm going to look for your wolves again tomorrow, follow those howls, and see if I can locate the pack. Night little sister, love you loads.

22

André was finding it hard to keep his contempt for Jamie showing through. As the small boat rode the undulating Atlantic rollers, the injured man groaned every time the slightest bump reverberated from the hull. It was still dark but the light of dawn was creeping over the eastern horizon casting the hills and the mountains of the islands behind them in sharp silhouette. André was also absolutely freezing cold. The temperature had plummeted through the evening and although the three men were fine in their cave, they had all felt the cold as soon as they made their way outside. Sandy had helped Jamie to the pick-up point while André had retrieved the boat. André had faked several calls to the boat captain to maintain the lie and keep Jamie and Sandy relaxed. While they weren't exactly close friends, André was unsure how Sandy would react and so could not trust the man to support his decision.

André had concealed ropes, nets and some heavy stones under the tarpaulin at the bow of the inflatable. He would use these to weigh the idiot's body down when he tossed it overboard. When they had arrived at the pick-up point, he had ordered Sandy to go back and break camp, pack everything up in preparation for moving on. They would be heading west and south, looking for any tracks they could pick up to identify where the wolves would be. Jamie had given them some helpful hints on tracking, luring and capturing the animals in his absence and André was convinced that he and Sandy could still achieve their aim.

André steered the vessel around a small headland, which he had previously identified on the map as being suitable for his needs. He cut the throttle back and allowed the boat to idle, the world silent save for the quiet rhythm of the engine. Jamie looked round at him in surprise and André pointed out to sea.

"Keep your eyes peeled. The captain's going to give a couple of flashes when he's in position."

Jamie nodded and turned to face the open ocean, peering through the dim light. André picked up the plastic bottle.

"Want a drink Jamie?"

Jamie nodded and gave the thumbs up to his colleague behind him. He felt the boat shift beneath him as André approached and heard the top being unscrewed from the bottle. The gunshot, while loud in the confines of the small craft, did not carry too far, André's use of the plastic bottle as a makeshift suppressor limiting the sound that the gun emitted. Jamie's head slumped at an awkward angle against the bow; the small entry wound oozing viscous blood that trickled through his hair. André worked fast, positioning the body so that the head and torso hung over the side of the boat, the blood running into the water rather than into the boat itself. He uncovered the ropes and nets and tied them around the corpse, leaving open pockets in the netting. He filled these pockets with the stones then secured them with smaller lengths of rope; testing the integrity of the macabre shroud once he had finished. Satisfied with his efforts he took a final look around him to ensure there was no reaction from landside. He knelt on the deck of the boat, slipped his arm under the legs of the body and scooped upwards. Jamie's net-wrapped, weighted corpse slid into the black water with barely a sound. André stood and watched as the body sank, slower than he would have imagined, bubbles streaming from the mouth, nose and exit wound as the sea claimed the corpse for itself.

André turned the boat around and increased the throttle, making his way back to land. He was pleased that all had gone well with his plan; he had got rid of an idiot who had threatened their whole enterprise with no fuss or trouble. And the remaining partnership would get a better pay-out, there being two and not three individuals for the final split. This fact cheered the South African somewhat but did not warm him any and he spent the remainder of the journey back to the drop-off point hunched over, hands thrust deep into his pockets and neck buried in his jacket. *Fucking Scotland!* He'd never take another job here again, no matter how well paid.

High on the slopes of the Ben, Finn watched the boat and its occupant. He had been too far away and the light too low to see any detail but it had looked suspicious. Angus had told him that there was only another old man who lived down this part of the islands and Finn had at least identified that the man standing on the boat was lean and tall, lithe movements eliminating the possibility that it was an old man. Unsure exactly as to what he had seen, Finn committed the location to memory and continued his way along the ridgeline, the morning sun lighting the way before him.

23

This place is stunning, Gary Finnegan thought to himself as they journeyed south past the smaller island of Benbecula. The early morning sun cast everything in a warm, golden glow that belied the freezing temperatures outside. Gary, Cal and Mhairi were following the Taylors and Rory, both groups in the comfortable Range Rovers the estate usually provided for well-heeled wildlife enthusiasts. Mhairi was driving and had kept the military policemen informed with a running commentary of the land, lochs and mountains they were passing. The road itself was really a road in name only, reclaimed by the grasses and ferns of nature. When Sergeant Callaghan had mentioned this Mhairi explained that the Taylors had re-wilded all aspects of the islands, and that included letting the access roads run to little more than passable tracks.

They'd each packed rucksacks of warm clothes, waterproofs and emergency equipment. The plan was to interview the old man and start looking for any trace of Sergeant Douglas based on that information. The Taylors had arranged for Angus to open up the bunkhouse for the three police officers and they would base their operation from there, returning in the evenings. The Taylors had provided them with a mountain of food and drinks to sustain them, which Gary had joked, made them look like they were preparing to climb Everest.

A movement beside some trees caught his eye and Gary pointed as a herd of red deer burst into the treeline seeking cover. Mhairi nodded.

"They're down off the hill tops because of the snow and the cold. You see how they ran from the sight of us just then? That's the wolves that have done that. Before they came the deer wouldn't bat an eyelid at people or cars. At anything really. When the wolves were reintroduced and the deer were being hunted, they remembered their place in the food chain and started acting like deer again."

"That's incredible Mhairi. I never thought of that before but I remember being near Fort William years ago and seeing people feeding deer from their cars."

"Yes, I've seen that myself. But that's not the only thing the wolves have changed; the whole ecosystem has been affected. The deer population are managed through natural predation, the saplings and shoots that the deer used to clear now grow to trees and stabilise the land, consequently there is less erosion as these now act as a wind barrier. It's called trophic cascade, where the introduction of apex predators has a beneficial effect right the way through the entire ecosystem. I'm not an expert on it but I'm sure the Taylor's could fill you in on all the details if you are interested."

Gary nodded in appreciation and continued the journey in silence, the beauty of these incredible islands dominating his thoughts. His eyes were drawn in different directions, as each location seemed to compete for his attention. A beach that would not have looked out of place in the Caribbean, a forest of ancient pines, a rocky outcrop dusted with snow, a golden eagle alighting from an old fencepost.

In the back seat Sergeant Callaghan was also quiet, sullen after his talking to earlier that morning. Gary had taken the Sergeant to one side after breakfast and informed him that if he couldn't behave like a professional then the Warrant Officer would have him removed from the investigation. The Sergeant had mumbled a vague apology and something about the beer going to his head. By then it had been time to leave and Gary had dropped the matter, taking his junior colleague at his word.

Cal couldn't wait for the interview to be done and the hunt for Douglas to begin. He only wished that he could be present at the interview, not convinced that Warrant Officer Finnegan and the policewoman were up to the task. Still, they would brief him on everything they got and at the very least, they were close to Douglas now, Cal could feel it. Without realising it his hand drifted to his side and he stroked the holstered pistol absent-mindedly as he looked forward to the day's progress. A rare smile broke across his face and he leaned forward.

"It's absolutely beautiful here, isn't it?"

The wisp of smoke drifting from the chimney of the whitewashed croft gave the only sign of human habitation. Gary watched as the leading vehicle pulled into a clear grassy area beside the dwelling. As their own vehicle slowed to a halt, the military policeman saw that the house was located in a spot of outstanding beauty. To their front was a small sandy beach bordered by rocky headlands that harnessed the clear blue waters and behind them the trees thickened as they rose towards the higher ground and became forests. As they approached the house Gary saw that it had a thatched roof, netted and weighed down with heavy stones looped on the ends of rope. Mhairi saw his puzzlement and smiled.

"We have winds the like of which you wouldn't believe up here, easily take the roof from a croft if it wasn't held down."

Paul Taylor had just reached the door when it opened before him and Gary watched as an old man greeted the Taylors, shaking hands with the pair. Paul introduced them.

"Angus, this is Mhairi Stewart, a police officer from Stornoway and Gary Finnegan, a Military Policeman who is leading the investigation." Taking turns to shake hands with the old man, Gary noted that in spite of his advanced years, his grip was strong. Angus beckoned them to follow him inside. Fiona Taylor stated her intention to check that the bunkhouse was fit for habitation and left the small group to attend to this. Gary turned to Sergeant Callaghan who was stood next to the journalist.

"We shouldn't be too long Sergeant so why don't you use the time to help Mrs Taylor get our stuff into the bunkhouse. Check the comms work okay and start having a good look through the mapping, see if you can narrow down any areas Sergeant Douglas might have gone to ground in." Seeing his subordinate nod in acceptance Gary stepped into the house, closing the door behind him. Several lamps that sputtered occasionally illuminated the small interior and there was limited seating, a small sofa and one chair. A fire warmed the room and the group waited in silence until Angus returned carrying a tray with a teapot and cups. Gary noted that the old man was also steady on his feet and there was no sign of any shaking or imbalance that he associated with most eighty-year old men. Angus told them to sit, his voice a soft, almost musical lilt. Gary was fascinated by the accent; the old man seemed to pronounce the letter b as a *p* and e as an *ei* sound, adding further to the soft brogue. He remained standing, allowing Angus, Paul and Mhairi to take the seats and watched as the old man poured the tea; again, hands steady not spilling a drop. Gary also studied the scar across Angus' head, an angry red line of swollen flesh locked together with a line of stitches. He was impressed with the handiwork.

As they had agreed in the car, Mhairi spoke first, introducing who they were once again and explaining the reasons why they were there. They had decided that Mhairi would concentrate on the assault and the poachers and Gary would take the lead on the Douglas aspect. Mhairi finished her delivery by asking Angus in his own words to run through what had happened. In the quiet of the warm room the old man settled back in his chair and in his singsong voice recounted the incident for them. As he spoke Gary and Mhairi scribbled occasionally in their respective notebooks but otherwise did not interrupt. Having never worked with Mhairi before, Gary was pleased to see that she knew how to interview a witness. You always asked the witness to tell the story in their own words first, never interrupting but making notes about the points you wanted to follow up on. Once they'd finished, the investigator would then question the witness in detail using the notes they had taken. Lastly, a good investigator would read back all the information to the witness in a summary, ensuring that they had all the relevant and correct information from the witness. This essentially gave the investigator three opportunities to gain the information as well as comparing versions to pick out lies or inaccuracies. Gary listened and nodded approval as Mhairi went through the whole procedure, thorough but without making it sound like an interrogation. Gary had just finished the sweet tea when Mhairi addressed him.

"Warrant Officer Finnegan, I'm quite happy with everything I have at this point. Would you like to ask Angus your questions about Sergeant Douglas now?"

Gary thanked her and addressed Angus directly. "Angus, I've been making some notes here while you were talking to

154

Sergeant Stewart so I'd just like to jump straight in there if that's okay with you?"

The old man nodded and shifted slightly in his chair. "Please Mr Finnegan, go on ahead."

For ten minutes or so, Gary questioned the crofter on every aspect of Finn Douglas that he could think of. What direction had he come from, what was he wearing, what was he carrying, what did he talk to Angus about, where did he say he was going, which direction did he go when he left. Even as he was concluding his interview, the military policeman was aware that the old man was not unsympathetic to Finn's plight. Gary asked if there was anything else he could think of that would help them find Finn. Angus stroked his beard and shook his head before looking up quickly at the soldier. "Oh yes! He has another gun you know. A rifle of some sort that he lifted from that brute who was going to kill me."

Gary raised his eyebrows. "Do you know what kind of gun?"

"I would say it looked like one of those American M16 jobs, but shorter and fancier if you know what I mean."

"Did you see if this weapon had any bullets with it?"

"Oh yes; there was a magazine attached when the lad took it." Seeing the military policeman's raised eyebrow, the old man chuckled and explained. "I wasn't always the old geriatric you see before you Mr Finnegan, I was once a soldier myself. Korea, Borneo, Aden, Cyprus."

Gary could see now why the old man had taken a shine to Douglas. He looked at his notes and at the final point he had underlined. "One last thing please Angus. Tell me more about the missing boat."

Leaving the croft, they blinked in the bright sunlight, a direct contrast from the small, dim room they had spent the past hour in. Paul Taylor remained in the doorway talking to Angus about getting him to a hospital and Gary grinned as he heard the old man shushing the landowner's concerns. He might be eighty but the old crofter was still as tough as they came. In silence, Gary and Mhairi walked to the beach where they stood for several moments looking at the groove marks in the sand where the old man's boat had been. Gary pointed towards the tip of the headland. "So, Douglas takes the boat and rounds the point there heading north. To where? There didn't look to be a whole lot of cover up that way when we drove past it earlier."

Mhairi stooped, picked up a stone and skimmed it across the smooth surface of the sea. "There's only really the sand and the *machair* all the way up to Hornish point."

"The *machair*?"

"Yes, the grassy coastal plain that extends north of here."

"That's pretty much what I thought. Why the hell would he risk the exposure?"

The policewoman smiled and barged him playfully with her shoulder. "Come on Warrant Officer Finnegan, you didn't fall for that tripe back there did you?"

Gary turned to face her, surprise giving him a comical countenance that caused Mhairi to chuckle. Gary shook his head. "What do you mean? The old man was lying? No. Absolutely not. Everything he said tallies up."

Mhairi threw another stone and walked slowly towards the rocky headland, waiting for the military man to catch up before explaining. "The whole way through that interview, Angus was still, hands folded over each other, calm and confident. The minute you drilled down into Douglas taking the boat he became animated, motioning with his hands, pointing north. A big change in his manner."

Gary thought back to the interview and realised that Mhairi was right. Gary had noticed it himself but had not assigned the same significance to it that the policewoman had. He looked at her as she continued.

"And after everything he told us about Douglas and how he couldn't kill the poacher, how he walked Angus home, buried Angus' dog, you don't think it's out of character that he would steal the crofter's boat? Leave old Angus unable to take the crabs and lobsters from his creels?"

"Well, I'll be..." He was cut off by Mhairi's laughter.

"Don't feel bad Gary. I've known these islands and their people all my life and it's a lot easier for me to spot these little inconsistencies. Right, keep up, there's something I want to check." They opened up their pace as they strode across the grass covered headland and scrambled up a large rock at the highest point. They were looking north along a sandy beach that curved all the way to another headland in the distance. Mhairi took off her pack and pulled out a pair of binoculars. She had scanned the area for only a minute when she gave a small exclamation of triumph. She handed the binoculars to Gary. "About three-quarters of the way up, just beyond the darker vegetation."

Gary took the glasses and swept the beach before him, zoning in on the area his colleague had indicated. He saw it at once: A boat. A wooden rowboat canted slightly to one side. Stunned, the military policeman lowered the binoculars and turned to his companion. "You don't think..."

"There was a very high tide last night but no real swell. My guess is the old man shoved that boat out on the outgoing tide well aware that it would drift north in the prevailing currents. Angus would know the boat would more than likely come ashore before Hornish Point on a calm sea."

Gary threw his head back and laughed. "The sly old bugger! Well, I certainly suspected that he had sympathy for Douglas and I would say this confirms it."

"Yes, I would have to agree. Now, daylight's wasting so let's get back and start this search while the trail is warm."

24

André had heard the sound of vehicles that morning but couldn't see them from the depths of the forest. He had to assume that they were responding to Jamie's attack on the old man and that, as such, he and Sandy would have to be extra vigilant from now on. Sandy had made only the briefest of enquiries over Jamie's return to the boat so André had not needed to construct any elaborate narrative to cover his actions.

And they had just had a big break: A crumbling bank of peaty earth at the side of a stream had given them their first signs of the wolves. Deep tracks, the pads and claws of adults and the small, more rounded prints of the cubs. Both men agreed that the tracks were very fresh, as they had not hardened in the overnight frost. André could feel the excitement of the hunt now. This was how he felt when they were getting to the crux of the mission. He remembered the same feeling when infiltrating Angola, assassinating guerrilla leaders in their own villages. Or the covert work in Guinea and Nigeria. The buzz was addictive, that heady mix of adrenaline and anticipation, blacked-up and armed to the teeth in some god-forsaken third world shithole. He missed those days badly, was not adjusting well to a life of retirement. Even though this job contained few of the risks he had faced on other missions, the buzz was back as he could feel them getting closer to the capture of the wolves.

They'd moved camp to the depths of the woods, well away from the area they had found the tracks in order not to spook the animals and scare them from the region entirely. Jamie had told them that the wolves would not take the cubs far from the den until they were around eight weeks old, when they would move with members of the pack to a rendezvous site. This apparently was an area where adults would guard the pups while the remainder of the pack hunted nearby. Both André and Sandy agreed from the tracks that they had found that the wolves' rendezvous site was somewhere nearby. Sandy had left André to set up camp while he retrieved the cached cages and other equipment and brought them to the new location.

André's plan was to get to the high ground and watch the area where they had found the tracks. They would attempt to identify the wolves' den by tracking their movements through the optics first of all then close in on foot for confirmation. After that they would come up with a plan that would allow them to get close enough to hit the cubs with the tranq darts. The guns were top of the range and could be relied on to hit a target at around fifty metres and the drugs would have the little animals out cold in just over a minute. All this was difficult enough but they would also have to keep an eye out for any police who had been dispatched to investigate the attack on the old man.

On Sandy's return they concealed the equipment under bushes and ferns in the unlikely event that anyone wandering through the area might see the kit. After a quick snack of cold bacon and beans, the pair made their way through the forest and on to the higher slopes of the area. They moved in silence, a small distance between each other, scrutinising the ground they traversed for signs of animal or human. André halted them at the edge of the treeline and pointed down into the lower ground below them. Sandy nodded agreement; from here they had a direct line of sight to the area where they had found the prints. André shrugged off the backpack while Sandy moved further back into the woods and began cutting some of the lower branches from the pines. As André set up the spotting scope, Sandy constructed the observation post, lining the ground with the branches before laying down the insulating mats on top. No words were needed, both men well familiar with the routine.

André gave the post a once-over but was happy with Sandy's work. He put the spotting scope on the low tripod and set it in place. He lay down behind it on his stomach and adjusted the focus until he was satisfied. Sitting up, he rummaged through his pack and pulled on a thick down jacket over his lighter one. Ramming a black woollen hat over his head he held up a finger to Sandy who nodded his understanding. They would take a one-hour stint at the scope; one watching while the other rested and listened for signs of any activity around them.

Settling behind the scope, André swept the optic slowly from left to right, looking at the stream and woods just over twelve hundred metres away. Nothing yet, but then he had not expected anything so soon. If they were right and they had identified a rendezvous site, then either today or tomorrow the wolves would return.

André had also not forgotten about the mystery man who had taken Jamie down. *Who the hell was he and what was his agenda on the island?* One thing André was sure of however and that was if he got any opportunity to find this stranger the wolves could wait. He wanted his bloody carbine back and to teach the stranger a lesson in minding his own business. A very permanent lesson.

25

With everyone so busy setting up the bunkhouse for the search operation, Rory Starkey had taken the opportunity to walk with the old man as he pottered around the outbuildings of the croft. Colleagues had often told Rory over the years that he was wasted as a wildlife correspondent, with his gift for getting people onside he should have been a *proper* reporter. Rory always smiled at the unintentional insult, but truth be told he'd never felt the urge to do the whole reportage thing. The best reporting inevitably came from elements of human misery; war, famine, disaster, terrorism, scandal, all areas that he was happy to steer well clear of. Nature was his love and he was fortunate enough to have been able to make a living from his one true passion. But he did have a knack for getting on with people, had never really had to work hard to get someone on record regardless of how difficult they were reputed to be. It wasn't something deliberate or anything that he could quantify but he'd always had it.

He handed the old man a hammer that he saw he would need to knock the ice from the stack of creels stood against the stone shed. The old man mumbled his thanks and knocked the ice from the concrete lumps within the netted traps. Without being asked, Rory worked alongside the crofter, moving the cleared creels and handing up the ones yet to be. Over the space of a half hour or so Rory learned a lot about Finn Douglas. He also learned that the old man had spoken to the marine a lot more than he had let on to the police officers. Once the creels had been done the pair moved back to the house where the old man put on a jacket, hat and gloves. He regarded the journalist for a moment seeming to make up his mind about something. "If you've the inclination you could walk with me along the *machair* towards Hornish Point."

"Sounds good. What are you doing there?"

"Well, there's a small chance that Sergeant Douglas may have beached the boat up there when he went his merry way."

Rory could see the undisguised twinkle in the old man's eyes as he spoke and found himself smiling. "Sure, why not. I'll just let the others know where I'm going."

The old man took the reporter's arm and guided him instead towards the outbuilding on the far side of his plot. "Ah now, there isn't really the need for that is there? They're all terribly busy with getting their operation up and running. Besides, then we'd have to explain how Sergeant Douglas got a boat all the way up to Hornish Point when you and I are carrying the only oars for the vessel."

Rory's mouth opened in shock before he laughed aloud at the old man's audacity. He watched as Angus reached up into the rafters of the shed and slid out a wooden oar then handed it to Rory. "Quiet now man. I know the law is worn without a tie in these parts but telling tales to the *Polis* is quite another thing entirely."

Rory shook his head and grinned, placing the oar on his shoulder and following Angus who was now carrying his own oar, behind the shed and into the long grass of the *machair* beyond. Looking back, he could see that they were out of sight from the group at the bunkhouse, yet another indication that the old man was as sharp as ever.

Mhairi, Gary and Cal stood beside the vehicles, their backpacks on with Mhairi tracing a route on the map with her finger, showing the military policemen her plan. "Okay, this is where Angus was attacked and the easiest way to get to it is using this old trail. I don't want to use the vehicles because if anyone is still in the area, they'll hear us coming for miles. We've each got a radio and you two are armed but I think we should stay together until we get to the location then fan out from there, see if we can pick up a trail."

Gary and Cal nodded, the priority to identify whether Angus' attacker was still in the area taking precedence over finding Douglas, though, as Mhairi pointed out, they would be looking in the same areas. Paul and Fiona remained behind, Paul getting the wood burner up and running and Fiona sorting out the kitchen area and food. The trio set off, following Mhari's lead and were soon among the young trees that heralded the beginning of the forests. It was a still day and the going relatively easy due to frost-hardened ground. Birdsong accompanied them as they progressed through the undulating woodland, crossed small streams and skirted boggy areas.

After some time Mhairi stopped and drew them in closer. "You see that deadfall lying on its side? Just past that is the clearing that Angus was talking about. The road is down to our right so if you get disoriented just head west, the sun on your left cheek, and you'll hit that okay?" The men nodded and Gary indicated the radio fitted to his jacket.

"Shall we dial down the volume on these now?"

Mhairi replied. "Yes, keep communications to a minimum unless we find something then let everybody know." With that, the policewoman stood and indicated with her hand that she was going straight ahead. Gary pointed to her right and looked at Sergeant Callaghan who nodded and with his own hand pointed to his sector to the left of the Mhairi. One by one the search party melted into the trees and out of sight of each other.

It didn't take Mhairi long to find the site of the attack. The grass remained flattened in the area and the dark areas on the ground she knew were blood. She called the others on the radio and they arrived within minutes. Without the need for words, each of them spread out from the centre of the clearing and examined the ground for any evidence they could find. Other than the bent and flattened foliage, Gary and Cal found nothing to indicate where the poacher had gone. Mhairi again called them on the radio and both men backtracked to her position. In a gloved hand she held up an object for them to see. A knife. Gary spoke. "That's a serious blade, a fighting knife. A Cold Steel Black Bear if I'm not mistaken." Seeing Sergeant Callaghan's raised eyebrows, the older man continued. "I once had a weapons nut from 2 Para I locked up for GBH and found one of those among his arsenal."

Mhairi pulled an evidence bag from her jacket pocket and placed the blade inside, taking care not to puncture the receptacle. "This is what he used to kill the dog and smack old Angus with. What are your thoughts gents? Would you consider this a typical poacher's knife?"

"I don't know about Sergeant Callaghan here but I would have to say no. There are far better knives on the market for butchering or dressing animals. That is a Tac knife; a tactical weapon, and not cheap either, that's a few hundred pounds for that model." Gary looked over at Sergeant Callaghan who was nodding his agreement.

"Yep. Must say I agree with the boss on this one. A typical poacher wouldn't spend the money on that when he could pick up a more appropriate knife in any Tesco or Asda."

Gary sighed. "Unfortunately, Mhairi, I've got to say that this, coupled with Angus' description of an assault rifle, puts these guys well outside the description of any poaching job that I'm aware of."

"Yes, I was thinking the same thing myself. But if they're not poachers then what are they? What do they want and more importantly, are they still here?"

Looking around them Gary pointed towards the direction of the road. "The main signs of activity into the clearing seem to come from there. It looks to me like whoever was here came in and out that way."

Mhairi nodded. "We know from Angus that he came in that way following the poacher's trail and that Finn took him back out the same way. Stands to reason that the poacher or poachers did the same. Let's follow that out and see if we can pick anything else up on the way back to the road." The group moved off again, three abreast and within touching distance as they followed the trail of crushed ferns and bushes along an old track. Other than the trail they were following, they discovered nothing else of significance and found themselves back on the old tarmac road.

Gary sniffed loudly, the difference between his body temperature and the cold, clear air causing his nose to run. "What are your thoughts Mhairi?"

The policewoman took a moment before answering, deep in thought as she pondered the question. "I think that after Angus and Sergeant Douglas left the area, at least one other poacher came back and helped the injured one. Think about it: a broken leg and unconscious, or at least a serious concussion. There's no way he got out of here on his own without dragging himself through the woods and if he'd done that, we would have found a lot more signs." She sighed and looked up at the forests and hills above them before turning out to face the sea. "Problem is; they could be anywhere. Even watching us right now. Or they could have been picked up by boat and taken the injured man to hospital."

Gary could feel the chill on his exposed face now that they had stopped moving. "Okay, what do you say we head back down to the bunkhouse, get warm and put all this together?"

"Agreed. I'll use Angus' phone to ring Stornoway and update them with what I have."

Grateful to be moving again, the group followed the road maintaining a brisk pace as they made their way back to the croft and the warm bunkhouse. As the disused thoroughfare curved inland, something caught Cal's eye; sunlight glinting off a reflective object. He almost said something but caught himself in time. *Douglas.* Finn bloody Douglas. He felt the excitement in his chest. He had just spotted the fugitive, high up among the trees on the side of the Ben. Had he been watching them? Had he seen Cal's face? Was he watching even now, seeing the gleam of excitement in the military policeman's eyes? No matter. Sergeant Callaghan Royal Military Police now had a lead on his man and he was going to get him. And Warrant Officer Finnegan and Sergeant Mhairi bloody Stewart could look for their own leads, Cal had no intention of handing over this information to them. They would only cock it up with their well-intentioned but utterly wrong approach to bringing Finn Douglas to justice. But Cal wouldn't. You could bank on that.

Back in the bunkhouse the three stood by the wood-burning stove, revelling in the warmth, hands wrapped around generous mugs of warm soup, courtesy of Mrs Taylor's efforts. Mhairi nodded to the map pinned on the wall. "Shall we have a look and see what we can come up with for tomorrow. I'm happy if we concentrate on the search for Sergeant Douglas now; I've got no trail or sightings for these poachers so unless something else turns up, we'll put Douglas as the priority."

The two military policemen agreed and the three walked over to the large-scale map, taking a moment to orientate themselves. Gary used the point of his pencil to indicate an area. "Right, his needs are few; food, water and shelter. On top of that he's going to want cover from view, somewhere that he knows he can't be seen from either the road or the occupied crofts." Moving his hand up and down the length of the map he continued with his briefing. "To the north, the forests thin out and he's channelled at Gramsdale unless he's got a boat, which we know now, he doesn't have Angus'." He gave a small smile back to his colleagues. "He did, however, have a kayak and may still have it and that would give him a lot more mobility."

Mhairi spoke. "True, but he'd also be taking a big risk exposing himself like that. While the islands are mostly free from people, there are regular boats and trawlers up and down the coast. A man in a kayak at this time of year would attract attention."

The military policeman considered this for a moment. "Okay. So, let's take it that he remains on land. Based upon the incident with Angus and what we know of the geography, where shall we start?"

Mhairi joined him at the map and drew a large circle over an area. "I think inland from Stoneybridge and up towards Beinn Mhor. There are some serious forests there, lots of water and the high ground behind them. If I was Douglas that's where I would head to first."

Gary agreed and looked to Sergeant Callaghan who nodded in assent. "I agree boss, that area seems to tick all the boxes that Douglas would need."

The older military policeman turned back to the map and studied it in silence for several moments. The area Mhairi had marked made the most sense but he could see from the bunched-together contour lines that there were also some serious ridges and crags on the higher ground. "Right, shall we go firm on heading up there at first light tomorrow? Get a full day to get up there and back before dark?" His companions agreed this was a good plan and gave them time to eat, rest and pack their equipment in readiness for the morning. Mhairi picked up her down jacket and put it on. "That works for me Gary, there's only about four hours of daylight left so we wouldn't achieve much by storming up there now. I'm going to use Angus' phone and update

Stornoway on the progress so far, see if I can beg, borrow or steal some more manpower."

As she left, Gary turned back to the map, familiarising himself with the lines and colours and interpreting these to what they represented on the ground. Sergeant Callaghan joined him and pointed to the area where they had just returned.

"Boss, if you've no objections I'm going to take a wander back up there, take a look around the beaches and see if there's any sign of crafts coming or going. I'm not going far and will be back well before dark."

Gary looked at the younger man in surprise. Callaghan's attitude had improved so much over the course of the day that he was almost a different person. He could only conclude that the threat of removal from the investigation had motivated Callaghan into pulling himself together. Even his deferential use of the term *Boss* was a welcome indication that he respected Gary' position as the lead on this investigation. "Good idea Sergeant, just take one of the radios with you in case you find something of interest or need to get a hold of us."

"No problems Boss, anything comes up I'll get on the blower right away."

Watching the younger policeman walk away, Gary reflected once again on what an about-turn of attitude had come over Callaghan. He was starting to enjoy working with the man for a change. He just hoped that it would last.

Cal waited until he was out of sight of the croft before he started running. With the down jacket and warm clothes he was wearing, it wasn't long until he was hot but he put his discomfort aside and continued with his quick pace. He stopped when he reached the treeline below the area where he had seen the reflected light. Breathing fast, he looked above him for a minute before leaning into the hill and beginning his climb through the woods. He would show Finnegan and Stewart what real police work looked like and couldn't wait to see their faces when he arrived back later with the fugitive in tow. He had no intention of handing him over to either of them however; when he got back, he would use the old man's phone to talk to headquarters directly and appraise them of the situation. The fact that they would be receiving this information from the junior member of the investigation would raise serious questions about Warrant Officer Finnegan's reliability. Questions that Cal himself was well prepared to answer.

He was breathing heavier now as he climbed higher, hands pushing on his thighs as he struggled up the steeper sections. He paused and leaned against a tree, panting with exertion. He knew he wasn't too far away from the location where he had seen the reflected light and reminded himself that Douglas was armed. *Well so am I.* He drew the pistol from his hip holster and cocked the weapon, making it ready. The harsh mechanical action shattered the stillness of the silent forest and he held his breath for a moment, shocked at how loud it had actually been. He remained still for several minutes until he was satisfied that there was no reaction to the sound. Checking that the plastic quick cuffs were open and ready for use, Cal took another glance around him before moving off. He continued moving uphill, slower and with more caution, the black automatic held at waist height and pointing to his front, ready for anything.

He could see through the trees that there was more light ahead and figured that he was approaching the edge of the forest on the northern side. He slowed his pace even further, knowing that Douglas must have been somewhere on that very edge for Cal to have seen the reflection. He rounded the large trunk of a spruce tree and stopped dead in his tracks, heart pounding and adrenaline surging through his body as he processed the sight before him. There, not more than thirty feet from him, was Douglas. The marine was looking out across the open ground, oblivious to Cal's presence. Cal attempted to calm down, convinced his booming heart would betray him. He brought the pistol up into a two-handed grip and advanced on the unsuspecting fugitive with great care and stealth, testing the ground beneath each footfall before placing his weight down on it.

Twenty feet and still Douglas continued to study the area to his front, no sign that he had detected the policeman. Fifteen feet and Cal could see the detail in Douglas' clothing, the stitching on his down jacket, the black gloves on the hand that operated the telescope. Ten feet and Cal felt a buzzing in his ears and a ridiculous sensation of needing to urinate as the excitement and anticipation coursed through him. He registered that there was no sign of a weapon and wondered where the marine had left it. Five feet and Cal halted, steadied himself and prepared for the capture of the marine when a movement beside him distracted him. Spinning towards it he shrieked at the face in front of him just as the man grabbed the pistol and punched him in the stomach. Cal dropped to the ground gasping for breath and unarmed. A boot to the shoulder laid him on his back and he felt the pressure of a foot placed on his chest pinning him down. Looking up, eyes wide in fear he saw a stocky man above him pointing Cal's own gun at him. *Not Douglas.*

As he processed this information another man joined the first and even through his panic-driven thoughts he recognised this individual as the man he had just mistaken for Douglas. This man knelt beside Cal and frisked him in a fast efficient manner, removing the maps, radio and spare magazines for the Sig. He then nodded to the other man who removed his boot from the policeman's chest. The searcher grabbed Cal by the chin and forced his head upwards so he could look him in the eye before speaking.

"Right you little bastard, where's my fucking carbine?"

Stunned by the question and still experiencing the shock of capture, Cal was aware of only two things. That this South African was nothing to do with Douglas and that he was in serious trouble.

26

It was the Spean pack, the smaller of the two groups, that Finn was watching. This was not the same group he had seen previously, as there were no cubs, but it must have been this pack that had initiated the howls last night. Finn lay prone, concealed in a natural hollow between a jumble of snow-dusted rocks. He watched from his high vantage point as the pack meandered through the bracken, heather and low scrub, their long legs covering the distance with deceptive efficiency. Finn couldn't tell which one the pack leader was but he had narrowed it down to two individuals; a big, rangy grey and a darker, almost black wolf. These two seemed to direct the remainder, leading from the front and disciplining the other wolves' infractions with short chases and a snap of their formidable jaws.

The pack slowed to a stop among a small stand of birch trees and seemed to be taking a rest. He watched as the younger ones chased, leaped and wrestled while the older ones were content to rest, lying down among the saplings. Finn could see now that the pair he had thought as leadership contenders were actually a male and female. He remembered Katy telling him that the initial theories about wolves and their social dynamic were all wrong. Finn recalled telling her that he knew all about the alpha male position and joked that half of the marines he worked with could be considered alpha males. A sad smile crossed his face as the memory of her correcting his notion came to him. Yes, she had said, there are alphas in a pack but not the way we are used to thinking. The alphas are actually more like parents than anything else. She had then surprised him with the depth of her knowledge when she explained that all of the previous observations on wolves had been done on packs in captivity. The wolves had been observed in an artificial environment and had not been acting naturally. Finn had been impressed, ruffled her hair and mocked her gently as a 'little professor', which he could see she had been secretly pleased with. She would have been a great naturalist, Finn had no doubt and a lump came to his throat at the thought of her amazing future cut so short.

He concentrated his attention on the wolves, picking out the details of the animals with the rifle's optical sight. The dense coats, the different colours and hues of the fur, the relationship dynamics. He laid the butt of the rifle down and reached into his white smock, pulling a document from a buttoned pocket. Unfolding it he turned several pages before he found what he was looking for: *The Spean pack*. He smiled as he read the names of the individuals and compared the older photos to the wolves as they were today. Lonach was the tall grey male and Borve the dark female and these were the pack leaders. The younger ones were Reiff, Brora and Broch, all born of the same litter.

Returning the pamphlet, Finn felt a sense of connection now that he was able to identify each animal as individuals rather than as part of the collective. He watched as, like any parents, Lonach and Borve observed the antics of the younger wolves, snapping on the odd occasion that the rough and tumble came too close to them.

Finn reflected that he had not felt a peace like this for as far back as he could remember. The action of sitting behind a rifle, concealed from view, he would normally associate with his tours of duty throughout the Middle East, watching insurgents' movements or in preparation for an ambush. Yet here he was, in this incredible place, observing these wonderful animals in their natural environment. Everything had changed for him also; he was sleeping well every night and waking refreshed each day, his feelings of desolation had dissipated to next to nothing but most of all he felt...quiet, at peace with himself and the world. The boy also remained absent from the island. Finn no longer found himself looking for the small figure in the dark corners of the cottage anymore.

He thought back to the incident with the poacher and Angus, the only thing that had interrupted his calm existence out here. He still felt the occasional burst of anger at the thought of the poacher's actions, defiling this place with his greed and violence. Finn knew he was taking it personally but calmed down when he remembered that it been the old man who had been hurt and not him. He hoped that the poacher and his accomplices had left the islands, was sure that they would not have risked exposure and arrest after Finn's intervention. *But then, who had that been in the small boat?* Maybe that had been an element of their withdrawal from the island; a smaller boat ferrying the men out to a larger one perhaps. Finn had not heard any shooting to indicate that there were deer being taken and as such was confident that the criminals had gone. Their C8 Carbine still nagged at him. It was such an unusual weapon for simple poachers to be using. Overkill really unless they weren't very good and were using the 'spray and pray' approach of automatic gunfire to bring the beasts down. Still, they wouldn't be using it again. Finn had wrapped the weapon in some old sacking and stashed it and the magazines among the makeshift rafters of the cottage roof.

The pack was on the move, Lonach and Borve trotting out of the trees and into the open ground. The younger wolves stood still for a moment before dashing out in pursuit of their elders. As Finn watched them lope across the clearing, he saw Borve lower herself to the ground and the others follow suit an instant later. Finn scanned the ground ahead of the wolves and saw the reason for the animals' reaction. Deer; a large herd foraging at the edge of a wood line. Their relaxed posture showed that they had not been alerted to the presence of the predators. Finn could see that there was little or no breeze to carry the scent of the wolves to provide any forewarning to the herd. Turning the scope back to the pack he watched as they moved forward in short increments, hugging the ground to keep their bodies from breaking the skyline and using small re-entrants and ravines to conceal their approach. He marvelled at their stealth and the way they moved as a group without any obvious communication. As they approached a small rise in the ground, Brora and Broch crept down a narrow gully while the remaining three wolves edged into the low bushes that crested the rise. Finn alternated his view between predators and prey and identified eerie comparisons between the wolves' preparation for attack and how he had carried out the same actions when in combat and closing with the enemy. There was a small noise that reached his ears and he turned to the source of it in time to see a huge stag bellowing in the direction of the younger wolves. As if on cue, Brora and Broch exploded from the forest, charging directly at the herd, closing the distance to the deer with ruthless efficiency. The herd panicked at the proximity of the wolves and splintered into three distinct groups, one that turned into the forest to their rear, the other taking the uphill option and the third group bursting through the heather and bracken of the moor. And straight towards Lonach, Borve and Reiff.

This smaller herd crested the rise and were instantly attacked by the waiting wolves. In the chaos and confusion of the ambush, Finn struggled to keep everything contained within the limited field of view that the rifle sight provided. As the animals began to separate, he saw that Lonach had taken down a young stag and was stood over it, tearing at the throat of the struggling beast. Borve was in battle with a hind, the dark wolf locked on to the rear leg and doing her best to avoid the flailing hooves of the terrified deer. Reiff continued to pursue the remainder of the herd but was well behind and soon slowed before turning back to his own group. Brora and Broch re-joined the pack and helped Borve with her struggling hind. Then the killing was over.

The pack relaxed and split themselves between the carcasses of the deer, gorging on the bounty of food. The wolves would snap and growl at each other whenever there was an intrusion to their feeding space and the interloper would back away then return to the feast, tail and ears lowered, to resume eating at a distant part of the carcass. Their faces and ruffs became bloodied as they shoved their heads deep into the deer's' cavities, tearing out intestines, meat and bones. Katy had told Finn that wolves would eat everything from a mouse to a moose and would gorge themselves at a kill to the point where they could hardly move after eating. This seemed to be what Finn was witnessing now as the hours went by and the predators continued to devour the deer. Feeling the cold now, Finn decided to call it a day. He collapsed the bipod legs of the rifle and crept slowly backwards until he was happy that he was well below the skyline. He stood, picked up his pack and began making his way off the hill, his legs a little unsteady at first from the hours of lying down. He looked at the sun starting its slow descent into the Atlantic, a burning orb in a clear sky. The sea itself was taking on the deep orange of the setting sun and Finn marvelled once again at the beauty of these islands.

Entering the forest, he stopped at the stream to fill his water bottles. It was dark in the woods with the last of the sun's light bringing only a dim glow through the trees. He made his way down to his small cottage and cursed his lack of judgement. It was too dark now for him to see if there were any signs of people being in the area, he should have left the mountain earlier. He leaned against a tree for several minutes, satisfying himself that nothing seemed out of place or suspicious and then entered his home. He worked fast, setting the fire, getting some of the venison and potatoes from the lean-to and preparing his meal. The room was warm soon enough, his food cooked and as he sat spooning the hot stew into his bowl he spoke to his sister as he waited for the meal to cool.

You should have seen it today Katy, it was incredible! I saw the Spean pack on the lower slopes of the Ben. They were all there too. Lonach, Borve, Reiff, Brora and Broch. They played in a small stand of birch for a while then they went hunting. They were so clever Katy. They sent Brora and Broch out to split the herd and chase them towards the others. It worked really well and they got two good-sized beasts, which they've been scoffing down all afternoon! You were right sis; they really gorge themselves don't they! It was so amazing to see Katy, your wolves are wonderful, this place is wonderful and I wish we'd come here together darling girl, I wish we'd done this together. He choked with emotion as he struggled to contain his anguish. *But we're doing it now sweet Katy; we're doing it now.* He wiped his eyes and took a mouthful of the stew before continuing. *And tomorrow I'm heading north, looking for the Freya pack. I'd love to see them again, especially the cubs. Anyway, I'll let you know how it goes but keep your fingers crossed for me; you know how hard these guys are to find! Goodnight sis, speak tomorrow.*

27

Cal stumbled out of the forest as the last of the light faded from the sky in an orange line on the western horizon. His breathing was ragged and his legs still felt unsteady, the shock of his ordeal still running through him. As he widened his stride to step over some boggy ground, he felt the sensation of pressure on his scrotum where, only half an hour before, the South African had held a blade to.

Unarmed and terrified, Cal had initially tried to bluster his way out of the situation, informing the men that he was a policeman and they were in serious trouble. Another blow to the stomach and the examination of his warrant card and military identification had given the men the truth of the matter. The South African had nodded to the other man and Cal had found himself hauled to his feet; arms locked behind his back as the other man restrained him. The South African had undone Cal's jeans and whipped trousers and underpants down past the policeman's knees. He had then stepped in close, held a fighting knife up to Cal's face and then placed the sharp blade under Cal's scrotum. The policeman had whimpered and begged the man not to hurt him, to be let go, promised that he wouldn't say a word about the men's presence. The South African had laughed and told Cal he had one opportunity to explain why he was following them; otherwise he would feed Cal his own balls. The policeman had blurted out everything: It was a mistake, they weren't chasing these men, they were chasing Douglas, and these men were only incidental to the investigation, of no interest to the military police. He told the men where they were staying, how many were involved in the search, what their plan was. The tall South African had kept the blade in place and regarded Cal with a cold stare that betrayed nothing. Once Cal had finished the man had spoken to him, but again, without lowering the knife.

"So, you're here to hunt down a soldier who's AWOL and you came up here because you thought we were him. What was your plan *mastermind*? Point a gun at him and walk him all the way back to your operations' centre? Might be that it's lucky you found us and not him. If I was him, I'd have killed you and buried you in a bog up here where no-one would ever find you."

The man had then lowered the knife and told Cal to dress himself. The policeman had collapsed to the ground once the man behind released his arms. He had struggled back into his clothes and stood up on trembling legs. The South African then told him to sit and listen without interrupting. Cal had been told what was now expected of him. He was given a satellite phone and charger, shown how to use it and the only number he would need to use, that of the South African's. His pistol and the magazines were emptied of their bullets and the neutered weapon returned. Cal would update the South African of the team's movements in advance, giving the poachers the ability to steer clear of the searchers. He was to call the South African at least twice a day with this information as well as any leads or sightings involving Douglas. The South African informed Cal that if he missed any of his updates then he would never leave the islands alive, that the South African had several teams operating and that they would shut down every exit point. He had promised Cal that it would not be a swift death for him, the knife reappearing in the man's hand to underline the nature of his potential demise. All Cal had to do was call in, as directed, with the information. One day, there would be no answer to his calls and this would mean that the men had gone and Cal was free.

He had asked for his bullets back, claiming truthfully that if his superior noticed them missing, he would demand to know where Cal had lost them and would initiate a search to find the ammunition. The South African had pondered this for a moment before tossing three of the gold-jacketed rounds back to Cal. "Here, one for the top of each of your magazines, just to keep up appearances." He had then pulled his jacket to one side and removed his own Glock, the weapon aimed casually in Cal's direction. "And don't try to be a hero; we'll be watching you and we'll know if you try to fuck us over. This is easy, just make the calls and we'll be gone before you know it and nobody will be any the wiser."

Stepping back onto the remains of the tarmac road, Cal knew that he had no choice. He didn't know who the South African and his companion were but the casual ministration of violence and their confidence had shown him that they were serious players indeed. As he walked, he shivered, the dropping temperature and the after effects of shock combining to add to his misery. He could feel the sat-phone pressing against his chest from the inside pocket of his jacket and he ran his hand over the outer of the coat to ensure there was no tell-tale bulge that would raise any interest back at the bunkhouse. He opened his stride, walking faster and trying to heat up. His mind was spinning as he sought ways in which he could extricate himself from the situation. He conjured up scenarios of being caught by Warrant Officer Finnegan or Sergeant Stewart, being found with the telephone or overheard talking on it. He then imagined being back in the hands of the South African and his companions. He was fucked; well and truly, but if he was careful, he could do this. He just had to exercise extreme caution when calling the South African. And after all, he reasoned, he was actually doing the team a favour when you thought about it: He was ensuring that the paths of the poachers and the searchers never crossed, thereby eliminating the potential for anyone getting hurt. And it was only for a couple of days at the most. *I can do this.* The lights from the croft were now visible a few hundred yards down the rough road and his hand absent-mindedly drifted to his scrotum as he made his decision: He would see this out. Nothing was worth risking his balls over.

Entering the door of the bunkhouse, Cal was engulfed in warmth, the wood-burner kicking out a welcome heat. At the sound of the door everyone present turned to look and Gary Finnegan gave a smile. "Well, well, the wanderer returns! Was just about to head out and start looking for you myself. Where have you been?"

The younger policeman strolled over to the wood-burner and held his hands to the heat radiating from the dark metal of the stove. "Sorry Boss, got a bit carried away and went a bit further than I meant to."

"No dramas, you're back now. Find anything of interest?"

Cal looked across the room at his superior and gave a casual shake of his head. "Nah. Nothing at all Boss. Anything new this end?"

Mhairi Stewart lowered the mug from which she was drinking and answered him. "No, nothing here either I'm afraid. Spoke to Stornoway and they've got no-one spare to send so just us for the foreseeable future. Mr and Mrs Taylor are going to stay down for another two days to help out though so that's a bit of a bonus."

Cal walked over to the map on the wall and studied it for a moment. "Still the same plan for tomorrow I take it?"

Warrant Officer Finnegan nodded. "Yes, we think that's the best option to start with and if we don't find anything, we'll discuss alternatives tomorrow night. Come and grab a hot toddy, just the thing to warm you up."

Smiling, Cal made his way over to the group, a sensation of something coiling and uncoiling in his stomach, as his betrayal of his colleagues was fast becoming a reality. As he reached for a spare mug, he reminded himself that his actions would be keeping them out of harm's way, preserving lives rather than endangering them. He settled on this thought as he sipped at the hot fiery liquid and joined the conversation, the weight of the sat-phone in his jacket pocket a damoclene reminder of his obligations.

Paul Taylor and Rory Starkey listened as Gary spoke about what Finn Douglas had gone through before his arrival on the islands. Paul shook his head in consolation.

"That's a lot of grief for anyone to handle. Can't say I blame the young man for going off the rails a bit."

Rory Starkey agreed. "It's all very well sending these young men around the globe to fight the wars but I sometimes think more should be done for them on their return. From what I learned about Sergeant Douglas he's seen a lot of action, even been decorated for it, Military Cross wasn't it?"

The military policeman nodded. "Yes, he was awarded it for bravery during a counterattack in Afghanistan. Saved his section by charging and fighting through a Taliban position. Was a pretty intense action, even by Afghan standards. Came down to hand to hand combat at one point."

The journalist gave a low whistle through his teeth. "That is pretty intense. What about you Gary? Didn't you get wounded in Afghanistan yourself?"

Gary Finnegan raised his eyebrows. "You have been doing your homework Rory! Yes, I caught up some frag from an IED. The body armour took the bulk of it but stomach and thighs took a bit of a pounding."

"Is that why you transferred to the Military Police?"

"Yes, pretty much. Once the rehab started showing results, I knew I'd never be strong enough to go back to the infantry so had to make a choice about where I wanted to go." He took a sip of his toddy and smiled back at the pair. "I've always been a nosy bugger so the Military Police seemed a natural choice."

Paul Taylor cleared his throat and addressed the policeman. "What will happen to the lad Gary? Will he go to prison for this?"

"Yes, he will Mr Taylor. Even with his extenuating circumstances, at the end of the day he went AWOL with a stolen rifle and ammunition. Very serious crimes, I'm sure you understand."

"Yes, quite, quite. Just can't help feeling a bit of sympathy for the lad after all he's gone through."

"If it's any consolation I feel exactly the same thing myself. It's my fervent hope that we can get Sergeant Douglas to give himself up and come with us. This will at least give him some brownie points when it comes to sentencing. My fear is that if we don't get him soon, they'll send some Special Forces team up here to hunt him down like a wild animal."

The journalist shook his head. "That would be a terrible end to what is already a very sad affair."

"Yes, it would Rory. That's why I'm doing everything in my power to get to the lad first, take him in quietly."

On the other side of the room, Mhairi was having a similar conversation with Fiona Taylor, who, like her husband, was curious as to what would happen to Finn when he was eventually caught. Mhairi told Fiona what Gary had explained to her earlier that day.

"Such a shame. A young man who's been at war all this time loses the only things dear to him in the world; family and friends. Little wonder he's gone off the rails a bit." Fiona Taylor bit softly down on her lip before engaging the policewoman with a melancholy smile. "We had a boy you know. Henry. A soldier. Just like Sergeant Douglas. He was taken from us in that awful bloody place. Seems we've been at war so long now we've all forgotten what it's like to have our young men home safe and out of danger."

Mhairi placed a hand on Fiona's arm. "Yes, I did hear Mrs Taylor and I was so sorry when the news came through. I didn't know Henry that well but we had mutual friends and acquaintances and everyone I knew thought he was brilliant."

"Thank you Mhairi. We're really only working our way through it. He was our only child you see." The older lady shook herself and smiled back at the policewoman. "I think that's why Paul and I are a little soft on Sergeant Douglas. Can't help but feel sorry for the boy."

"I know Mrs Taylor and to be fair, I think we all feel the same way. Well, most of us." Looking over at Sergeant Callaghan, Mhairi thought the military policeman looked flushed. He was stood beside Gary and the others but a little apart and lost in his own thoughts, not listening to or joining in the conversation. As she observed him, he looked at his watch then walked to the door at the end of the bunkhouse. *Probably tired*, Mhairi thought. Out in the cold air all day and it had been an early start that morning. She turned back as Mrs Taylor was informing everyone that dinner was nearly ready, a hearty stew with potatoes and bread. Mhairi felt her stomach rumble at the thought of the food and made her way into the kitchen.

Cal walked behind the outbuildings and into the long grasses that covered the dunes. Looking around to confirm that he was alone, he took out the sat-phone and turned it on. As briefed, he waited until the reception status in the illuminated window had finished then he dialled the pre-programmed number the South African had shown him. His pulse raced and breath quickened as he carried out his clandestine actions. After only two rings the phone was answered by the familiar voice of his captor who spoke only one word: *What*. Cal briefed the South African on the timings and movements that the searchers would be involved in the next day. The voice on the other end said nothing more until Cal had finished and there was a brief pause. "That it?"

"Yes, that's all today."

"Okay. Speak tomorrow."

The call was terminated and the tone beeped from the handset until Cal turned the device off. He felt a little disgruntled at the South African's lack of appreciation of his information. Still, it would be over soon. He pocketed the phone and stood, deciding to take the opportunity to relieve himself while he had the privacy. As he finished, he touched his scrotum, exploring the area gently with his fingers. He could still feel a faint crease where the knife had been but there was no blood or punctures. He shivered again as the memory of the incident returned to him with full clarity. Zipping his fly back up, he hurried through the *machair* and back to the bunkhouse, ready for food.

As the figure strode past him, Angus could see that it was the younger of the military policemen. The old man had just turned the light out in the boat shed when he had caught sight of someone leaving the bunkhouse and heading for the dunes. He had closed the door and started to walk after the person when he saw the yellow glow and the shape of a face. The sound of someone speaking drifted to where he was standing in the shadows but he did not hear any details. As the figure had walked past him, something had stopped Angus from calling out. He couldn't say what it was but he was a big believer in listening to his gut instinct. It had saved him quite a few times over the years so he wasn't going to ignore it now. Walking back to his own home the old man pondered what he had just seen. According to the policewoman and the Warrant Officer, none of them had telephones that would work because of this silly computer problem on the mainland. That was why they were using his landline, as apparently the old-fashioned system had been the least affected. Why then, would it be, that the younger policeman was sneaking out and making calls on a telephone that no-one knew he had? As he passed the grave of his Eva he knelt slowly and placed his hand on the cold mound. "Well girl, it's a strange time right enough. A very strange time. Let's hope Sergeant Douglas comes out of this okay. If it weren't for him, we'd both be buried in a bog in the forest somewhere with not a soul the wiser. Sleep well old girl." He paused outside his door as he thought again about the younger policeman's actions. Maybe he would tell the Warrant Officer in the morning, but as he thought it through, he decided to keep it to himself for the time being. Maybe the Sergeant had a good reason for having a telephone and keeping it from the others. Well, wasn't really for Angus to say. He would bear the incident in mind and bring it up if circumstances dictated.

28

Sandy leaned across and whispered in André's ear, keeping his movements slow and silent. "I reckon straight down there where we saw the prints on the first day. They obviously use that trail and cross the stream there on a regular basis."

André remained still behind the spotting scope, watching the pack make their way through the stream and up the edge of the peaty bank. The men were very close to the wolves; a matter of two hundred yards at most and André could see every detail of the pack as they entered then left his field of vision. The cubs stumbled and rollicked as they followed the adults, their chubby bodies and downy hair in contrast to the lean and graceful elders. André did not reply until the last of the animals had trotted up the bank and disappeared into the woods beyond. He sat back from the scope and nodded to his companion. "I agree. That's the spot we want. Let's give them a few minutes to get out of earshot then we'll take a walk down and look for possible firing points. We'll need to identify a few as we're not going to know what the wind is doing until tomorrow." Sandy agreed and the men stashed the scope and the insulation mats into their packs before making their way down to the stream.

André had come up with three positions he was happy with. Each one afforded good cover behind a bank of earth and bushes but gave a clear view of the target area. He and Sandy walked around the positions and cleared deadwood, twigs and any debris that could risk exposing them to the wolves' sensitive hearing and compromising the whole operation. André was satisfied with their preparations. All that remained would be to get the equipment ready in the morning and move into whichever position was downwind from the stream's crossing-point. Each man would take two tranq guns, charged and ready to go. André knew that as soon as the first dart was fired the wolves would take flight and the men would have the briefest of opportunities to make the second shot.

Sandy came up with the suggestion of baiting the stream crossing with some game to encourage the pack to linger there, extending the men's narrow window. André raised his eyebrows in surprise; it was actually a smart idea. With that, the men left the area and continued on foot in the opposite direction of the animals. They'd reached the area early that morning, wanting to observe the stream as soon as daylight broke, maximising the likelihood that they would catch the wolves transiting the trail. It was afternoon now and André was starving. Deciding to kill two birds with one stone he directed Sandy to go and check the snares for game and meet him back at the camp. He would prepare a fire to cook the meal and set the equipment out ready for checking.

The men parted ways without a word, Sandy remaining on the high game trail he was following while André dropped down into the lower forest. André stopped short of their camp area and knelt down for several minutes, listening and observing. Other than birdsong and leaves rustling in the breeze there was no sign that anything was amiss. He walked into the small clearing and dropped his pack, stretching upwards at the relief of having shed the load. Taking a long drink from his canteen he swept the area with his eyes, identifying suitable firewood and examining the tree cover above, noting with satisfaction that it would disperse much of the smoke into different directions.

The fire was ready and the equipment laid out in neat lines by the time Sandy returned carrying four large mountain hares. André grinned. "Good hunting bru, that's exactly what we're after!"

Sandy smiled and dropped his own pack before taking the hares over to the small stream where he skinned and dressed the game, ready for eating. He returned to the fire and passed three of the beasts to André who took them and laid them on some ferns. Sandy hung the remaining carcass from a length of cord he had tied to a tree branch. "We'll keep that one for tomorrow's bait. I'll leave it up there out of the reach of foxes or anything else." André grunted his understanding and continued with placing the hares on the wooden skewers he had cut from some of the greener branches. The fire was going well and he placed the meat on an angle above the embers, feeling the heat on the back of his hands. He nodded towards the tranq guns and both men ran through the familiar series of checks. The cages were then inspected and the radios given a confidence check with a few clicks and quiet words.

André took out his sat-phone and called a pre-set number. After a brief moment he spoke, making his way to the edge of the clearing. "It's on for tomorrow. No firm timing as yet but details will be given as and when. Just make sure you are in the area ready for fast extraction on my mark, understand?" He listened as the voice on the other end confirmed his instructions then hung up. Although there was no longer anyone on the other end of the line André kept speaking, making his way back into the clearing as he did so. "And Jamie got back okay? Good, good...no I don't need to know the details, just checking he got back that's all. Yep, okay, speak tomorrow." He ensured the ring tone was set to silent before putting the phone back in his chest pocket. He avoided eye contact with Sandy but monitored him discreetly. He could see no apparent reaction to the conversation and was happy that Sandy had bought into his lie. How he would react when the truth came out, André wasn't too sure but he would deal with that when it happened. At the moment he was torn between getting rid of Sandy completely or paying the boat captain to support his narrative. Well, no point dwelling on it now, there was food to be eaten. He smiled at Sandy and pointed to the cooking meat. "Grab a pew man, won't be long now."

29

Finn had risen early, keen to get over to the northern ridge and find a good spot to lie up before the wolves entered the area. Dawn was breaking in the east as he left the cover of the forest and strode across the flanks of the Ben. His breath steamed in small white clouds ahead of him as he traversed the higher ground, eyes watering in the biting cold breeze. He would have to take that into account once he spotted the pack, need to ensure he was downwind of the animals.

Another night of untroubled sleep had left him refreshed and rested and he soon covered the distance, warming up in the cold morning. He was dressed in his cam-whites and facemask and knew that he would be difficult to spot from a distance, blending into the wintry background. The rifle was slung over his back, leaving his hands free to assist in scrambling over the frost-rimed rocks that occasionally impeded his path.

Finn felt good: Lean and light, a stripped-down version of the Finn Douglas who had first set foot on these islands. His mind felt more at ease too. He was sleeping well, eating well and burning up any excess energy through the physical efforts he indulged in on a daily basis to secure food and firewood. The grief still assailed him, he did not think that would leave him at any point in the near future, but it certainly had diminished in both frequency and intensity. The wolves provided him with a sense of purpose as well as a link to his dear, sweet sister. Finn had always loved wildlife, not to the same level as Katy but was finding his fascination with the creatures growing daily. He admired their physical traits, the strength, stamina, power and speed that the animals had displayed during their hunts.

He had a lot of ground to cover in order to get to the area where he had last spotted the Freya pack but the thought cheered rather than demoralised him. Finn felt truly alive in this elemental world, finding peace with himself through physical effort and subsistence living. His pack was lighter today, stripped of all but the essentials in anticipation of the long trek he was intending and he moved fast across the flanks of the hills.

Now and then his thoughts returned to his dead friends and fellow commandos but he found that the pain of memory had diminished somewhat from the dark days back in Arbroath. He smiled as he recalled a particularly eventful night in Plymouth in which Nick Davies had sprinted along Union Street stark naked, pursued by the Naval Regulators, the Navy's own police force. Finn shook his head at the memory. Nick Davies, a real wild-man. Always popular with the ladies but never could settle down. Good bootneck too, very fit and switched on and would probably have gone all the way to Warrant Officer. Finn hoped Nick's death had been swift and painless, a crumb of comfort against the loss of a well-loved friend.

Crossing the featureless moor, Finn allowed his mind to drift back to his old life when he had been a leader of men. He remembered the heady mix of fear and excitement on his first deployments to Iraq, the welcome baptism of contact with the enemy and the adrenaline-fuelled chaos of his first firefight. He thought about the pressure he had felt when first promoted and being responsible for a section of marines at war, recalled the odd mix of pride and relief he had felt at getting all his lads home safe. It hadn't lasted. His first tour of Afghanistan saw Finn lose two of his marines to an IED just outside the village of Loy Mandeh. Young lads. Cresswell and Baker, both nineteen. On their return to Arbroath, Finn had ordered the troop to meet up at the Central Bar where he had charged their glasses with rum and toasted the fallen marines. He had given a short speech lauding the courage, humour and loyalty of the two men before the troop downed their drinks and saw off their comrades with a suitably drunken night of mayhem.

Although sad, Finn did not feel the deep-rooted sorrow he had experienced in his first weeks on the islands. He found that, without any conscious effort, he was able to concentrate more on the happier memories he had of his men rather than the dark ones. He imagined his mum and Katy watching over him and wondered what they would think of his actions. His mum would no doubt be worried that he wasn't eating enough and would hurt himself scrambling over cliffs and mountains. Katy would just be ecstatic to see him roaming the islands with her wolf packs. Finn paused for a few moments, standing in a small copse of spruce trees. He noticed movement near the shore below him and slipped the rifle from the pack, looking through the sight towards the area of old Angus' croft. He saw several figures moving around outside the buildings and focussed his attention on their activities. Two men and a woman were wearing backpacks while another man and woman stood speaking to them. Goodbyes were said and the three with the packs on walked away from the croft and began following the old road south. Finn tracked their progress, curious who these people were. They clearly weren't poachers, unarmed and making no attempt to conceal themselves. Police, looking for Finn after the old man had called them? Perhaps, but there were no police cars near the croft that he could see. That left the possibility that the trio were part of the wolf conservation group or something related to it. Finn studied their packs, noting that they were too light to be carrying anything other than a day's worth of gear with which to survive with. The group left the road and veered into the woods where Finn lost sight of them. He would have to be careful on his return to his cottage as the group would be somewhere in the area. He was not unduly worried, confident that his skills and field-craft would keep him hidden from all but the well-trained observer. He strapped the rifle back on to his pack and continued walking through the small stand of trees and began climbing the steeper slope, heading north towards the area he had last seen the Freya pack.

30

The day was a cold one and Gary Finnegan pulled his woollen hat down over his ears as they walked along the edge of the forest. Mhairi noticed his actions and smiled. "Freezing today, isn't it?"

Gary nodded and rubbed the tip of his nose, which was stinging in the cold. He turned to check on the younger military policeman and saw that he was lost in his own thoughts as he followed on behind. Gary had noticed that Sergeant Callaghan had been quieter than usual and wondered if perhaps his subordinate was losing his appetite for the search. He decided not to say anything but to monitor the Sergeant discreetly for the next few days, make sure there was nothing else bothering him.

Cal was tired. He hadn't slept well, had tossed and turned all night, wrestling with his conscience over his deal with the South African. He was a *Military Policeman* for crying out loud! He upheld the law, not twisted and perverted it. He could not however, see any way out of the situation other than complying with the poachers' demands. He'd considered going to Warrant Officer Finnegan and telling him everything but could not face the prospect of his superior's disappointment in him. As he followed the others through the thickening forest, he concluded that there was nothing else for it but to stick with it, give the poachers what they wanted and it would soon be over with no need for anyone else to become involved.

Leading the small group, Mhairi was heading for an old track she remembered from before the island had been a wildlife refuge. She had not been in the area for many years but the occasional rise in the ground or stream crossing resonated with a feeling of familiarity. The breeze had abated somewhat now that they were in the cover of the trees but the day remained freezing, one of the coldest days of winter so far. Her thoughts turned to Sergeant Douglas and what they would do if they encountered him, either by accident or design. Gary wanted to talk to Finn, convince him to surrender himself, give up his weapon and return to face the music. He seemed sure that he could reason with the marine; explain that his circumstances would be brought into consideration, particularly if he cooperated with the military policemen.

In truth, Mhairi wasn't so sure that they would find Douglas. His training, skills and experience were far in advance of any of theirs and they were only aware he was on the islands due to his intervention on Angus' behalf. He had been on the run for months prior to this without even a sighting of him reported. No, unless they were very fortunate, they wouldn't see hide or hair of Sergeant Douglas unless he wanted them to. The ground was rising as the forest clung to the slopes of the hills of Hecla and

Beinn Mhor and Mhairi revelled in the burn in her thighs as she powered up the incline. Throwing a quick look over her shoulder she could see the two military policemen starting to struggle keeping up with her. She reached a small clearing and stopped, taking off her pack and pulling out a water bottle. As Gary and Cal drew level she spoke. "Five minutes?" Gary nodded and both men dropped their packs, their heavy breathing loud in the quiet hush of the glade.

No one spoke for several minutes, each enjoying the rest and the peace of the forest. Gary watched as his breath fogged in the frigid air then dissipated gradually, leaving no trace it had ever been there. He took a last swig from his canteen and replaced it, put his pack on and turned to Mhairi. "Where are we now?" The policewoman stood beside him and using the tip of a pine needle indicated their position on the waterproofed map. "We're here, with Hecla to our east and Beinn Mhor south east. We'll climb a bit higher to the point where the trees thin out and then make our way south looking for any signs of our guy." Gary nodded his agreement and checked to make sure Sergeant Callaghan had heard everything and was gratified to see his subordinate nod to him as he donned his own pack. With Mhairi at the front again, they made their way up the steep incline towards the edge of the forest.

The snow crunched beneath their feet, a thin crust from the overnight frost collapsing onto the softer powder below. With the forest on their right side and the high ground to their left, the group continued, eyes searching the landscape for any sign of Sergeant Douglas. The bright snow on the high ridges contrasted with the stunning blue sky behind and Mhairi felt the familiar appreciation of being among the mountains. Her last trip had been some time ago, a quick two weeks in Yosemite for some technical climbs. She sighed as she thought back to her more carefree mountaineering days, when she would just take off at the drop of a hat for an exped to the high places. Like everyone she knew, work and life in general had eventually taken priority and the travel became less and less to the point where even a dash to the mainland for a weekend's climbing seemed a luxury.

When Paul had transferred to Glasgow, she had considered joining him, doing the whole big city thing. She had soon realised though, that the act of him leaving the job at Stornoway was also the end of their relationship. It had been on the cards for some time, but both of them had seemed to be reluctant to say the actual words. She was grateful it had ended in an amicable manner as she still bumped into Paul's family from time to time around the islands. Paul would also drop the occasional e-mail, giving her all the gossip from the big smoke, talking about the challenges of policing in a big city. Mhairi had heard from Shona McLeod that Paul was in a relationship with a female officer down there and that they had just bought a flat together in the west end. She was pleased for Paul; he was a nice guy and deserved to be happy. Mhairi had not been in a relationship since the split almost two years ago, had not found anyone she considered suitable. She'd had the odd flirtation with visiting colleagues from the mainland and a brief, drunken snog with a Swedish climber in Glencoe, but that was it. She loved living and working on the islands but knew that the price to pay for her lifestyle was a limited supply of suitors. *Slim pickings in Stornoway*, as Shona would often lament.

Mhairi wondered about the two military policemen. *Were they in relationships?* She didn't think it likely as there had been no rush to Angus' telephone to talk to wives or partners back home. She would be surprised if Sergeant Callaghan was in a relationship. He was a bit intense and seemed to have a temper on him. Gary was nice though. He was one of those mellow guys, good at their job but without the need to broadcast it to all and sundry. He hadn't mentioned a wife or girlfriend back home but Mhairi could imagine him in a long-term relationship with an equally nice partner. As she looked at the ground ahead of her she slowed her pace and dropped back to keep step with the military policeman.

"Beautiful up here isn't it?"

Gary nodded and smiled. "It certainly is. This is one of the most stunning places I've seen. And you're from here, right?"

"Yep, guilty as charged! Born and bred on the islands and now living and working them for my sins!"

"You're lucky; this is a pretty special corner of the world Mhairi. Hell, I might just move up here myself!"

Mhairi saw her opportunity. "Yes, but what would Mrs Finnegan think about that?" She watched as a sad smile played on Gary's lips.

"Well, there's just me now Mhairi. Mrs Finnegan passed away a few years ago now."

Mhairi placed her hand on the policeman's arm. "Oh Gary, I'm so sorry. I had no idea."

"Please Mhairi, don't apologise, you weren't to know." As they walked, she listened as Gary explained how Sinead, his wife, had contracted cancer some years into their marriage. It had been a long, drawn-out process by all accounts but the policeman gave no hint of self-pity, rather a sense of gratitude for having had the time with his wife. "Got it right first time round you see, not a lot of fellas can say that." Mhairi could not imagine what it must have been like for Gary to endure such a horrific ordeal afflicting someone who he clearly had loved so much. He turned to look at her and gave her a playful nudge. "What about you? No PC Plod to go home to at night?" Mhairi laughed and began talking about Paul and their relationship, finishing with a funny remark about settling down with one of the old crofters to avoid being a crazy spinster who kept cats. A yell from behind them made them turn around in surprise.

Cal stood with his hands on his hips and addressed the pair to his front in a patronising tone. "If you two have quite finished with the girly chat, any chance we can take a look at these footprints?"

210

31

André and Sandy sat together, looking out at the stream before them. Both men were relaxed, backs against tree trunks, arms resting on knees. They could see a long way up the valley from their position and would be able to spot the wolves well before the animals could see them. Once they spotted the beasts, both men would retreat into the cover of the bushes behind them and wait with the tranq guns for the wolves to arrive at the crossing.

André burrowed his neck down into the warmth of his jacket. He was freezing despite the layers of clothing he was wearing. He was done with Scotland and its miserable bloody weather, couldn't wait to get back to his home in South Africa, back to the warmth. Still, if all went well, they would be off these islands today and on their way back to Glasgow with the goods for the client. He'd had a call from the boat captain just after first light telling him that the boat was anchored up in the Sound of Barra and ready to come north on André's command. *Good.* Everything was now in place and ready to go as soon as the wolves made their appearance.

He stood and stretched, looking up into the valley. Still no sign of the animals. He walked over to the tranq guns that were stacked against a tree to their rear and ran a last cursory check to ensure they remained good to go. Content, he strolled further into the forest and relieved himself against a bush. The breeze was at his back and he was happy that the wolves wouldn't smell his urine, as they would be downwind from the men's position. Walking back to Sandy he paused and squinted, looking up to the head of the valley. He thought he had seen a flicker of movement up where the trees came close to the rock face. He caught it again and shook his head. *Just a crow.* No sign of the wolves. He sat back against the tree and resumed his hunched position, thinking about what he would do as soon as he got home. *Beer and braai. Yes man, that's exactly what he would do. A nice cold one and a couple of steaks on the deck.* Perfect. And with any luck it would only be a couple of days away. Despite the cold he could feel himself nodding off to sleep, eyelids becoming heavier and his breathing slowing. He looked up and caught Sandy's eye. The Scotsman nodded and indicated that André should sleep while he took watch. The South African nodded back, closed his eyes and stretched out his legs. He was asleep in less than a minute, a soft, rhythmic snoring sound indicating the depth of his slumber.

André woke, as he always did, alert and ready for anything. Sandy was stood over him holding a thermos mug of coffee. "Hey boss, been a couple of hours now." André accepted the coffee with a grunt of thanks and sat up against the tree.

"No sign yet?"

"Nah, nothing. A couple of birds, a hare, but no bloody wolves."

André cleared his throat and spat into the bushes. "They'll come. They use this area a lot so it must mean something to them. We just need to be patient. You remember that ambush in Maiduguri we did? Four bloody days before the ragheads went through it. I was going out of my mind with boredom, nearly packed it in and walked off the job!" Both men chuckled at the memory and began swapping anecdotes of operations and ambushes they had been involved in. André checked his watch at one stage and saw that they had been talking for nearly two hours. Sandy was in the middle of a story about a black operation in Angola when André held up his hand to silence the Scot. Keeping his movements slow, the South African stood, bringing the binoculars up to his eyes. *There they are!* The wolves were leaving the cover of the forest and beginning their descent into the valley and towards the waiting men. They were still some distance away and André turned to Sandy and pointed in the animals' direction. The Scot nodded and stood, joining André and taking a turn with the binoculars. Handing them back both men made their way to the tree behind them to pick up the tranq guns. Which had vanished.

32

Finn was breathing hard, having sprinted most of the way back to his pack. He'd slung the tranquiliser guns into the small loch beside the forest, leaving his arms free to pump and drive him forward.

He'd spotted the poachers that morning, just as he'd crested the hill at the top of the valley. Studying them through the rifle's sight, he'd seen the guns stacked against a tree behind the men. Finn had decided to get closer to the men, to try and find out what they were doing and what the strange looking weapons were for. He'd cached his pack and stalked the men's position for over an hour through the forest. He had covered the last fifty feet on his stomach, clearing the ground before him of all loose twigs and debris. The men hadn't been speaking and after a few moments Finn identified the sound of light snores coming from behind a tree. He had manoeuvred himself into a better position and soon had a clear view of both men from about ten feet away. One was asleep against a tree, nothing more than a body in a down jacket struggling to cover every inch of exposed flesh. The other man focussed his attention up the valley, sweeping it occasionally with a pair of binoculars. Then Finn had studied the weapons. There were four of them and he saw that they were tranquiliser guns, the gas cartridges and darts providing the clues. They were after the wolves.

Finn had felt a cold fury take root within him and thought about unslinging his rifle and taking the men prisoner, marching them to old Angus' house and sending for the police. He had decided against this, unsure if there were any more of these criminals in the area and not wanting to get the old crofter involved more than he already was. So, he had taken the tranq guns instead. He'd crawled to the guns and taking two at a time, made his way silently back through the forest where he could stand, out of sight and earshot of the poachers. He'd made fast progress and was passing the small loch when he made the decision to ditch the weapons there.

With the pack on his back, Finn maintained his breakneck pace, knowing that he had to put as much distance between the poachers and himself as he could. It was likely that the poachers had some tracking experience and Finn needed to be far enough away from the area to have the time to lay down some false trails. He panted as he ran past another small loch and crested the rise of the ridge, dropping downhill on the eastern side of Hecla's flanks. He changed direction, turning south now, keeping the hills between him and the poachers, a natural barrier providing him with cover while he made good his extraction.

A glance over his shoulder brought some hope: A storm coming in from the north. Broiling black clouds advanced over the sea, the dark curtain beneath them an approaching wall of snow that would cover Finn's tracks once the storm hit the islands. This was good news. He slowed his pace a little, no longer running but taking wide strides, head down, focussed on covering the distance. He wanted to get back to his home before the storm broke in earnest. He had more than enough food to sit tight for a few days during which he hoped the poachers would pack up and leave the island. He hoped.

33

They followed the footprints well into the forest but were struggling now to find any more, the hard ground and rocks yielding very few clues to assist the searchers. Mhairi turned to the military policemen who were examining a scuff on a lichen-covered rock and arguing about whether or not it had been made by Douglas. "Guys, it's getting pretty dark in here and I think we have to face up to the fact that we've taken this as far as we can."

Gary Finnegan nodded and looked around the area they found themselves in. "Yeah, I agree Mhairi. We're not going to be able to see anything soon." He turned to Sergeant Callaghan and watched as the younger policeman continued scrutinising the forest floor for further traces of the fugitive. Gary was about to say something when the younger man swore and looked up.

"It's here. I've found a trail!"

Gary and the policewoman looked at each other then made their way to Sergeant Callaghan who was now following the small trail he had discovered. Gary saw that the younger man was correct. It was not an established trail by any means but someone or something had been using this route on a regular basis. Gary felt the excitement build within him. This was Douglas. He could feel it. Sergeant Callaghan looked up and met his eyes. Gary smiled at him. "Good work Sergeant, bloody good work. Let's follow this as far as we can or until the light goes completely. This has to be him; both Angus and the Taylors were adamant that there's no-one else out here."

Cal basked in the praise of his Warrant Officer. He too was excited; Sergeant Finn Douglas Royal Marines was now very close to capture and all because of Cal's hard work. He listened as Mhairi spoke to the men.

"Yes, I agree. This is Sergeant Douglas. Let's keep the chat to a minimum though; we have no idea how near he could be. We've got about two hours of daylight left so let's make the most of it."

As their eyes adjusted to the gloom, they found it easier to pick up the trail when it was lost due to hard ground or water. They would look around the adjacent area and identify spots where they would have stepped or leap from and could usually pick up Sergeant Douglas' trail from there. Gary noticed the breeze was increasing and the forest seemed to darken faster than usual. He looked at Mhairi and she indicated with a flick of her head to the sky above.

"Storm. From the north, that's why it feels colder. Probably snow coming."

Gary cursed silently. Snow would cover the tracks and trail they were following and just when they were making real progress. He was mulling this over when he stopped in his tracks and sniffed the air, a frown wrinkling his brow.

As quiet as he could manage while ensuring the others heard him, he spoke.

"Anybody else smell smoke?" All three stood silent and concentrating, sniffing softly and looking into the depths of the woods around them. Mhairi looked at Sergeant Callaghan and nodded just as he gave Gary a nod of his own to indicate that he too could smell it. The group closed in to discuss this new development and spoke in whispers. Mhairi pulled out the map and Gary produced a small torch with a red filter that allowed them to see but without being prominent enough to be seen at any relevant distance.

The policewoman used a small twig to orientate the military men. "Okay, we're about here, in this part of the forest. There's no homes or crofts in the area other than an abandoned house over to our north, just behind that rise." Looking up she pointed to a spot through the trees. "By my calculations it can only be a hundred metres or so in that direction." A silent consensus saw the military policemen draw their weapons and proceed with exaggerated care through the darkening woods in the direction Mhairi had shown them.

When they first saw the cottage, they were so close that it surprised them, so well did it blend in to the environment. Kneeling behind a large spruce as they considered their options. Mhairi leaned across to Gary and whispered in his ear.

"Someone's definitely been living here. Look at the roof repairs, they've taken care to cover the wood in mud to make it blend in but that's definitely new wood."

Gary agreed and wondered about the next course of action. The trees around them were creaking and groaning as they were buffeted by the increasing wind. Gary realised that the temperature had dropped while they were following the trail and knew that the storm would be upon them soon. He pulled his colleagues close to him and whispered his plan.

"Okay, I'm going to have a look around. You two stay here and whatever happens, stay calm. Douglas isn't going to hurt me, let me talk to him and bring him in that way. If he's not here I'll come back and we'll talk about what are options are then." He stood, holstered his weapon and walked towards the cottage.

Cal watched his superior walk to the building. He didn't think Douglas was there but you never knew. His hand was feeling cold, as he'd removed his glove so that he could handle his weapon properly, even though he only possessed three bullets. The wind was picking up and a whistling noise accompanied the groans and creaks of the wind-blown trees. He raised his eyebrows in surprise as he saw Gary returning after only a few moments. The older man said nothing but beckoned them to follow him away from the cottage. They crossed a small stream and carried on for a few metres until Gary stopped them and told them what he'd seen.

"It's Douglas right enough. There's some of his kit left in the room but no pack or rifle. He's set up a bed, a cooking area and a chair. He's also got a stockpile of food hanging in a larder so I think it's safe to say that this is his base and that he'll be back. So how do we want to take it from here?"

Mhairi pulled on a woollen hat and tugged it over her ears as she spoke. "Well, I think we wait here till dark to see if he returns. We know where he is living now and I think he'll be back here before the storm hits which is anytime now." Gary turned to Cal and looked at the younger man for his thoughts on the matter.

"I'm with Mhairi boss; we wait. This could all end tonight if Douglas returns to the cottage." Gary nodded his agreement and ran through his plan.

"Right, we'll go back and cover the cottage from where we were before. When Douglas arrives, we let him go into the cottage and get settled. I'll approach and knock on the door, telling him who I am and what I want and ask him to listen to me. Let's remember, he's got a gun but he's shown his absolute reluctance to use it so bear this in mind. We don't want any unnecessary gunplay; that's when people get hurt or killed. So, follow my lead okay?"

"What happens if he runs boss? I'm damned if I'm just going to shout at him to stop and risk losing him again."

"Fire a warning shot into the air and order him to stop. Unless he's pointing his rifle at one of us, he is not a threat and you do not have the legal right to engage him with a weapon. Do I make myself clear?"

221

The younger policeman nodded, his expression sullen and grim. He looked at his superior who was discussing with Mhairi how they would get Douglas to Stornoway if he surrendered. Cal turned his attention to the dark forest around him and smiled. *Hell, in these dark woods with snow falling and the wind blowing a hoolie, who could tell whether or not Douglas would be carrying a weapon?*

With a jolt the military policemen remembered something. "Ah boss, I'm just off for a call of nature." Gary gave him a dismissive wave and Cal walked some distance into the forest before he stopped and pulled out the sat-phone from inside his coat. He shielded the display screen with his hand and waited until the reception bars were full then he pressed the pre-recorded number. It rang several times before the familiar Boer twang answered. Taking a wary look back towards his colleagues Cal whispered into the handset, updating the South African with their progress that day.

34

André had just finished dragging Sandy's body into the woods when the phone vibrated in his chest pocket. He looked at the screen and saw it was a call from the military policeman and pressed the button to accept it. He had listened without any real interest until the policeman mentioned that they had found their fugitive's hideout. André had sparked then, all senses on alert and brain racing as he assimilated the information. He let the military policeman finish then demanded the exact coordinates of the hideout's location. He sensed the reluctance at the other end and growled his demand a second time. There was no further hesitation.

He terminated the call and looked again at Sandy's body lying in a small ravine on a bed of pine needles. The loss of the tranq guns had sent André into a furious rage. The reality sinking in that the operation was now over, that they could not hope to get the wolf cubs without the tranquilising equipment. He had screamed his frustration into the hills, challenging whoever had taken his weapons to come back and face him. Sandy had placed a hand on his shoulder to calm him down and André had spun, faced him, and smashed the edge of his hand into the Scotsman's throat. Sandy had clutched at his throat and collapsed to his knees, eyes widening and face turning purple as he struggled to get air through his crushed windpipe. André then kicked the kneeling man hard in the face, causing him to crash to the ground. Mad with rage André had leapt on the prone man and sat astride him, pinning his arms. He had then punched the Scotsman in his puce-coloured face. Punched him over and over until his knuckles hurt and his arms felt tired. It was only then that André emerged from his rage-induced blackout and looked at his handiwork. Sandy was a mess. A *dead* mess. His face a bloodied, purple pulp of tissue, sinew and bone. André had stood on shaky legs and cleaned himself up at the stream, wincing at the cold water on his lacerated hands. He had then dragged the Scotsman's body into the cover of the forest.

He searched Sandy's body and took a map, wallet and the binoculars from it. Looking down at his sat-phone he scrolled through the menu and retrieved the military policeman's message. He found the coordinates on the map and checked them once again before turning off the phone. By his reckoning it was some distance away and he would not make it there on foot before nightfall. Which presented the South African with a problem: He couldn't flail around in the woods at night trying to find this hideout; he would only give himself away. But he didn't really want to wait until tomorrow to deal with this bastard who had humiliated him on two occasions now. First Jamie and now André himself, although, truth be told he placed the blame for this debacle squarely with the dead Scotsman. It had been his duty to watch over them when he took the sentry role. The thought of Jamie brought something to mind and André smiled, realising with a jolt that he might make it to the location before dark after all. But there was no time to waste.

He rummaged through Sandy's rucksack and took the food and spare jacket, stuffing the goods into his own pack. He shouldered his load and set off at a steady trot towards the old road. Despite the fact that his actions were now solely concerned with revenge, André felt calm and clear headed. It reminded him of his early days with the Recces, his country's elite Special Forces unit. Every one of them had experienced the same thing; that the more desperate and fucked-up the mission was, the calmer and more confident you became. And the thing was, this mission had just become completely fucked up: There would be no payday for this one and a black mark would be against André's name when any similar work was being touted on the circuit. So, this mission was well and truly over. But the *new* mission was just beginning. André was going to find this marine and kill him. Slowly and with as much pain and agony as he could inflict upon a human being.

He smiled at the thought and soon settled into a steady jog, lulled by his rhythmic breathing and the cadence of his footfalls. When he reached the road he turned north, opening his stride and increasing his pace on the firmer surface. He hoped that he had enough time. The old man's place was only a couple of clicks along the road. Where André would get himself a vehicle and cover the distance to the marine's hideout in no time at all. The thought of this spurred him on and by the time he could make out the old man's cottage in the distance, André was running as though completely unencumbered.

35

"I think it's going to be a bad storm." Paul Taylor turned back from the door of the bunkhouse and looked at his wife. "Anything from the gang yet?" Fiona Taylor shook her head and pointed at the radio set, which had been silent all day.

"No, not a thing. Could be they're out of range or just in a bit of a black spot." Paul moved closer to the stove and warmed his hands. "Well, here's hoping that we hear from them soon. It's getting dark now and they really want to be off the hill before that storm hits us."

"Should we take a drive out and go looking for them do you think?"

"No, I'm sure they're fine. Mhairi's a mountain girl and she knows the islands well enough to get them down before the storm hits." The pair were silent for several minutes until the door opened and Rory Starkey entered, rubbing his hands together and shivering.

"Cold night ahead I'm thinking." He closed the door behind him, a shriek of wind protesting as the door was secured. "Any news from the searchers?" He made his way to the stove as Paul Taylor nodded to the coffee warming on the plate.

"We were just discussing that actually, but no, nothing yet." The journalist poured himself a mug of the thick, dark brew and sipped noisily, sighing as the hot liquid warmed his insides.

"I've been talking with old Angus quite a bit and he's told me a few things about Sergeant Douglas that he didn't feel were relevant to the police investigation." Paul Taylor raised his eyebrows and Rory held up a hand to allay his concern. "No, nothing about where to find the lad, more about his frame of mind and why he's here of all places." Turning to face both of the Taylor's he briefed them on what he had learned, pausing regularly to drink from the chipped enamel mug. "Sergeant Douglas is here because his dead sister, to whom he was very close. She adored wolves and had always wanted to come here to see them in the wild. He also believes that what happened to his family is some kind of retribution for the lives he has taken over the years in the wars he has been fighting. From what the old man told me, I would say that Sergeant Douglas probably has on-going PTSD issues; Angus noticed that some of Sergeant Douglas' fingers seemed to have regular tremors. When he mentioned that to Douglas, he apparently brushed it off as 'another part of the price to be paid'."

"What do you think he meant by that?"

"The old man wasn't sure but suspects Douglas mistakenly believes that he deserves whatever is coming to him. Angus agrees with the PTSD theory, although he refers to it as shell shock. They didn't have the medical name for it back in his day but he'd seen enough of his colleagues in Korea with similar symptoms."

Fiona Taylor shook her head. "It's just so terrible. He's a young man who has endured so much and is in need of medical help rather than a jail sentence. I hope with all my heart that he gives himself up tonight, ends this now and gets the help he needs." She turned to her husband. "We could speak up for him Paul; inform the authorities that he isn't the criminal they believe him to be, get a statement from Angus about how he saved his life yet still didn't kill the poacher."

"Yes, we will do that Fi. I'm with you on this; that young man needs help not incarceration."

Rory Starkey placed the empty mug down on the table. "I'm going to do my bit too. I've got all the information from Angus and he's happy that my paper runs with it as long as it's in support of the lad and not some salacious red-top rubbish, which it would never be. Once the police have got him, I'll get the details of how it all happened and look to get my editor to run his beady eye over it."

Paul Taylor raised an eyebrow. "You think it will help Sergeant Douglas, Rory? I only ask as the public seem fatigued with all the coverage of the war and there isn't quite as much support for the troops as we've seen in other conflicts you know?"

"You're right Paul, the public is tired and not particularly Forces-friendly. But this is a story about a broken man, someone who has lost everything and just wanted to be left alone in peace: A fugitive surviving in a wilderness of mountains, forests and wolves: Saving an old man's life without taking another's, even when that would have been the easier thing to do: A man seeking peace and redemption through isolation and the renouncement of violence. This is an amazing story that I think will generate public support for leniency for Sergeant Douglas. His story will resonate with the families and friends of all those affected by war and its cost to their young men."

"Well, when you put it that way, I can see where you get your optimism from. I'm still not so convinced but I think it could at least generate some sympathy for the lad."

Fiona Taylor stood and was about to pour more coffee when the door opened and all three turned to see who had entered. The figure slammed the door closed behind them, their face not yet visible but Fiona frowned when she saw that it was a stranger, their height and clothing different to anyone currently on the island. Paul Taylor had taken one step towards the individual when the man turned from the door, pulled down his hood and pointed a gun at him.

"Sit down on the chairs, keep your hands where I can see them and nobody will get hurt."

Paul retreated and joined his wife on the two-seater. Rory Starkey followed suit, lowering his long frame into one of the canvas camping chairs by the wood-stove. Rory studied the stranger as he advanced into the room. He was South African by the sounds of it and familiar with weapons as there was no hint of nerves or uncertainty as he covered them with the pistol. He carried a large pack but seemed unaffected by the weight, indicating he was accustomed to carrying loads. *Ex-soldier or mercenary perhaps?* As he watched, the stranger looked at the map on the wall and strode across to it, taking the two sets of vehicle keys that had been hanging on the hooks beside the board.

Paul Taylor cleared his throat. "Who the hell are you and what's the meaning of this?" The man turned to face him with an amused smile. He moved closer to the group, the matt-black muzzle of the pistol never wavering from its position.

"Never mind who I am, that's not important. It's what I want that's important. I need to get to that bloody marine you are trying to arrest and I need to get there now. So, you're going to take me. Do as I say and you'll live. Defy me and you'll die."

Rory Starkey continued to study the South African before speaking. "I'm afraid we can't help you there old bean, haven't had any contact with the team for most of the day."

The shot was shocking in the confines of the bunkhouse, the harsh echo reverberating around the room as their ears rang. Paul recovered first and looked over at Rory, stunned to see the dark stain flowering on his chest. The journalist sat, wide-eyed and blinking rapidly, unable to process what had just happened. He brought his hand to his chest and touched the area, lifting his palm to his face to confirm his worst fears. Seeing the dark blood sticking to his hand he

231

moaned and tried to sit up in the chair but found he had no control of his body. Paul made to stand but was barked at by the Afrikaner. "Sit fucking still or the woman gets it next. I told you before, you help me or you die. It's fucking basic people." Fiona Taylor began to sob, bringing her hands to her mouth as she watched the dying journalist before her. Paul put his arm around her shoulder and pulled her in against him as he continued to watch the killer in front of him. Paul could feel his own legs shaking and his breathing quicken as shock engulfed his body. The killer gestured with the pistol, waving it towards the door.

"Get up. You, fella; you're going to drive me to where I tell you. The woman is in the back with me. One wrong move from you and I'll shoot you both in the guts then let you watch as I cut her into little bits." He held out one of the sets of keys to Paul with his free hand, keeping the gun well out of reach. Paul took the keys in his shaking hand and walked towards the door, his arm around Fiona. As they reached the door his wife stopped and looked back at the journalist in the chair, his entire chest now drenched in blood. She pleaded with their captor. "Please, let us get some help for him. We'll do whatever you want but don't let him die."

André Voster gave a brief glance back at the man in the chair then shoved the woman over the threshold. "Get going. He's already dead, he just doesn't know it." The wind whipped their hair and battered their faces as they made their way to the Range Rover. Paul opened the driver's door and was climbing in when he leaped back in shock as two shots rang out. He turned to Fiona, fearing the worst but saw that the man had shot out the two front tyres on the remaining vehicle. His heart hammering in his chest, Paul took his position behind the wheel and waited while his wife and their captor climbed into the rear. The doors closed and the man looked at a map with a small torch, his face highlighted as Paul looked into the rear-view mirror. The man looked up. "Drive. Out of here and right until I tell you otherwise." Paul started the engine and engaged the automatic gears to drive mode. He switched on the headlights, released the handbrake and moved off, turning right at the end of the drive and on to the island's main road.

Angus had just finished his bath when he heard the shots and the vehicle leaving. Dressing as quickly as he could he loaded his shotgun and turned off the lights before leaving through the back door of his croft. The wind was shrieking around the building and the cold attacked his bare hands that clutched the weapon. One vehicle was gone and the other was resting on two flat tyres. The old man had no idea what had happened but he knew that it wasn't good. Bringing the shotgun up into his shoulder he advanced towards the bunkhouse, heart pounding in anticipation of what he might find. He stood behind the wall at the side of the door and with one swift movement, turned the handle and shoved hard. The door opened with ease, assisted by the force of the wind. When there was no immediate reaction, the old man brought the shotgun up again and entered the bunkhouse. The journalist's chest and stomach were soaked with blood and his arms hung listlessly over the sides of the chair. His head was collapsed upon his chest and the old man hurried to his side. Angus lifted the journalist's head, the chin warm against his cold hand, and heard the sound of breathing: Laboured and struggling but breathing none the less.

Refusing to give in to panic, the old man grabbed his shotgun and half ran, half shuffled back to the house. He burst through the door and made his way to the telephone. It was dead, no dial tone whatsoever. Angus knew that the storm hadn't been strong enough yet to be bringing down telephone lines and wondered what the problem could be. He grabbed the torch from the table at the front door and walked around the side of his croft where he shone the light against the wall there. His suspicions were correct; the wire had been cut. And not just severed; whoever had done it had cut a whole section away to ensure that the wire couldn't just be reconnected. Cursing in Gaelic the old man dashed back inside and began grabbing the limited first aid essentials that he had in the house. There was no prospect of help for the poor reporter. No one would be coming any time soon, there was only a stubborn old man with a handful of bandages and iodine and barely-remembered medical training from decades before. Rushing back to the bunkhouse, the old man recalled how the journalist's entire torso had been soaked in blood and wondered if indeed there was anything that could help him.

36

The first flurries of snow were just hitting Finn as he entered the cover of the forest. The wind was in full force, the forest alive with shrieks and groans as the tempest increased. He was hot from the running he had done that day and was looking forward to some food and rest. He slowed his pace now that he was in the cover of the woods. It was almost dark with little ambient light and he had no wish to injure himself by falling or running into a tree branch. His thoughts returned to the poachers and he allowed himself a smile as he imagined their stunned surprise when they found their tranq guns had disappeared. They would be angry, he guessed, but also keen to leave the islands before they were caught. Finn intended remaining close to the cottage for the next day or so before venturing out again to confirm that the men had gone.

He stopped at the small stream and replenished his water bottles, ready for the night. Some of the snow was filtering through the canopy and into the forest, limiting his visibility and he moved on, keen to be inside. Making his way over the small ridge he could just make out the shape of the cottage, a shade darker than the forest around it. The tension slipped from his shoulders as he took the final few steps to the door, pleased that the day, with all its potential for confrontation, was over.

Gary Finnegan watched, heart pounding in his chest as Sergeant Douglas emerged from the forest like a silent wraith, clad in his white winter camouflage. He held his breath as the marine strode past his position and watched as he entered the cottage. After several minutes a small chink of light became visible at the base of the door. Gary turned to Mhairi and Sergeant Callaghan and held his splayed hand up to indicate that he would go in five minutes. His colleagues nodded their understanding and turned their attention back to the dwelling.

He had been involved in similar situations throughout his career, which, like this one, were rarely straightforward. He had tried to think of all the variables, the 'what ifs', Douglas' potential reactions to the policeman's presence. He was sure that Finn posed no threat to him but could not discount the possibility that the marine would run the second Gary announced himself. He had altered his plan a little to cover this eventuality and briefed Mhairi and Cal earlier. Gary would now make his way to the door and Mhairi and Cal would cover the entrance from the safety of the forest. Gary would then open the door and walk straight in, closing it behind him. The others would then leave their cover and take positions directly outside the door, ready in case Douglas should overpower the military policeman inside and try to escape.

The five minutes were up and Gary took a final look at the cottage door and stood, pulling his hood down so that when he entered Douglas would be able to see his face. The wind buffeted the policeman and snow flurries stung his face. With every step he half-expected the door to fly open and Sergeant Douglas to come bursting out but all remained still within the building. Reaching the door, he took a deep breath and before nerves could take hold, he grasped the handle and shoved, stepping quickly into the light of the room and slamming the door closed behind him.

Finn tripped over his pack, such was his shock at the intrusion. Even as he scrambled across the room to get his weapon, he was anticipating a bullet in his back from the poacher. His fingers had just touched the stock of the rifle when the voice boomed around the small room.

"Sergeant Douglas, I'm Warrant Officer Finnegan, Royal Military Police. Please stop and look at me." Finn ignored the command and grabbed the rifle, clambering to his feet and facing the intruder. His chest heaved as his breathing quickened, the shock of the situation now kicking in. Finn pointed the rifle at the man before him and studied him. The man was older, dressed for the hills and had his hands up, talking to Finn all the while.

"Listen Finn, I'm Military Police. I'm the lead investigator in the search for you and you need to listen to me. Please just hear me out and don't do anything stupid."

Finn looked over the policeman's shoulder at the closed door. "I'm taking it that you're not alone?"

"No Sergeant, I'm not. My team's out there but I've told them you'd come quietly, without the need for guns and handcuffs."

Finn gave the policeman a sad smile. "Well, I don't want to seem rude but it wasn't really your place to give them that assurance was it?"

The policeman pointed to the floor beneath him. "Look, I'm going to plonk down just here. No tricks or funny business, I just need you to hear what I've got to say. You're the one with the gun in here, the one with the power. All I have is my words. You're a smart man Finn and I know you'll do the right thing here."

Finn's mind raced as he struggled to think of a way out of his predicament. *Could the policeman be lying? Had he come here on his own?* No, that's not the way they operated and besides, Finn was an armed fugitive so it was likely that the policeman had some serious support outside. He could feel tears of frustration welling in his eyes at the thought of being taken from this place, his sanctuary, and the wolves. He would lose his link to Katy and a lump came to his throat as he considered this. He too slumped against a wall and slid down until he was sitting on the floor, weapon still aimed at the policeman. His voice cracked as he spoke. "I can't go back Mr Finnegan. This is where I belong, out here. It's the only place I feel at peace."

Gary nodded and lowered his hands so that they were resting on his knees. "I know mate, I know. The problem here is that if you don't come back with me tonight there's only two ways that this is going to end for you. One, my colleagues outside will shoot you when you try to run and two, you somehow get past them and escape then a team of SAS or SBS will be up here with orders to take you down. You're a soldier, and a bloody good one by all accounts so you know I'm not bullshitting you."

Finn nodded. "I know you're not bullshitting me. But I have no choice. This is where I belong. I go back now and they'll throw me inside for a couple of years at least. I stole a rifle and other military property and have been AWOL for months so they're going to make an example of me."

Gary shook his head and leaned forward. "Yes, under normal circumstances that's what would happen but after what you've suffered between the death of your family and your friends there will be a fair bit of leniency shown. *But only if you do things my way.* If you give yourself up now that will be a huge factor in any sentencing considerations."

Gary watched as the tears rolled unchecked, down the younger man's face and into his beard. There was no hint of menace or threat from the marine, only sadness and melancholy. The military policeman continued his plea. "We've spoken to the old man you saved from the poacher and taken a statement from him. Got it in black and white that you saved him from certain death while exercising proportional force against his assailant. That's a good start Sergeant Douglas, but not enough on its own. Come with me tonight and any court martial will look at both these things in a positive light."

Finn shook his head. "I'll still be sent down for a while and even if I got through that, what do I do after? I'll never go back to the marines and I'll just be as fucked up as I am now."

The military policeman pointed across the room. "Look at your hand Finn. See those little shakes on your left fingers? That's trauma lad. PTSD, shell shock, battle fatigue, call it what you will. You aren't well Finn and that's what's pushed you to where you are now. It's nothing to be ashamed of; it's an illness and like anything else it can be treated. Again, I think that once you've been examined and diagnosed this will explain a lot of what you are going through and why you've done the things you have."

Finn looked at the fingers the policeman had indicated. He had noticed the tremors himself of course but had accepted them as part of the legacy of his war-fighting days and nothing more. He looked up as the military policeman continued talking.

"You've probably been having nightmares, yes? Talking to yourself, drinking heavily, hypersensitive to things? Okay, maybe not here where you feel at peace, but back home I'm pretty sure you must have experienced most of these things." Gary watched as the marine lowered the weapon and rested it across his thighs, wiping his eyes with the sleeve of his white smock.

"That's why I can't go back Mr Finnegan. I did feel all of those things, back in my old life, but I don't get them here. The boy didn't follow me here either so I know that I'm

240

doing good. Almost back to normal with all of that shit behind me. Well, except for the talking. But that's a private thing and I'm not talking to myself." Seeing the policeman's puzzled look, Finn smiled sadly and explained. "I talk to Katy, my sister and tell her how amazing this place is and how wonderful her wolves are. She wanted to come here so much and I want her to hear that it's as amazing as she always said it would be."

Warrant Officer Finnegan felt his throat tighten as the younger soldier shared his raw emotional state. "Finn, I lost someone very dear to me once and I went through some of what you're going through now. I lost it for a little while until a good friend gripped me one day and asked me that if my wife could see me, and what I was becoming, what would she say to me? Now I'd had all the platitudes, condolences and best wishes that you always get, but this was the one thing that got through to me. Because she would have been disappointed in me. Hurt and disappointed that I was throwing away the one precious thing that she had lost: Life. I was drinking hard, messing up at work, alienating myself from friends and family, a proper downward spiral. For the very first time throughout that whole process I felt ashamed of what I'd become and what I was throwing away so I changed. Talked to friends and family, took some time to travel and get my head straight then chucked myself back into work. And I'm still here now, mate."

Gary paused to monitor the marine Sergeant's face and was pleased to see none of the expressions that might indicate a sneer or rejection of the policeman's story. "My point is Finn, if your mum and Katy have been watching you and could speak to you tonight while I'm here, what do you think they would say?"

Gary knew that there was an inherent risk that Finn would rebuff this approach and be furious with the policeman for getting personal with the mention of his mum and Katy and how they might judge him. He watched the marine closely for any hint of an adverse reaction and saw that Finn was staring off into the space between them. There was silence for a moment before the younger man spoke. "Do you believe in fate, karma, or whatever you want to call it? I didn't, but the more I thought about it the more I thought yeah; mum, Katy and the lads, their deaths are all payback for the people I've killed over the years. God or whoever, letting me know that there's a balance to address. Then there's the boy: That little lad in Libya that I killed. He used to follow me around everywhere, just watching, letting me know what I'd done." He turned his attention back to the military policeman, the sad smile again playing on his lips. "Even the bible says thou shalt not kill doesn't it? But I did kill, and I did it many times. And I killed a child. I'm sure there's a special hell reserved for that alone."

Gary stood up slowly, rubbing the area around his buttocks where the cold of the floor had seeped in. He was pleased to see that Sergeant Douglas did not react to his change of position and was confident that his message was getting through to the marine. "No Finn, that's not quite right. The bible actually says 'thou shalt not murder': quite a difference. And if you've read the bible, you'll have seen for yourself that it is full of wars and killings. God isn't punishing you Finn. *You're* punishing you, and it would devastate your mum and Katy to see you like this. Come on son; let's end this now. Let's get you out of here and back where we can get you some help. Please Finn."

Finn sat in silence and reflected on the policeman's statements. The professional soldier within him recognised that all was lost, that whether he went with the policeman tonight or not, his capture on the islands was inevitable at some point. And there was nowhere else that he wanted to go, no fall-back position or alternative hiding spot. The grieving, personal Finn was devastated at the thought of leaving his sanctuary and returning to everything that he had turned his back on. But there were no other options. It was over. He stood and looked at the military policeman and nodded his head in resignation and acceptance of the situation. He took a couple of steps across the room and held out the sharpshooter to Gary who took the weapon from him and checked that the safety catch was applied before slinging the weapon onto his shoulder.

The military policeman put his hand on Finn's shoulder. "Thank you, Sergeant Douglas. I give you my word that this is the best thing you could have done and that I'll make sure

243

all of this is documented for the court martial to see. I know it's hard son but this is the right thing to do." He could feel the relaxed muscles in the marine's shoulder and the dejected expression on his face and knew that this wasn't a ruse. He spoke again. "I'm going to open the door now and let my colleagues know we're coming out. They're armed and I don't want to risk any misunderstandings okay?"

Finn nodded and Gary opened the door, admitting an intrusion of snow flurries carried on the howling wind. He shouted to make his words heard above the din. "Okay, it's me. I'm coming out with Sergeant Douglas so don't bloody shoot!" After a brief pause, he put his hand on Finn's back and applied some pressure to indicate that the marine should go before him. Both men left the cottage and Gary pulled the door closed behind him. He squinted as his vision readjusted to the dark night and eventually could make out the sight of his two colleagues standing some ten feet from the door. Both had their hoods up and were covered in a dusting of snow and Gary could see the relief on their faces that the situation was over.

He beckoned them closer. "Put your weapon away please Cal, Sergeant Douglas is coming with us of his own free will. Cal, take this rifle and Mhairi, will you go in and get Sergeant Douglas' pack please?" Finn watched as the younger military policeman took the rifle and slung it over his shoulder, staring at Finn with a look of undisguised contempt. "Well, well, well. The great Sergeant Douglas

244

Royal Marines. I told them we'd get you. Was only a matter of time."

Gary took a step towards his subordinate and vented his fury. "Sergeant Callaghan, you will shut your stupid mouth and from now on will speak only when spoken to. Do you understand?" The younger man stood in open-mouthed astonishment and made to reply but Gary closed the distance and grabbed him by the front of the jacket, surprising Cal with the strength he exhibited. "DO YOU UNDERSTAND?" Cal nodded, shocked and off balance by the verbal assault. Gary turned to the marine who had been observing the proceedings with a bemused detachment. "I'm sorry Sergeant Douglas, please forgive that unprofessional outburst from my colleague."

Mhairi returned to the group who were waiting for her at the edge of the forest. She dragged Finn's pack along the ground as she still had her own strapped to her back. Finn looked at the Warrant Officer who nodded his assent and the marine took the pack from the policewoman and shouldered it with ease, tightening then fastening the padded waist belt. Gary turned to Mhairi. "Let's get out of here. You happy taking the lead again?" He had to repeat himself as his words were torn away by the force of the wind and the snow but she heard him and nodded to show she understood. She took a torch from her pocket and shone it into the trees, the fat flakes of snow reflecting the light back against the darkness. They had just taken their first steps away from the cottage when the pale face of

Fiona Taylor appeared like a spectre from the depths of the forest. Mhairi stopped and let out a gasp of surprise and shone the beam of the torch directly at the woman. A tall figure stood directly behind her and Mhairi could now clearly see the automatic pistol being held against Fiona's head. The man spoke, shouting to make himself heard above the scream of the wind.

"Which one of you bastards stole my guns?"

37

For a brief moment there was only the sound of the wind's relentless assault on the forest then André repeated his demand. "I said, which one of you bastards stole my fucking guns?" He punctuated the end of the sentence with an increase in the pressure of the weapon against Fiona's head. Fiona cried out in pain and in reflex Gary reached for his own pistol but was halted by another yell from the man. "Stop right now or she gets a bullet. All of you now take out your guns and throw them as far into the woods as you can. One wrong move and I'll blow her highness' fucking brains out okay?"

Gary struggled to process the scene in front of him but knew that they had no choice but to comply with the stranger's demands. "Do it." Cal turned to him for confirmation and he nodded while taking his own pistol from his hip holster and slinging it into the darkness. His colleague followed suit but just as Cal was about to throw the rifle into the trees the man bellowed again.

"Not the rifle Sergeant Callaghan. Bring that one to me." Cal looked first at André and then at Gary, noting the puzzlement on the Warrant Officer's face. André walked

Fiona closer to the group while remaining tucked in behind her, exposing as little of his body as possible.

Cal spoke. "Wait. You don't need us. He's the one you want. That's the one I told you about, the marine." Finn stared as the policeman pointed to him across the small gap. Mhairi and Gary looked at the younger military policeman in astonishment. Gary shook his head to clear the snow that was clinging to his brows.

"Sergeant Callaghan, who the hell is this man and how do you know him?" Looking back at the stranger, Gary watched as a smile crossed his face.

"Oh, the Sergeant and I are old friends, aren't we Cal? Cal's been helping me keep a tab on your movements around the place in case it got in the way of my business. Which you certainly bloody did."

Gary turned to his subordinate, shaking his head in disbelief. "Cal, please, say this isn't true." The look on the younger man's face told him all that he needed to know. "Why?"

Only once before had Cal felt as wretched as he now did and he had never resolved that situation. Never had gotten over his humiliation and professional embarrassment. Amid the howls of the wind and the driving snow he decided that this time it would be different. He could still make this right. He looked over at Gary, Mhairi and Douglas and noticed their stunned expressions as they registered the impact of his deceit. He turned his attention to the South African who was now standing a little apart from Mrs Taylor, holding her with his free hand while he beckoned Cal forward with the pistol.

"Come on boy, bring me that rifle and then you can be on your way." Cal nodded and walked towards the man, unslinging the rifle as he closed the distance. As Cal took the rifle in both of his hands, he dropped suddenly on one knee and brought the weapon up, aimed it at the South African and pulled the trigger. At the same time André reacted instantly, grabbing Fiona and propelling them both from the line of fire and into the doorway of the cottage. The rifle did not fire.

Gary was frozen to the spot as he watched the whole scenario unfold before him in surreal slow motion. Cal looked down at the rifle with surprise and realised that the safety catch was still applied. As he moved his left hand to release it, a shaft of light caught Gary's attention and he saw that the Afrikaner had stumbled into the cottage with Mrs Taylor in front of him like a human shield. Two flashes sparked over the woman's shoulder and the bark of the shots carried through the howling of the wind. Gary turned to see Sergeant Callaghan fall to the ground at the same instant the shaft of light vanished and the cottage door was closed. Spurred into action, Gary ran to his fallen colleague and dropped to his knees, noticing instantly the dark entrance hole on his Sergeant's temple. Gary called Cal's name and cradled the Sergeant's head, turning it over and gasping as he saw the exit wound on the other side. Sergeant Callaghan was dead.

He had no time to process this as Mhairi and Finn grabbed him and hauled him to his feet. The marine picked up the rifle but Gary took it from him, a cold efficiency now starting to emerge from his initial shock. "No. I've got this. I'm going to talk him out as he's got nothing but a pistol and I've got the sharpshooter. You two get back there and try and find the pistols. If he doesn't come out, we'll need to look at other options. MOVE!"

André squatted in a corner of the room well away from the doorway. He ran a hand through his hair and cursed aloud, frightening the woman and causing her to cry out. He was fucked. That little bastard had seen to that. André hoped that he had managed to get a bullet into him although his shots had been wild, as he'd struggled through the doorway. He only had his Glock and they had that bloody big rifle with its telescopic sight. And they were probably looking for their pistols that they'd thrown into the trees. *Fuck, fuck fuck!* He scanned the room a second time, searching in vain for an escape exit that he might have overlooked but there was nothing but the front door and four walls. In desperation he looked to the roof, wondering perhaps if he could tear a way out.

His eyes were drawn to something stashed in the low rafters and he stood and walked over to the area beneath it. Glancing at the woman to ensure she wasn't going anywhere he stretched up and lifted the sackcloth-wrapped item down, a huge smile breaking across his face as he immediately identified the object within. The carbine; he had found his C8. He lifted the weapon from the sack and then took the spare magazines from the bottom of the hessian bag. He checked that the weapon remained loaded and stashed the magazines in the pockets of his jacket. One hundred and twenty rounds of 5.56mm ammunition. Plenty to get him out of this mess and deal with that interfering marine. He turned back to the woman slumped on the floor. He now had a plan.

Gary stood covering the doorway with the sharpshooter rifle as he yelled at Mhairi and Finn behind him. "How you doing back there?"

Mhairi's faint reply came and instant later. "Nothing yet!"

Gary swore and began running courses of action through his head, how he could talk this maniac into giving up without putting Mrs Taylor at risk. He thought about his dead colleague and wondered again what the hell the lad had been mixed up in with this bloody South African psychopath. His thoughts were halted by the door opening a fraction and the sight of Fiona Taylor's face in the small aperture lit from within. She shouted out at the military policeman, her voice breaking with strain and emotion. "Don't shoot, we're coming out. He wants to talk." Gary raised the rifle to his shoulder and yelled back his reply. "Okay, come out slowly and no-one will get hurt."

After what seemed like an age the door opened fully and Gary watched as Mrs Taylor again was used as a shield to cover the man behind her. There was no gun at her head this time and Gary assumed that it would be stuck into the small of her back. The sight on the rifle was of no use at such a close range and Gary looked over the top of it, keeping the barrel pointed towards Fiona and her captor. He did not dare risk the shot and the South African was cunning, ensuring that his head was never in full view as he shuffled forward, covered by Fiona's body. The South African's voice boomed across the small distance now separating them. "I'm going to throw down my gun but I want your word first that you won't shoot me."

Gary looked for signs of trickery but could see nothing to support his suspicions. "Okay. Throw down your gun. You have my word. I won't shoot. I'll arrest you and you'll be taken into custody but you must throw down your weapon now." He watched, alert for any deception as the man raised his arm and held it aloft behind Mrs Taylor, the pistol dangling from his fingers, everything silhouetted in the backlight of the cottage's lamp. Gary spoke again. "Throw the weapon out to your side. Do it now." The South African complied without hesitation and the pistol spun through the night air and landed by the roots of a spruce tree. "Good. Now I want you to step away from Mrs Taylor and put your hands on your head."

He barely heard the man's reply but made out the query within it. He repeated his command. "Step away from the woman and put your hands on your head." The pair had now moved closer to Gary and he could see that the South African was cupping a hand to his ear, straining to hear

Gary over the wind. Gary screamed his directions again and realised too late that he had allowed the man to get very close to him in the confusion of getting his orders across.

André shoved the woman as hard as he could directly at the policeman, dropped to one knee and swung the carbine that he had concealed behind her up into his shoulder. The woman crashed into the policeman and careened off to one side, her momentum carrying her flailing into the trees. The policeman also stumbled backwards and was just regaining his balance when André fired a burst from the carbine. The harsh BAAARPP and the flare from the muzzle dulled his senses and he stood, advancing on the now prone form of the military policeman. André looked down through the falling snow and saw the holes in the chest of the down jacket the man was wearing. He noted that the rifle was shattered from some of his shots and would be of no use to him but wasn't concerned now that he had the C8. He could see the policeman was struggling to breathe but that he was still alive. He fired a further two rounds into the policeman's face, the muzzle flash briefly illuminating the pale features, and ended his existence. Pausing only for a moment he turned back to the clearing and retrieved the Glock from where it lay on the ground, placing it back in his holster.

From the cover of the dark forest Finn pulled Mhairi to her feet. They had dropped to the floor at the sound of the first burst of gunfire and looked up in time to see the South African follow up with the kill shots. They stared at the scene before them in disbelief until Finn pulled her close and looked her in the eye. "They're dead, there's nothing we can do. We have to go."

38

Paul Taylor opened his eyes and struggled to make sense of where he was. He was cold and realised that he was sitting in the driver's seat of one of the Rovers. The car was being buffeted by strong gusts of wind and a small accumulation of snow had settled on the windscreen and windows. He leaned forward to turn on the ignition and immediately lost all sense of balance and direction and vomited over the steering column. Spitting out the vile substance from his mouth, he raised his hand to the side of his head where he was experiencing terrible pain. He flinched and cursed as his hand made contact with the area and looked at his fingers in the dim light. The dark, shiny coating was obviously blood. Had he crashed the car? Had an accident? With a sudden fear he turned to the back seats, hoping that he was alone. His head spun and the nausea struck again but he bit back on the urge to be sick again. The rear of the vehicle was empty and he turned back to the steering column, found the keys in the ignition and started the vehicle. The headlights came on automatically and he saw he was parked by the side of the road near the start of one of the old forest trails.

Then, in a rush of jumbled images, everything came back to him. The South African, Rory, and Fiona. Fiona: *Where the hell was she?* He recalled the South African leaning forward from the rear seat and telling Paul to pull over and turn the ignition off. That was the last thing he remembered. The bastard must have knocked him out cold. Paul turned on the interior light, tilted the rear-view mirror and examined the side of his head. There was a large gash just above his temple and a trail of the dark, viscous liquid running down his face. The wound itself looked like it was beginning to clot and the blood flow was oozing out, rather than flowing freely.

So, the South African had taken Fiona. *But where and why?* What could he have needed her for if his sole aim was to kill Sergeant Douglas? He leaned across and opened the glove compartment, pulling out the ordnance survey map. He unfolded the document and ran his finger along the features until he identified where he was according to the map. The old forest trail was marked on it, a dotted line running through the forest and up towards the higher ground of the Ben.

What the hell was he looking for? His finger tracked the route of the path as it left the old road and followed the contours of the forested slopes, over the small stream and onto the high ground above Coire Dubh. With a burst of clarity, he sat upright and slapped the steering wheel. He remembered Mhairi's assertion that this area would be a very attractive one for Sergeant Douglas to base himself in. Returning to the map, he examined it with greater care than previously and saw what he was looking for within seconds: the small square symbol that represented a house or a dwelling. That's where the South African had gone. That's where Fiona would be.

Paul opened the car door and stepped out into the raging storm. The cold was immediate and he gasped, shielding his eyes as the snow was driven against his face. He opened the back door of the Range Rover and gave an exclamation of joy when he saw that the contents had not been disturbed. The equipment box remained closed and he wasted no time in undoing the latches and opening the lid. He removed one of the down-filled jackets and put it on, zipping it up and pulling the hood over his head, tightening the draw-cords. He found some gloves but put them to one side and reached into another compartment, pulling out two small items: a radio handset and a battery.

Attaching the battery to the clips on the bottom of the handset, Paul knew the likelihood of it having a full charge was low, but even a small charge might be enough to get some help out here. With the battery attached he turned the channel to the one they had been using at Angus' place and, taking a deep breath, turned the volume knob, hearing the click as the power came on. The small green LED light showed that there was at least some charge left in the battery and he knew better than to waste this. Pressing the transmit button on the side of the radio, Paul spoke clearly into the device. "Anybody listening, this is Paul Taylor, east of Stoneybridge and needing assistance, over."

He grabbed the gloves, closed the door and ran back to the front of the vehicle, jumping in the driver's seat and struggled to pull the door behind him against the force of the wind. Once the door was secure, he turned the heating up to full and the fan to maximum. He brought the radio back to his face and repeated his statement, keeping the handset beside the uninjured side as he listened for a reply. The static and muted cackle seemed to mock his efforts and he tried again. "Anybody listening, this is Paul Taylor of Monach Hall and we are in trouble, I repeat, we are in trouble, over."

More static and white noise were the only sounds emanating from the radio and he gripped the device hard in frustration. He repeated himself several times and waited, ear jammed next to the speaker, all attention awaiting a reply. It was useless. Nothing was coming back and he did not even know if his transmissions were getting out. He was just about to give up when the burst of crackling voice came through.

"Paul, Paul, this is Mhairi, Mhairi. Where are you? Over."

39

Angus was pressing hard on the gauze pad when the burst of transmission came over the radio. Hearing both Paul's and Mhairi's voices he bound the pad to the journalist's chest and grabbed a radio. "Hello, hello, Paul, Mhairi, this is Angus, over." There was nothing but the crackle of static in reply to his message. "Hello, anyone. This is Angus at Grogarry and I have an emergency, over."

A garbled voice came from the speaker and the old man placed his ear closer to the radio, face scrunched up in concentration. He swore in frustration, unable to make out what the person on the other radio was saying. "Hello anyone. This is Angus from Grogarry and I have a medical emergency, over."

"Angus, Angus, it's Mhairi. What's going on? Over."

The old man brought the radio to his mouth, eager to reply to the transmission. "The newspaper man has been shot in the chest. It's pretty bad. Over." There was a brief crackling once again before a new voice came over the airwaves.

"Angus, it's Finn. How is his breathing and have you stopped the blood flow? Over."

"Finn, there is still a lot of bleeding but I've stopped the worst of it with gauze and bandages. His breathing is bad though; sounds like he's gargling. His chest looks really big and his lips are blue as well. Over" There was silence for several moments and Angus thought he had lost the connection again until Finn's voice came through, faint but clear.

"Angus, I need you to lift his head up and check the position of his throat. Once you've done that, let me know." Puzzled, the old man put down the radio and gently lifted the journalist's chin, his eyes widening in surprise at what he saw. He lowered the chin and replied to Finn's request. "Finn, it's Angus. His throat is in the wrong position; it's moved to one side now. Over."

"Okay Angus, he's got a sucking chest wound and you need to listen to me so we can save him as he doesn't have much time. You need to get bandages or cloth strips, some tape and a hard bit of plastic or even a credit card, do you understand me? Over."

The old man wasted no time, taking the radio with him as he ran back to his house through the heavy snow. He pulled drawers open and located some sheets, scissors, masking tape and a plastic folder. Back in the barn he closed the door against the blizzard and laid the items out on the table. "Finn, it's Angus. I've got everything you told me. Over"

Finn's reply was broken due to the poor reception. "Okay. Make some bandages up from strips of the cloth.

They need to be long enough to wrap around his torso. Use a square of the plastic to cover the exit wound but seal it only on three sides, I say again, only on three sides. Confirm, over." The old man replied his understanding and began making his improvised equipment. Once he had finished with his efforts, he pulled the journalist forward in his chair, allowing him to fall against him in an intimate embrace. The strained breathing became louder and Angus made soft soothing noises as he cut the journalist's shirt from him, exposing the horrific wounds. Maintaining his hold on the reporter, he used his free hand to clean the exit wound with some cloth and could finally see the ragged hole where the bullet had left the body.

Casting the cloth aside, Angus picked up the plastic square he had cut from the folder's flexible cover. Reminding himself of Finn's instructions, he placed the square over the wound and firmly pressed down on the masking tape on the three sides of the cover. He understood now what he was doing. The plastic cover on the exit wound would act as a valve, becoming a seal when Rory breathed in, but allowing the air to leave the chest cavity when he breathed out. Some long forgotten medical lecture returned to the old man as he applied a pad and bandage to the wound at the front of the chest. The journalist's chest cavity had been filling with air as a result of the wound, collapsing his lungs and, in effect, suffocating him slowly. The improvised valve would now allow this air to escape, deflating the chest and allowing the lungs to re-inflate and get the oxygen back into the body. Satisfied with his work, Angus placed the journalist into a sitting position, ensuring that the rear wound was not pressed hard against the back of the chair. He wiped his shaking hands on another cloth and picked up the radio.

"Finn, it's Angus. It's done. Over."

"Roger that Angus, well done mate, you've probably just saved his life. You should start to see some improvement in his breathing soon and his chest should also go down."

Angus looked at the slumped reporter and thought he could see a little improvement already, although he knew that it could also just be his wishful thinking. Finn's voice startled him from his reverie.

"Angus, it's Finn. Keep him warm, monitor the bleeding and try to get help."

The old man gripped the handset in frustration. "Finn, he cut the telephone and the vehicles are no good either. Over."

"Sorry Angus, I can't stay on any longer. We've got some problems here so I'm going to have to go silent for a while. Stay safe old man. Out."

Angus sighed and placed the radio down and felt a weakness in his legs now that the adrenaline was leaving his system. *Try to get help? From where? And how?* The telephone was gone, the vehicle's tyres had been shot out and there was a raging blizzard outside. He really couldn't think of anything. He ran his fingers through his white hair and decided that the best thing he could do was to look after the reporter. He could see an improvement already and hear that the breathing was less laboured than it had been. Angus walked over to the spare equipment and picked up a couple of down jackets, which he placed over and around the journalist's body to keep him warm. Looking around the room he spotted what he was looking for and made his way to the table beside the stove. Without preamble he lifted the bottle to his lips and took a long drink of the fiery liquid, feeling the burning sensation slide down his throat and warm his chest. Putting the whisky back on the table he sat down on one of the chairs and began thinking about how he could get some help.

40

Finn clicked the radio off; keen to preserve whatever power remained in the batteries. He was glad that he'd managed to talk Angus through the treatment of the reporter's wound, as the man would have died otherwise. Tension pneumothorax was the medical term but Finn, alongside many soldiers who had seen it first hand, usually referred to it as a sucking chest wound. He tucked the radio into an inside pocket of his jacket to keep it warm, again, doing everything in his power to retain the charge in the batteries.

He followed Mhairi through the blackness of the forest, stumbling and tripping as they sought to put some distance between them and the South African. The last time they had seen the man was at the cottage when he had killed Warrant Officer Finnegan. Finn had been shocked at the man's casual application of violence and knew that they had to get away from him or they would both be dead alongside the military policemen. As the gale whipped snow at his face, Finn shook his head at the memory of the policemen's deaths. The Warrant Officer had seemed like a decent bloke, genuine and keen to end Finn's situation without violence. He hadn't deserved to be murdered like that. Mhairi stumbled in front of him and Finn thrust out an arm and steadied her. She stopped and turned in to face him, shouting to be heard above the shriek of the wind.

"Where are we going?"

Finn leaned in and yelled beside her ear. "I don't know. We need help. We've got people injured and who will die unless they get medical attention."

Mhairi wiped the tears from her eyes, the murder of the military policeman still vivid in her memory. "I know, but how? We can't lead him back to Angus and there's no phone or vehicles we can use there anyway."

"Look, we've got the cover of the forest to our advantage. We can hardly see anything here so he's in the same boat and the snow's covering our tracks in any open areas."

"How long can we keep this up for? If we don't get help Rory is going to die. And what about Mrs Taylor? I saw her get smashed against a tree and not get back up. And Paul? What's happened to him? We've heard nothing since that first transmission"

Finn shook his head in frustration. "I know, I know. We need some way of getting help but I can't see how."

Mhairi looked towards the steeper slopes. "What about the old radio mast up on Beinn Mhor? The old buildings are still up there."

Finn raised his eyebrows in surprise. "What about it?"

"There might be something there we can use to contact Stornoway or the mainland. Even if there isn't any equipment we can use we might get through to someone on that." She patted the lump where the radio bulged from Finn's jacket. "I've had amazing reception up there when I've been on climbing trips. We're too low here to reach anyone except each other."

"What about this storm? It's crazy to go up there, at night in this blizzard."

"You have a better idea?"

Finn didn't. Mhairi drew the map from her jacket pocket and, shielding the light with her hand, highlighted the area with a torch. "Look, we're about here. I say we follow the glen up past Loch Iarras then through the corrie to the foot of the Ben. Then we take this re-entrant and tackle the ascent here – short and sharp."

Finn shook his head. "That's a tough climb, and at night, in a blizzard…. I don't know, Mhairi."

But the policewoman was already stowing the map away. "Yes, it is. But I know it well, done it quite a few times. And we're not exactly spoilt for choice, are we?"

Finn was about to reply when a burst of gunfire tore through the forest, ripping shreds of bark and splinters from the trees around them. Dropping to the ground beside the policewoman, Finn grabbed her by the arm and made eye contact. "Let's do it. *Now.*"

41

Paul Taylor stood above the bodies of the military policemen and put his head in his hands. He was about to check that both men were dead when his eyes were drawn to a patch of colour beside a tree. He let out an involuntary moan as he recognised his wife's clothing and rushed to her side, stooping beneath the branches of the tree that were being thrashed around in the wind. Taking off his glove he touched her face and was shocked at how cold the flesh was against his fingers. Fearing the worst, he reached to check her pulse but stopped when he saw her eyes open. "Darling, it's me Paul. Are you hurt?"

Fiona Taylor moaned and pulled her arms into her sides and tried to sit up. Paul helped her, leaning her against the trunk of the tree, his eyes drawn instantly to the dark wound on the side of her head. She groaned again and touched the wound, wincing at the pain. Putting his hand on her shoulder Paul repeated his question.

Fiona shook her head. "No, no, he just shoved me against the tree when he…." Her voice trailed off as she looked at the bodies in the small clearing. "Oh no…"

Paul hugged his wife as she sobbed into his jacket. She began shivering hard against him and after several moments he disengaged and leaned in close to speak to her. "Come on Fi, we need to get you out of this cold." He stood and lifted her to her feet, putting his arm around her shoulder and leading her into the cottage, closing the door behind him. He sat her in a chair and working by torchlight, lit the lamp then added kindling and wood to the fire. As the blaze took hold, he moved his wife nearer to the warmth and looked at the wound on the side of her head. It had stopped bleeding, probably as a result of the cold but he would need to clean it and get a bandage on it. Looking around the room he saw a pile of equipment in the corner and among it, a small medical pack. He unzipped the little case and took out some sterile swabs, gauze and a bandage. He returned to his wife and placed the items on a table beside her chair. She looked at the equipment but said nothing, giving Paul the briefest of nods to indicate that she acknowledged his intentions.

Paul cleaned the area of the wound with the sterile swabs before applying the gauze pad and bandage. He choked a little at his wife's stoic acceptance of the pain and discomfort, which she accepted with silence. He threw the soiled swabs onto the fire and summoned up a false smile. "Well, you're still a tough old bird Fi, I'll give you that. How do you feel?"

His wife looked back at him with a rueful smile of her own. "I feel like I've been slammed into a fir tree and half frozen to death."

He knelt beside his wife and embraced her, feeling his eyes well up with the emotion. She hugged him hard for several seconds then pulled back. "Paul, what are we going to do? That mad swine has killed Rory and the Military Policemen and he's probably got Finn and Mhairi by now."

"No darling. Rory's alive; I heard it on the walkie-talkie. Finn talked Angus through a procedure and it seemed to have worked."

"Angus is okay as well? Oh, I'm so glad, I hadn't even thought of him."

Paul took her hands in his. "Darling, we need to come up with some way of getting help. Rory might not last the night without it and Finn and Mhairi need all the help they can get. The Rovers are no good, he shot out the tyres on the one at Angus' and must have done the same to mine while I was out cold."

"No, he did that with a knife. Probably didn't want to alert the policemen and Mhairi that he was here. Oh, he's got another gun as well. I think it's that automatic thing that Finn took from the other poacher."

Paul swore softly. Now the killer had an automatic rifle to add to his arsenal. Stalking two unarmed people on the side of a mountain in a blizzard. *God help them.*

42

André Voster knelt against a tree and waited for his eyes to adjust after the blinding flash from the carbine's burst. He didn't think he'd hit either of them as they were gone within seconds of him reaching the point where they had been stood. He cursed aloud, raging at the snow and howling wind that kept him from tracking his prey. He rose and removed his pack, opening the flap and rummaging inside until his fingers found what he was after. Closing the pack, he left it to one side as he fiddled with the straps and buttons of the item he had retrieved. Once he had donned the item, he toggled the small switch and smiled as the low-pitched whine became audible. He lifted his hand to his forehead and lowered the tubes until they were in front of his eyes. His world was now a luminescent green, his view into the forest expanded tenfold. He chuckled as he donned his pack and continued on his way. Night vision goggles. He was pretty sure the bloody marine didn't have any of those!

He tried to put himself in the shoes of the marine and the woman. What would he do if he was them? They would be trying to get help. They had no weapons and were being pursued by an armed man who was going to kill them so they needed help. *Okay, how will they get it?* They don't have a sat-phone and André had taken out the old man's landline. The cars are both fucked so they can't drive them. *A boat?* No, the seas were raging earlier and if anything, would be worse by now. *So, what would they do?*

The goggles were already giving André an advantage over the marine. Even though the snow was falling heavily, in some of the thicker areas of the forest, the South African was picking up occasional footprints. Finding a prominent set where it would appear the pair tripped, André stopped and took a minute to study his map. The tracks seemed to indicate that the marine was heading higher, up towards the mountain. He frowned; this didn't make any sense. *Why would they leave the cover of the forest and risk exposing themselves on the slopes of the mountain?* Scrutinising the map, he had almost given up when a small detail caught his eye. On the eastern side of the summit of Beinn Mhor there was a small square object on the map, barely noticeable against the scrum of contour lines. There was some tiny writing beside the symbol that he strained to make out as the map flapped in the gusting wind. He turned his back to the gale, shielding the map and stared hard once again, at the small symbol and the writing alongside.

Clever bastard. As he tucked the map away and turned his goggles back on, he felt a grudging respect for his adversary. The marine was going to climb the mountain, at night and in a blizzard in order to reach the disused radio buildings. He must think there is a way of contacting someone for help. André couldn't be sure that there wasn't and needed to start closing the distance and fast. He studied the map and identified the obvious route that the marine would take to the foot of the mountain but after that, he couldn't say. It was sheer rock faces without any apparent easy climb. André needed to get to them before they started climbing or at least catch them on the rock face and pick them off with the carbine. That, however, left him with a hollow feeling. He really wanted the marine to suffer, pay for his interference. Yes, André wanted to get him before the climb. Go to work on him with the knife; see the fear and agony in his eyes before he killed him.

The South African increased his pace, the goggles giving him confidence to stride through the forest. He knew the marine and the woman couldn't possibly be going at the same pace and was sure he could catch them before their ascent. Maybe he would wing the marine and play with the woman, make him watch her suffering first. The thought warmed him and he smiled as he strode between the wind-whipped trees.

43

Paul Taylor handed the steaming mug to his wife who cradled it in her hands, blowing on the hot tea before raising it to her lips. Paul poured some for himself; his in a small bowl as there had only been one mug in Sergeant Douglas' belongings. The radio lay on the table, Paul's efforts to raise anyone unsuccessful.

Fiona sighed as the tea warmed her from within. "Paul, what are we going to do? I feel so bloody helpless just sitting here knowing that Mhairi's being hunted by that psychopath."

"I know dear, I know. Look, I'm going to go back down to the car and get some flares from the safety box. I'll bring them up here and set them off from the clearing. Maybe a boat will pick them up and report them."

"Oh Paul, there's no boats out there tonight. They'll have all come in well before the storm hit."

Paul knew Fiona was right but couldn't face the prospect of doing nothing. He slurped his tea and was lost in thought, struggling to come up with any viable suggestions. After some time, he placed his empty bowl down and looked at his wife. "How are you feeling now darling?"

Fiona touched the bandaged area gently and nodded. "I'm okay. Still a bit sore but not too bad all things considered."

"Right. The way I see it we have two options. One, we stay here where it's warm, there's shelter, and we wait for help to arrive. Two, we bundle up, walk back to the car, warm up again then walk on to Angus' and reassess the situation from there. Thoughts?"

"I don't want to stay here. There's nothing to say that murdering swine won't come back whether or not he gets Mhairi and Sergeant Douglas. Let's go with your plan to get down to Angus. If we can't find help, we can at least assist him with poor Rory."

Paul felt a sudden, deep affection for his wife. Even in the direst of situations she looked beyond her own predicament and to what she could do for others. "You're an amazing woman Fiona Taylor. Utterly amazing."

"Well, let's try and stay alive long enough for me to enjoy that appreciation dear husband."

They spent several minutes dressing in the warmest clothes they could find and ensuring that they had the torch and the radio. Paul opened the door and was pushed back as wind and snow forced their entrance. Hoods up, husband and wife staggered into the clearing, buffeted by the gusts. Paul felt a gloved hand on his arm and turned to his wife. Fiona pushed her face against his.

"What about them?" She indicated with her head to the bodies of the military policemen. Paul thought for a moment and nodded. "Hold the door open for me." As she carried out his command Paul approached the body of Gary Finnegan, a heavy cover of snow masking the details of the body beneath. He took a deep breath and grabbed the boots of the dead policeman, dragging him across the clearing and into the cottage. As he hauled his funereal load past his wife, he heard her sob and saw that the snow had been blown from the body and the awful sight of the imploded face was now clear. Settling the corpse in the middle of the room, Paul put the arms into the side and the legs together before placing a cloth over the face and covering the horrific injuries.

Giving himself no time on which to dwell upon his awful task he went straight back out to retrieve the body of the younger policeman. He repeated the process and dragged the lighter body inside and placed it alongside that of his colleague. He placed another cloth over the younger man's face and was about to leave when something caught his attention. He bent down, unzipped the jacket and reached inside shivering at the realisation that there was absolutely no body heat under the jacket. He heard Fiona behind him.

"Paul, what on earth..."

His wife's query was cut short as he stood and studied the object he had retrieved from the sergeant's corpse. He looked at his wife who had her hands cupped over her mouth in astonishment. Investigating nothing more than a misshapen lump in the sergeant's clothing, Paul had found a satellite telephone. Now, they had a chance.

44

Leaving the cover of the forest behind them, Finn immediately felt the full assault of the blizzard. He'd paused briefly at the edge of the treeline and improvised a harness from some of his climbing rope for Mhairi and then fastened his own harness and connected a short length of rope between them. Visibility was poor and communication all but impossible unless they shouted in each other's ears and Finn realised that they could easily become separated or lost.

Mhairi led, breaking a trail through the snow some six feet in front of Finn. She had taken a compass bearing while Finn constructed her harness and was following it religiously, given that the blizzard allowed them only several feet of visibility. The snow was already thick on the ground and some of the drifts almost knee deep. He was pleased with the progress they were making, much quicker than their stumbling advance through the forest. He hoped Mhairi was right about the radio reception from their handsets as he had little faith that there would be anything to assist them in the old radio shack.

Mhairi stopped and turned her back to the wind, waiting for Finn to close the short distance. She took hold of the rope and pulled Finn to her, pulling his hood to one side and shouting in his ear. "Loch Iallas is to our right and we're now in that wee valley between Bheag Tuath and the Ben up to our left. I'll take another bearing and get us to the small loch at the bottom of the two Bens then we can decide on the climb, okay?"

Finn gave the thumbs up and Mhairi turned her attention to her map and compass, having difficulty keeping her feet against the howling assault of wind and snow. Finn watched as she stowed the map back inside her jacket and set off once again. Turning to look behind him Finn could see there was little point to his vigilance: The South African could be twenty feet or half a mile away, Finn still wouldn't see him through the whiteout. He turned when he felt the tug on the rope and followed Mhairi, her back just a dark lump appearing between sheets of snow.

Slipping on an exposed rock Mhairi realised that they couldn't be far from the small loch as they were now encountering the boulders and rock faces that bordered the water. She advanced with exaggerated care, fearful of twisting or breaking an ankle on the snow-covered rocks. Finn took his lead from the policewoman and was careful with his own progress, testing each foot placement before committing his weight to it. He bumped into Mhairi's back, unaware that she had stopped due to his attention being focussed on the ground. She pulled him close and shouted in his ear once again. "We're here; that's the loch to our front and Beinn Mhor to our left. Let's look at finding a route up."

Finn pointed to a large rock looming out of the snow beside them and Mhairi nodded, both taking shelter in the lee side of the monolith. Mhairi pulled out the map and torch and used her finger to orientate Finn. "Okay, we're here and that's the Ben there. I think our best option is to go straight at this; follow this stream up to where it goes between these two features then get on this ridgeline here and walk to the base of these rock faces. I've done them many times before and they're not bad." She watched Finn, his moustache and beard crusted with snow and ice and waited for his reaction.

Finn held the other side of the map and studied it for several moments. "I agree. I think that option gives us the least amount of climbing. What's the climb like?"

"Moderate mostly with a difficult bit on the last pitch. In this weather though you can probably guess it will be a bit tougher."

Finn nodded and handed the map back to her. "Okay, let's do this. There's no point roping up; I've only got a couple of karabiners, no protection whatsoever. You lead, I'll follow and just stay close. Keep looking back to check I've made the pitch because we're not going to be able to talk much up there."

Mhairi nodded and stood, untying the knot on her harness and handing the rope to Finn. She waited as he packed the rope away and put his pack on. He clapped her shoulder to let her know he was ready and they set off, maintaining their careful progress as the ground became steeper beneath them. The gradient soon increased and the going beneath them became treacherous, much of the stream haven frozen and coated the rocks with ice. Mhairi could feel her thighs burning and her breathing become ragged but knew that it would abate soon enough once her body adjusted to the increase in effort. She glanced back over her shoulder and saw that Finn was right behind her. She cursed as a blast of wind and snow hurled her to one side. Catching her balance, she wondered if she'd underestimated the danger of the climb. Yes, she had done it many times before but never in these conditions. But there hadn't been any other options.

Finn watched the policewoman struggle to keep her balance and thought about the climb for the summit of the Ben. It would be more exposed up there and the wind much stronger. They would have to be very careful; one wrong move would see serious injury or even death. The last notion prompted him to remember they were being pursued and he glanced back over his shoulder but could see nothing beyond a few feet. Wiping the snow that had been driven into his face he continued to follow the policewoman as she scrambled up ahead of him.

45

André smiled and dropped behind the rock, occupying the indentations he had spotted that the marine and the woman had left. He pulled out his map and traced various features with his little finger, murmuring to himself as he did so. Although unfamiliar with the area and the mountain, he applied his many years of experience to identify which route the pair would take to the radio shack. There were several options that he could see but one stood out from the others because it explained why they had travelled to this location, rather than taking a straight climb from the edge of the forest. Yes, that stream would take them to a decent ridge and then it was only a small climb to the summit and the shack. He knew he had no time to waste and thrust the map back into his pocket and stood, pulled his glove back on and left the protection of the rock, swaying in the winds that battered him.

Although the night vision goggles had limited visibility because of the blizzard conditions, they still enabled André to identify and navigate around the natural hazards of rocks and crevices. He knew that he had to be making better progress than the marine and the woman, and had this assessment confirmed when he saw a patch of deep snow that had recently been disturbed. The tang of adrenaline flooded his mouth as he anticipated the imminent capture of his prey. *Yes, very close now*. He could only be a matter of minutes behind them. Surveying the luminous green world that the goggles provided, André began to think in detail about what he intended for the interfering marine.

46

The darkness and the blizzard denied Finn any chance of seeing for himself how difficult the climb would be. He shielded his eyes from the driving snow with a cupped hand and looked up the rock face in front of him. Nothing. Only the dark stone and its draping of snow. Mhairi pulled on his sleeve and led him further along the base of the edifice. She pulled his head to hers. "This is where we start. The first pitch is pretty much straight up for about twenty feet, loads of holds and good rock. Then there's a change of direction to the right and onto a similar pitch for another twenty or so feet. I'll stop at each juncture and make sure you're with me okay?"

Finn nodded and tightened the waist and chest straps of his pack. It was colder up here and the wind made even standing still an effort. He watched as Mhairi started the climb, noting her confident movement and ease of balance. He waited until she had gone about six feet up the face then he began his own climb. He was gratified to find that it was exactly as Mhairi had described: not too difficult and with plenty of hand and footholds. Finn ensured he maintained three points of contact with the rock-face, never moving a hand or a foot until the other three appendages were secure.

The wind tore at the pack on his back, unbalancing him on a couple of occasions. Looking up, the snow stung his face as it was funnelled between his body and the rocks. He saw Mhairi looking down at him and then change direction towards the second pitch.

Mhairi was finding the climb quite easy but had been shaken when a gust of wind caught her and peeled her back from the rock, leaving her with the utter conviction that she was going to fall. She had managed to regain her balance and return to her climb but she had been spooked by the experience. She slowed her ascent somewhat, taking time to ensure solid hand and foot placements before moving. Finn was right behind her and didn't seem to be having any difficulties. She stopped; realising with a jolt that she had reached the third pitch where, from memory, she knew things became more difficult. She waited until Finn was stood next to her and then pointed in the direction she intended.

Finn gave Mhairi a little distance then followed her route. He had only been climbing for a couple of minutes when he realised that this pitch was much more difficult than the previous two. He watched Mhairi as close as he could to identify which hand and foot holds that she was using. His feet slipped several times as they struggled to find a purchase on the icy rock, and his mouth flooded with the coppery taste of adrenaline as the fear of falling assailed him. He was also being unbalanced by the wind buffeting his pack, adding to the difficulty of the climb. Looking up, he had almost reached Mhairi when the policewoman slipped, her foot skidding out from under her. Finn could see that she was reaching for a handhold but couldn't make it and was sliding from her position. Wasting no time, Finn tested his foot holds were solid, bent his legs then released one of his hands. He shoved his gloved hand under Mhari's foot and thrust upwards, halting the policewoman's descent. He felt the resistance as Mhairi realised what he was doing and pushed down on his hand, gaining the leverage to haul her body back up the rock-face and secure the hand holds.

Mhairi looked down at Finn, her heart hammering in her chest and gave him a thumbs-up to assure him she was okay. She watched and waited as the marine made his way up the pitch and past the point where she had nearly fallen. Finn was taller than Mhairi and made the pitch with none of the difficulties that she had experienced. Mhairi continued with the climb, taking even more care in light of her recent experience. She recognised the prominent crevice in front of her as the start of the final pitch and felt a sense of confidence for the first time since they'd started the climb. This last section was longer but easier than the previous one, the exposed rock fractured and broken with lots of opportunities for secure holds. With a renewed sense of determination, she reached up for the first hold.

47

André glared through the green of the goggles at the rock face above him. He had found where the pair had started their climb by following the disturbed snow and knew they were just ahead of him. In the driving snow however, he couldn't see shit. And he didn't know what route they would take up the rock-face so he couldn't be sure that he would remain on their tail. *Fuck.* There was only one thing for it and that was to climb from this point and follow the path of least resistance. One or other of the pair must know this route, they wouldn't have picked it at random and logic dictated that they would have picked the easiest ascent they could, particularly on a night such as this. André secured the carbine to the side of his pack, took a deep breath and began to climb.

It was actually easier than he thought. Lots of holds, and good, clean rock, none of that crumbling shit. Through the goggles he could pick out the options for each section and was progressing quickly. He'd climbed a lot in the Drakensbergs all through his life and although it had been some years since his last visit, he was pleased to see that he had lost none of his skills. The route was pretty obvious, each change of direction easy to identify by being the easiest option. As he reached a large crevice in the rock face, André looked up to identify the next pitch and almost yelled with excitement as he caught site of a leg disappearing into the darkness above him.

Spurred on by the sighting, André climbed faster, the thrill of closing with his quarry energising him. The climb was becoming easier with much more holds available and André knew he would catch the pair soon. He cautioned himself after slipping on some ice, slowing his advance a little, keen to avoid any threat of injury when he was so close. He maintained a steady progress, securing each hold before committing to it and was pleasantly surprised when he realised that he had reached a rock-covered ridge. The climb was over. He was a few hundred metres from the summit and the radio shack. His euphoria was short-lived when he realised that the marine and the woman were even closer to their objective. He tore the carbine from the side of his pack and strode hard up the ridge, staggering against the driving snow.

He had only been walking for several minutes when he saw the marine appear out of the blizzard above him. He raised the carbine to shoot but by the time he had the weapon in his shoulder the figure had disappeared into the freezing maelstrom once again. Cursing, he started running as best he could up the steep slope, skirting boulders and shattered rock formations. Looking up once again he saw the pair of them, standing together up ahead of him. In one fluid motion he swung the carbine up into his shoulder, released the safety catch and fired a burst, blinded by the shock of the light through his night vision goggles and ears ringing from the sound. He moved forward slowly until his vision returned but saw no sign of his target. He started running again.

48

Two things happened at once for Finn: A shower of sparks bounced off the rocks around him and Mhairi screamed. Over the shriek of the wind he heard the burst of gunfire and instantly understood what was happening. Mhairi fell to the ground and Finn dropped down beside her, noting the policewoman was clutching her leg. Finn grabbed her and examined the area, shaking his head when he saw the ragged, seeping hole. He turned the policewoman over, deaf to her screams of protest and saw the exit wound: A through and through. Mhairi was lucky; the round had passed through her upper thigh missing the femur and artery. She was in agony but nothing vital had been damaged.

Finn worked fast, knowing that the South African was right behind them. He dragged Mhairi to the cover of some rocks and sat her against one. He could barely hear her over the howling wind but knew that she would be moaning with the pain. He shrugged out of his pack and pulled the small medical pouch out, grabbing several items then putting it back into the main pack. He put a packet to his mouth and tore off an edge with his teeth. With great care, he shielded the wound from the wind with his body and applied the gauze, discarding the empty sachet and winding the bandage around the policewoman's leg and securing the end. He looked over his shoulder at where they had just been but saw nothing other than the dark and the snow. He put his face against Mhairi's and shouted above the shriek of the wind. "How you doing?"

Mhairi had been clenching her teeth hard together when Finn was treating the wound. She relaxed her jaw and found her voice shaking with emotion. "I'm in agony Finn. What's the leg like? Is there a lot of damage?"

Finn cupped her chin and lifted it, making sure she was looking into his eyes. He shouted again to make himself heard. "No: You're really lucky. It's a through and through. No bone or artery damage, just the muscle. I've put quick clot and a bandage on to control the bleeding but we need to move now."

Although it was the last thing Mhairi wanted to do she nodded her understanding. She felt Finn grab her under her armpits and haul her to her feet. She screamed as she put some weight on the leg and felt it collapse under her. Finn steadied her and thrust his arm under her own, underpinning and supporting her injured side. He leaned his face into hers. "Okay, let's go. I've got you. We can do this Mhairi."

She clenched her teeth once again in anticipation of the pain and lurched alongside Finn as he half dragged her back up the mountain. The pain was incredible, the shock of it robbing her of breath and making her stomach muscles rigid with tension. Her head whipped around as she looked for the killer to emerge from the depths of the storm and finish them off. She screamed as her leg bumped against a rock, a stab of unimaginable pain consuming her. *There's no way I can do this. No way. We're both as good as dead.*

Finn turned his head towards her but said nothing, focussing everything on getting them off the mountain and into the safety of the radio shack. It could only be a couple of hundred metres away and although it was a steep walk, he was convinced they could make it. The policewoman was quite petite and Finn knew he could carry her if it was necessary. He turned his head, looking behind them for any sign of the killer but saw only snow. This guy was going to catch them. They just couldn't move fast enough to evade him. Finn tried desperately to come up with something to give them a fighting chance. Anything just to give them that vital space to get some distance. His options were limited as he was unarmed and carrying an injured person but he had to think of something. Thinking back to when the killer had shot at them Finn suddenly had an idea. It wasn't much of one but in the circumstances, it was better than nothing. He leaned into the slope of the mountain, grabbed the policewoman tighter and propelled them up the hill as fast as he could manage.

49

André swore and fired a burst into the darkness. He had found no sign of the marine or the woman. He had run up the steep slope, legs burning and lungs on fire until he had reached a point where he was certain that they could not have been so far ahead. He had backtracked then, made his way down to where they had been standing when he fired at them. There were no tracks or signs here, the ridge being completely exposed to the fury of the storm. They must have run off to one side to get out of his line of fire. Wasting no more time he stalked into the darkness, his world a glow of green, the rifle in his shoulder and ready to fire. He had spent several minutes searching the area for the pair before realising they could not have come this way as it ended in a sheer cliff. In a fit of rage, he had fired the weapon into the void.

I'm losing them. He turned back in the direction he had just come and ran back to the clearing on the ridge. As he reached the spot with the disturbed snow from his own trail he paused and looked at the side he had not searched and saw a small depression. Moving closer he saw that as fast as the blizzard was covering the trail, it was a very deep and wide one and he smiled with the realisation that one of the pair was wounded and being dragged along. *Good*. That would slow them down.

André knew that the pair couldn't be far ahead; they must have re-joined the ridge while he was searching the eastern side, barely missing each other. His excitement grew as, between blasts of snow, he saw the disturbed snow the pair were leaving in their wake. His breathing was ragged now with the exertion of running up the steep slope but he did not slow down, the knowledge that he would have his target any second now, driving him forward. And there they were. The marine was above him, between two large rocks, his back to André and completely oblivious to his presence. Grinning, André put the rifle to his shoulder and taking careful aim, fired two shots into the marine's shoulder, watching as the body toppled forward and out of sight. André didn't want to kill him, just wing him enough so that he could go to work on him with the knife. Keeping the carbine in his shoulder André began climbing towards the body.

50

Finn watched as the tall man made his way up the steep slope towards him. He could see that the man was cautious, the rifle still in the alert position, but he was also confident. *Good.* That's what Finn was counting on.

Finn had raced up the slope, dragging Mhairi along, knowing that for his plan to work he needed to buy a little time. He had reached a spot he thought of as being suitable and took Mhairi to one side, propping her against a cluster of rocks. He had then raced around like a madman, collecting large boulders and placing them in a pile. Jamming his pack between two large rocks, Finn had then stripped off his jacket and put it over the pack, zipping it tight and pulling up the hood. He had just finished when the two shots had hit the decoy, toppling it forward. From his position behind another rock Finn had stared hard into the storm and watched as the man emerged from the darkness.

Finn held his breath as the South African continued his steady advance beneath him. There was something strange about his appearance and it took Finn a moment to work it out: Night vision goggles. No wonder this guy had managed to track them down. There was now only around ten feet between them and Finn knew that he would only get one shot at this. As the killer reached a long slab of rock, Finn stood, raised the boulder above his head in both hands and hurled it as hard as he could at the man. The sound of something smashing and the scream came at the same time to Finn's ears and he watched as the South African crashed to the ground and slid down the slope and out of sight. He couldn't be certain that the man was dead but he was definitely injured and his night vision goggles destroyed. Finn had bought the time they badly needed.

Working as fast as he could, Finn retrieved his pack and put his jacket on. He ran to Mhairi and saw that she was almost sleeping now that the shock had worn off. He roused her, hauling her to her feet and taking control of her once again. Putting his face against hers he yelled. "I got him. I don't think he's dead but he won't be coming after us. Let's get some shelter and some help." He saw that she had understood what he was saying but replied only with a slow nod. Tightening his grip, Finn began the last climb up the hill towards the disused radio shack.

Relying on memory and a general sense of direction, he drove them towards the old shack. The dark and the blizzard constrained visibility to only a few feet but he could tell from the way the slope beneath him dropped to the east that he was close to the building. He stopped at a clump of rocks and laid Mhairi down in their shelter. He heard her moan as his head came close to hers and he yelled above the wind to make himself heard. "I'm going to go forward and find the shack. I'll only be a minute, don't worry." Wasting no time, he staggered off, fighting the wind as it howled around his body. In less than a minute he caught a glimpse of something tall in the near distance, and after several steps was confronted by the gable end of the shack. Finn turned and made his way back to the policewoman, lifting her to her feet and half-dragging, half-carrying her to their destination.

As they arrived at the building, Finn examined the lock and was gratified to see that it was a standard padlock and bolt affair. Sitting Mhairi against a rock, he took the ice axe from the back of his pack and inserted the pick-end through the padlock hoop. Taking a firm grip of the handle he gave a hard thrust downwards and was rewarded with a faint clatter as the broken lock bounced against the metal doorway. Finn opened the door and threw his gear inside then grabbed the policewoman and carried her into the building. Settling her into a corner, he pulled out his torch and illuminated the small room. Closing the door behind him he searched the room in the light of the torch.

The main item of interest was an old radio set, dusty from lack of use. Finn made his way straight to it and studied the equipment for a moment until he had identified the roles of the various dials and knobs. He reached forward and toggled the power switch. *Nothing*. Cursing, he flicked the switch off and on several times but still, no life emanated from the contraption. He turned to Mhairi who was watching him, her face pale in the glow of the torch.

"Mhairi, you any idea how to get this thing up and running?"

The policewoman beckoned him over and Finn obliged, helping her to her feet once again and hearing the intake of breath as her injured leg took some of her weight. He helped her to the radio set and sat her in one of the chairs, watching as she familiarised herself with the apparatus. Finn could see that she had used this type of radio before and was impressed to see her pull the set forward and examine the cables at the rear of the device, ensuring everything was connected. She sighed and leaned back, pulling her hood down and looking at Finn. "There's no power getting to it. Maybe the connection is completely severed, but I'm pretty sure I remember someone saying it was all intact, just not used anymore."

Finn sighed and lowered his own hood, brushing the ice and snow from his beard. "Okay, let's try the hand-held, see if we get anything from that."

The policewoman nodded and Finn took the small radio from the pocket inside his jacket and handed it to her. Turning the power on, their hopes were lifted by the reassuring crackle of static. "Hello anyone receiving, this is a police emergency and we require assistance, over." The speaker emitted a burst of squelches and beeps but no other response. She tried again. Hello, anyone receiving, I have an emergency, I repeat, an emergency, over." After a brief pause, the static was interrupted by a broken voice and some unintelligible words. Finn clapped his hand on her shoulder and the policewoman smiled at him before speaking again. "Hello, hello, say again your last, over." The faint, broken speech was drowned out in the sea of static and Mhairi cursed. "Hello anyone receiving, this is a police emergency, the summit of Beinn Mhor and we need help, I say again, we need help, over."

Finn strained his ears but heard nothing more than the crackle of static and the bursts of interference. Mhairi kept trying but there was no repeat of the earlier words. Finn pointed to the old radio set on the desk. "Mhairi, where did the power come from this? I'm assuming it would be a generator?"

The policewoman nodded. "Yeah, they used to keep one in that small room on the northern side."

"What do you mean *used to*? Do you know for sure it's no longer there?"

Mhairi's brow furrowed as she contemplated the question. In truth, she had only assumed the generator would have been taken away. There was a possibility that the generator had been left, much like the old radio, on the off chance that it might be required for use in the future. She felt her excitement rise at the possibility. "You're right! It might still be there. I just thought it would have been taken away but I don't remember it actually happening come to think of it."

Finn nodded and thought for a moment. "Okay, here's the plan: I'll head out to the generator room, get in and see if there is anything there. If there is, I'll try to get it going.

If not, I'll climb up the mast with the hand-held and see if the added height gives us a better reception. Someone was trying to reply to us before and maybe some extra elevation will give us a better signal."

"Finn, you need to be careful. That mast will be treacherous in these conditions."

"I know, I know but I'll tether myself to the ladder with some rope and a karabiner, give myself a fighting chance."

Mhairi nodded her head towards the door. "What about him?"

Finn placed his hand on her shoulder. "Look, I hit him pretty hard. I heard him scream and watched him slide down the rock face. Now, he might still be after us, but if he is, he's probably in worse shape than you are. We don't have a choice here; we need to get the comms working and get some help out here."

"Yes, I know, I know. I just hope he's as bad as you think he is."

Finn knelt so that he was level with the policewoman and took her hands in his. "I wouldn't leave you here if I didn't think I had a chance of either getting the generator running or getting through on the hand-held. Once I leave, you'll barricade the door and not open it for anyone else but me. I'll leave you my ice axe as well, just in case."

Mhairi smiled sadly and allowed her head to drop forward and rest against Finn's own. "The irony hasn't escaped me in all of this you know. I came here to track down an armed fugitive and bring him to justice and now

I'm being hunted and shot by at by an armed fugitive but being saved by the very person I was chasing. It's insane." Finn lifted her head until she met his eyes. "Listen, you'll be safe Mhairi, I won't let anything happen to you, I swear. Let's have another look at that leg before I head out." Finn removed his gloves and turned Mhairi's leg gently to expose the side where the entry wound was. Satisfied he repeated the same for the exit wound and was pleased to see the dressing was working well. He gave her a smile. "That's doing the job. You'll be good as gold in no time, back on the beat, swinging your truncheon or whatever it is that you police types do!"

Mhairi smiled at the marine's levity and reached out a gloved hand and stroked his face. "Thank you, Finn. I'd be just another dead body on this mountain if it wasn't for you." Finn returned the gesture and she leaned into his hand as it touched the side of her face.

"Yeah but let's face it Mhairi, you wouldn't even have been on this mountain if it wasn't for me." Mhairi saw the pain in his eyes and tried to think of something to say but the marine was already on his feet, pulling his gloves back on and preparing for the task ahead.

He picked an old wrought-iron poker up from the disused hearth and hefted it in his hand. This would break up any lock that the generator room might have. He delved into his pack and pulled a length of climbing rope from it and deftly fashioned a securing line to his harness. He swept the torch around the small room as he searched for items that they could use to barricade the door but saw nothing of any significant weight or bulk. A couple of smaller items near the doorway caught his eye and he smiled as he identified that they were exactly what they needed. Door wedges. The radio operators would probably have used them to help in keeping the door tight in the frame whenever the howling gales had hit them. He picked them up and showed them to Mhairi. "These are perfect. Once I'm out just smack them into place, bolt the door closed and you'll be fine. Here's the ice axe. I'll prop it against the wall here for you." He walked back over to her and put his hand on the back of the chair. "I'll pull you over to the side of the door and you can sit there till I return, keeping the weight off that leg."

Mhairi nodded her assent and Finn dragged the chair across the stone floor, the wooden legs screeching in protest. She watched as Finn placed the ice axe within reach and slid the wedges along the floor to rest against her feet. He grabbed the hand held radio and the poker then pulled his hood up.

"Right, let's do this. When I return, I'll give five slow knocks with the poker on the door so that you know it's me, okay?" Finn could see that the policewoman was fearful; not relishing the prospect of being left alone in the dark and injured while that madman was still potentially coming for them. "Mhairi, it's cool. I'll be back before you know it."

"Like you said before Finn, it's not like we have any other options open to us. You be careful out there, Finn Douglas. There are already far too many people dead or hurt on this island and you're not joining them. Do you understand me?"

Finn smiled, gave a nod and opened the door, a flurry of snowflakes blowing past him in a shriek of wind. The door clattered closed behind him and Mhairi bolted it then hammered in the wedges as Finn had directed. Grimacing as the pain from her wound protested against her activity, she settled back into the chair clutching the ice axe and thought about the marine outside. *Come on Finn. You can do this. You can get us out of here.*

51

André screamed as the cold air met with the nerves of his shattered teeth. He dropped to his knees in agony and cupped his hands to his mouth to cover the bleeding orifice. The rock had hit him on the forehead and face, smashing the night vision goggles and his nose and mouth. His front teeth were broken and the nerve endings exposed to the freezing air, a torture almost beyond endurance. He sobbed and gathered his thoughts, breathing with difficulty through the blood and mucus in his nose. Rage dominated his entire existence: He could not believe he had been ambushed and hurt in this way. He, André Voster, former South African Special Forces and world-renowned mercenary, taken out by a bloody marine with a rock.

The need to kill the interfering marine was now the driving force in André's mind. The pain from his wounds a distraction. In a moment of rare clarity, the South African tore the pack from his back and rummaged in the front pocket until he had found what he was looking for: Painkillers. Good ones too. Shielding the blister pack from the gale he popped several of the capsules from their beds and scooped them into his mouth, swallowing with some difficulty. He put his pack on once again and stared up into the darkness above him. It was only his forehead and mouth, for fuck's sake! The freezing cold was taking care of the flesh wounds, reducing the bleeding and numbing the exposed area. The painkillers would soon kick in and take care of the worst of the pain in his teeth and allow him to concentrate.

The loss of the carbine was a blow. The rock had smashed the weapon from his hand throwing the rifle down the mountain and out of sight. He had tried to locate it but to no avail. He still had the Glock and his knife; didn't really need anything else but he would miss the comfort blanket of the larger weapon. Still, spilt milk and all that. *Look forward and not behind man.* He wiped some of the sticky blood from his eyelids and pulled himself to his feet, bracing himself against the relentless assault of the wind.

Staggering up the mountain it occurred to André that he had not even considered an extraction plan. He frowned as this thought took hold and suddenly realised that his pursuit of vengeance had become all encompassing, blinding him to reason and rationality. He shook his head and dismissed the distractions. He needed all of his concentration focussed now: Find this marine and the woman and make them pay for their transgressions. They would die in agony; full of pain and regret for the day they had dared fuck with André Voster.

Stumbling over some small rocks, André stopped and looked around him. There was nothing to see but the sheet of snow being driven by the wind against the darkness. He could feel the slope veering off to his left and remembered from the map that the radio shack was on this eastern slope. Taking great care, he negotiated the rock field, moving back towards his right when the slope steepened. Then it was there, directly in front of him: The radio shack.

André stopped and breathed deeply through his nose, hearing the wheeze as the breath made its way through the clogged nasal cavities. The pain in his teeth was easing into a throbbing ache but he was also feeling a little spaced out from the effects of the painkillers. He would have to monitor that. Didn't want this bloody marine getting the jump on him when he wasn't able to concentrate fully. He drew the Glock and checked the chamber to confirm the weapon was still loaded. His gloves felt too cumbersome when handling the weapon so he removed them, immediately feeling the cold bite against the warm skin.

He followed the wall of the building, turned a corner and saw the door. Creeping forward he held the Glock in front of him and stood ready to one side of the metal door. There was no lock but a long, fresh scrape against the surface of the door told him that the marine had probably broken the lock as they made their entry. André placed his hand gently against the door and applied pressure in a gradual manner, confirming that the door was shut fast but without alerting whoever was inside. He thought about his next course of action. If it was locked from the inside how would he get in? He couldn't say for certain where the lock was so shooting it to pieces wasn't an option. The hinges were on the inside, so again, he couldn't get access to them either, and besides, they were much more difficult to destroy with only nine-millimetre rounds. He cursed the loss of the carbine once again.

André decided to survey the whole of the building, identify any other entrances or weaknesses. Keeping close to the walls he advanced around the perimeter slowly, wiping the snow from his swollen eyes as he examined the structure. The western wall of the shack yielded nothing; a blank canvas unbroken by even a window. André stopped for several minutes in the lee of the wind, the building shielding him from the roaring gale. He had to get in and soon. They were probably trying to raise some help even now and André needed to be away from here before that help arrived. *How am I getting away again?* He raised his head at his own question and acknowledged a sense of detachment from the situation. He didn't need to get away as long as the marine and the woman were dealt with. Shaking his head to clear these thoughts he felt a stab of concern at his lack of focus. He must have taken too many painkillers. He just didn't feel......right?

He moved further along the wall and turned the corner, looking along the northern edge of the shack. The wind hit him head on and he was driven back several steps before he regained his balance and lumbered forward once again, head down against the onslaught. A smaller room appeared in front of him and just as he reached it a dark object manifested from the dark and disappeared into the gloom ahead of him. André's eyes widened in surprise at the sight. The marine. And only five or six feet in front of him.

Opening his stride, André caught up with the shambling figure as it walked away from the building. The figure stopped and seemed to be adjusting something around their waist. As André advanced, he saw now that the marine was stood at the base of the radio mast and was adjusting a harness and a rope. At least he now knew that they hadn't made contact with anyone. Smiling with satisfaction he raised the Glock, took careful aim, and fired.

52

Finn fell to the ground stunned and in great pain. He had just been readying his rope to climb the mast when he had felt something slam into his shoulder and spin him around, knocking him off balance. He pulled his hood back and looked down at the area, his heart hammering in his chest as he took in the sight of the protruding down-feathers from the holes in his jacket. He had just processed this information when the South African appeared out of the dark, gun in hand and his face a macabre mask of dried blood and gouged flesh. He yelled something at Finn but Finn could not hear him over the shrieking wind. He could also now feel the pain of the wound and the blood trickling down his back. *This is bad. Really bad.*

The South African stepped forward and motioned for Finn to stand, keeping the pistol trained on him as Finn laboured to get to his feet. His shoulder was a fire of agony now and he screamed as the wound stretched and contracted under his exertions. Finn stood, hunched over and clutching his shoulder, mind racing at how he could escape from this madman and keep Mhairi safe. He had no weapon; the poker was back in the generator room next to the empty fuel cans that had so disappointed him. As he watched, the South African approached him, smiling in an awful rictus displaying a row of broken and bloodied teeth. He said something else that Finn couldn't understand and as the marine leaned forward the butt of the pistol smashed against his forehead, splitting the skin and knocking him to the ground once again.

Finn rolled. Instinct took over as his mind recognised that he would die in this place unless he fought. He stood quickly, gasping in pain and faced the man before him. Moving as best as he could, he bobbed and weaved from side to side, making himself a harder target to hit. He could see the South African trying to keep the gun on him but having trouble doing so. A bang and an instant flash told Finn that the man had fired again but this time failing to hit him. Finn watched as the South African wiped his eyes and that was all he needed. Taking advantage of this slightest of distractions, Finn threw himself headlong down the eastern slope of the mountain.

53

André screamed at the night sky as the marine disappeared into the maelstrom. His shot had missed and the clever bastard had used the distraction to throw himself down the mountain. Wasting no time, André stumbled down the slope in pursuit, tripping on rocks and slipping on ice. His numbed senses identified too late that he was careering out of control and the fact only became apparent when he found himself airborne then crashing to the ground, bouncing along a cluster of rocks. Struggling to stand, he knew he had hurt himself badly. His breathing was ragged and he was in pain every time he drew a breath. He placed his hand on his ribcage and applied a gentle pressure, howling in agony at the sensation. He had broken his ribs. *Fucking great, as if this night wasn't bad enough.* As he cursed his fate another more important factor came to him and he looked at the hand he had used to examine his ribs. It was empty. He had lost the Glock.

Finn watched as the killer dropped to his knees and screamed at the night skies above him. He was a matter of feet from the South African but he had not been noticed yet, the crazed man more concerned with his injuries than on locating the marine. Finn knew that would change, and soon. This bloody mad man was fixated. He realised that he had to come up with a plan fast; his strength was ebbing due to his wounds bleeding freely. As he watched, the South African stood up and pulled a knife from his belt then began scanning the area around him. It was only a matter of time before he spotted Finn in his exposed position. Taking a deep breath Finn struggled to his feet and met the killer's eyes just as he spotted Finn.

André stepped forward, his stomach muscles clenching hard against the pain of his broken ribs. He saw that the marine wasn't doing too good either, pale and slumped, hand on one thigh supporting his weight. As he advanced, André could see that the marine had no weapons, no pack, just a harness with a few coils of rope. He watched as the marine was pushed back by a sudden gust but André felt none of it. He was immune to all outside interferences now that he was closing with his prey. It had always been his gift: that ability to shut down all but the instincts he needed when finishing the kill. He raised his free hand before him, keeping the knife lower and a little further back. The marine moved to one side with difficulty and André darted forward slashing the blade across his foe's chest.

Finn gasped as the shock of the cut hit him. It felt like his chest was alight and he risked a look downward. His jacket lining was slashed open and a combination of feathers and blood were immediately evident. Looking back at the South African he saw that the man was in no hurry to kill him and Finn felt a real fear encompass him. This man was going to draw this out and make Finn suffer. Then he would do the same to Mhairi. Finn had never felt so useless. Wounded and unarmed against a psychopath who didn't seem to care whether he lived or died. Finn continued to move in a circle, trying to make things harder for his adversary but then tripped against a rock and lost his balance.

André sprang forward and spun the knife into an underhand grip, ducked low and slashed the marine from hip to shoulder, hooting with pleasure as he revelled in the scream of his enemy's agony. He watched as the marine staggered backwards and looked behind him, obviously searching for some route of escape. *No way bru, no escape tonight. Just you me and uncle André's knife.* He giggled at this. *Uncle André's knife! Where had that come from?* His smile wavered as he recognised that these were not perhaps coherent thoughts to be having at this point. *Get back to work Voster: This job isn't over!*

Finn felt faint. He knew he was bleeding badly and that he was dealing with a bona fide lunatic. The mad bastard's hoot of victory had confirmed that. Finn became aware that he could now see things more clearly and realised that dawn must be approaching. He also knew that, at some point soon, this would be over for him and just beginning for Mhairi. He couldn't let that happen. All of this was his fault. His curse. He had to make it right for those who were left. He looked behind him and realised that he knew exactly where he was, having initially lost his bearings as he had

311

tumbled down the slope. He pushed himself upright using the rope knot on his harness and stared at the murderer in front of him. He beckoned with his free hand, smiling as he yelled over the tempest. "Come on then you cowardly South African bastard. Come and see what a real soldier can do."

André laughed at the marine's audacity. You had to hand it to him; the interfering bastard had some balls. Still, he wouldn't be so cocky once André had cut those same balls off and showed them to him as he died. He stalked forward, noting that the front of the marine's jacket was saturated in blood. It was getting lighter too and André could make out more details on his adversary, the split forehead, blood streaming down the side of his face, the exhausted and pale features. André decided to stop playing with his food. He feinted a strike to the chest but dropped low and struck at the marine's stomach with a straight stab. He felt immediately that the knife had not found its target by the lack of resistance and saw that the marine had turned his body at the moment of impact and that the knife had passed harmlessly through his jacket. And then a heavy blow to his injured ribs made him scream.

Finn drove his elbow as hard as he could into the side he had seen the South African checking earlier and was rewarded by the scream, confirming he had hit his target. To his credit, the South African did not collapse or drop the knife but went with the impact, pulling away from Finn and any follow up blows. Finn swore. This bastard was good.

He watched as the man straightened with obvious difficulty and saw for the first time, the utter madness in his eyes. His face was blank and emotionless and Finn saw that the time for games was over: The South African was coming to finish him.

André felt calm and serene as he circled the marine. He felt no pain anymore and just wanted to finish the job and get paid. *Who was this guy again? Why am I supposed to kill him? And where the hell am I?* André felt a small flicker of fear as these questions came to him but they were quickly quashed by his desire to finish the mission and deal with such irrelevancies later. He slashed at the marine's right side and missed. Recovering quickly, he stabbed at the abdomen area but again, missed his target. Humming an old Boer hunting melody, he circled, stalked, thrust and slashed but still did not find his target. He needed to be closer. He narrowed the distance of his circle, determined to finish this kill.

Finn watched the South African edging closer and knew that he would have one chance at this. If he failed, then he and Mhairi were dead. Finn didn't care about himself, he had earned that death, but Mhairi had not. As he dodged the thrusts and stabbing attacks, Finn discreetly coiled his rope into a series of loops in his hand. He stared hard at the knife, watching and waiting for the moment. He was feeling slightly off balance and knew that this was from the blood loss and that he was rapidly running out of time. *Come on you South African bastard, do it!*

André grew frustrated with his lack of success and decided to end it here and now. The marine was weakening rapidly and André wanted to kill him while he was in full possession of his senses. Wanted him to suffer as he died. *Okay, it's time my friend.* Feigning a slash to the chest André stepped closer to the marine and changed the attack into a sudden thrust and felt the resistance as the knife stuck fast into the body. The marine did not react in the way André had imagined and indeed, stepped closer to André so that their chests were touching. André pulled back on the knife but it wouldn't come. Frowning he glanced down and his eyes opened wide with surprise when he saw the blade of the knife grasped hard in the marine's bleeding hand.

Finn clamped down hard on the blade of the knife, ignoring the searing pain of the gash in his hand. As the South African looked down in puzzlement, Finn quickly used his other hand to drape the loops of rope over the man's head and jerked down hard. The South African choked and dropped the knife as he reacted instinctively to the ligature constricting his breathing. Finn threw his own body down the slope and pulled hard on the rope behind him. As Finn landed on the ground, the South African stumbled over him, remaining upright as he staggered down the steep slope, both hands grasping the rope around his neck. Finn arrested his own momentum and wedged himself between two large rocks, the rope reeling out between them.

André threw his legs out in front of him as he tried to loosen the choking noose around his neck. His eyes bulged and face darkened but he felt a glimmer of hope as his fingers pried loose one of the coils. He looked ahead for somewhere to throw his body to the ground then his mouth opened in a silent scream as he flew over the edge of the precipice and into thin air.

Finn tensed as he waited for the inevitable but still screamed in agony as his body was jerked hard and smashed against the boulders. He sobbed in both pain and relief as he realised that his plan had worked. The South African was now hanging in the abyss just beyond the rocks that Finn had wedged himself against. Finn had seen how close they were to the sheer drop and understood that if he could get the killer close enough, he could grab him and take them both over the edge. As he had hauled on the rope, luck more than judgement had been his saviour and he had realised that he did not need to go with the South African to his death. He could live.

Finn felt the greyness at the edge of his vision begin to extend its progress and his breathing deepen with a long wheezing note every time he inhaled. The weight of the hanging man pinned him against the rocks and he did not have the strength to release himself from his macabre umbilical. The pain was almost gone though and he just felt tired. *So tired.* He was warm and comfortable and he wanted to have a bit of a sleep before he told Katy about his latest adventures. She would be cross with him for hurting himself but her wolves were safe from the bad men now. As his head dropped on his chest he could feel and hear his heart beating as it struggled to pump dwindling blood to his vital organs. Lulled by this rhythm, he recalled the sound of the rotors on his last helicopter ride in Libya and dreamed that he was looking out once again at the crowd of villagers. In this dream however they were waving to Finn and as his consciousness faded, Finn raised his bloodied hand to return the wave of the smiling boy pushing his wheelbarrow of fruit and bread back towards the village.

54

Rory Starkey leaned on the railing and took a couple of minutes to regain his breathing. He'd chosen the stairs over the lift, going on doctor's orders to continue rebuilding his fitness levels. He smiled as he recalled days climbing the peaks of the Hindu Kush and crossing deserts, his long legs eating up the distance with little difficulty. And now here he was, puffing and wheezing like an old man after only three flights of stairs. Still, it could certainly have been a lot worse.

Finn's directions to Angus over the radio had saved Rory's life. The journalist had survived what would have undoubtedly been a certain death because of this. The Taylor's had arrived at some point later that night and helped Angus care for the injured reporter. More importantly, they had managed to procure a satellite telephone from somewhere and called for help from Stornoway and the mainland. Just after first light, the storm had abated enough for rescue and police helicopters to deploy to the island and assist the group. Rory would never forget the feeling of relief on seeing the neon-jacketed medics barging through the door of the bunkhouse and opening their medical holdalls. Their calm, efficient actions providing him with a sense of safety. He remembered also the tears that had rolled down his cheeks, a manifestation of the relief he was feeling and Fiona Taylor's soothing voice as she held his hand.

The Taylors and Angus had been fine, although Fiona was taken to the mainland for a twenty-four-hour hospital stay as a precautionary measure in light of her bump on the head. Rory had been flown directly to Raigmore Hospital in Inverness and operated on as soon as he arrived. The surgery was a success but the journalist had lost a lot of blood and had been very weak. His recovery, consequently, had been a slow one but eventually he progressed from patient to convalescent, working hard to regain his former physical abilities.

As soon as he was able, he'd reached out to his editor, relaying with undisguised fervour the importance of getting the full story of Finn Douglas on the front page of *The Times*. His editor had visited him personally and brought along Ben Chivers, the Scottish crime correspondent. They had produced the traditional hospital gifts of grapes and flowers as well as their standard banter, jokingly referring to Rory as 'the malingerer'. Both men had listened to him in silence; Ben taking copious notes while the editor merely nodded or shook his head at relevant junctures in Rory's narrative. Ben had asked a lot of detailed questions about the poachers, gleaning every piece of information that Rory could recall. His aim, he had explained, was to use these details to get some more information from his vast network of contacts on both sides of the law. Look to identify exactly who the poachers were and what they were doing. After Ben had left, the editor had asked Rory if he felt up to the task of writing the story himself. Rory would not have had it any other way. He wanted this young man's story to be told to the country as it had happened and only he could do that.

Mhairi had visited Rory on a regular basis. She too had received surgery at the same hospital for her gunshot wound. Rory took advantage of one of these visits to debrief her on the details of what had happened to her and Sergeant Douglas that night on the mountain. He took notes and asked detailed questions to confirm he was accurately recording the facts. Once again, the Royal Marine had saved yet another life through his actions. Mhairi then explained how she was rescued from the radio shack that morning.

Finn had left the shack to attempt to get communications up and running and had told Mhairi not to open the door to anyone but him. The policewoman had found herself drifting off as she sat behind the wedged door and had lost all track of time. She had been awoken by the door being banged from the outside and voices that she did not recognise shouting. Frightened and wary, she had sat wide-eyed, heart pounding until she heard a snatch of Gaelic being spoken. She had yelled herself then and wrenched the wedges from the door, admitting a group of armed police. Two were colleagues of hers from Stornoway, the others from the armed response unit in Inverness. As

319

they were attending to her she told them about Finn and when she had last seen him. Two of the mainland police officers had glanced knowingly at each other and she had demanded to know what they had seen.

Hector, her Stornoway colleague, explained that as the helicopter had swept over the summit of the Ben that morning, the pilot had sworn into the microphone and turned the machine around, making a second pass above the eastern ridge. They had all been stunned into silence by the sight of a body hanging from a rope over the abyss; the dark, purple head giving all the confirmation required that they were looking at a corpse. Once they landed the police had divided into two groups; one had come to search the radio shack and the other to investigate and retrieve the hanging body. A fresh dressing was applied to her leg and the arrangements made to transport her to Inverness.

By her own admission she had become a little hysterical then, refusing to move until they had found Finn. Hector had placed an arm around her and told her that, while there was a chance Finn had survived, the police had only seen one body from the helicopter and that was the one hanging above a two-hundred-foot drop. He convinced her to at least allow them to carry her to the helicopter and get her comfortable and ready for the journey. Reluctantly she had agreed, numbed by the dawning realisation that Finn was dead.

Mhairi was just being carried over the threshold when a burst of transmission came over the policemen's radios:

The search team had located another body, attached to that of the hanging man. There had been a long pause before another squelch of static preceded the next call. This body was alive.

55

Finn Douglas looked out of the window, taking in the view of the manicured lawn and the neat row of spruce trees that bordered it. The crisp, clear morning air gave everything a sharpness of definition and he couldn't wait to be enjoying the day for himself rather than just looking at it. He looked at his watch and saw that he still had an hour to go before the doctor's final visit. Sighing, he sat down in the small chair next to his bed and pulled a magazine from the open bag on his bed. Looking around the small room, he grimaced in distaste. He'd had enough of hospitals. While the room was comfortable and private, it had been nothing short of an open prison for him. Still, it was over now.

Finn still had no clear recollection of his rescue. His last clear memory was of drifting to sleep and thinking about his last helicopter journey in Libya. During the subsequent interviews and chats with military and civilian police, he concluded that on that last morning on the mountain, he had not been imagining the sound of rotor blades but was hearing the rescue helicopter as he lost consciousness. His next memory was of waking up in Inverness hospital having been treated for his life-threatening injuries.

As soon as he had been deemed strong enough the interviews began from the military police. He left nothing out, cooperating fully with the investigating officers. To their credit, they had not been unsympathetic to Finn despite the fact that they had lost two of their own at the hands of the South African. Their attitude had surprised Finn. He had anticipated hostility from Warrant Officer Finnegan and Sergeant Callaghan's colleagues but received nothing but professional courtesy. Police Scotland had concluded their interviews in a similarly professional manner, even going so far as to praising Finn in his actions that had saved the lives of Angus, Rory and Mhairi.

The Taylors had also been very generous to Finn: His private hospital room secured and paid for by them. They had also used their considerable influence to ensure that Finn was not transferred to a military hospital and instead he had spent his whole recovery at the Inverness facility. A pair of military policemen took turns to sit outside his room as he was deemed a flight risk, despite the fact that for the first month of his recovery he was exhausted walking to the bathroom and back. He had been provided with a military solicitor which the Taylors had promptly sacked and employed their own family lawyer to represent him.

Mr Campbell, as Finn always referred to him, was a jolly, red-cheeked bear of a man whose loud bonhomie masked a deep and sharp intelligence. From the onset he had directed Finn to put his cares aside and that Finn would not spend one day of his life behind bars for anything that had happened to him since his return from Libya. Mr Campbell retained the services of some of Britain's finest psychiatrists and leading experts in Post-Traumatic Stress Disorder or PTSD as it was referred to. Initially Finn was loath to engage with these authorities, feeling uncomfortable with the suggestion that his mind was too weak to cope with the responsibilities of a professional soldier. It had taken one of the PTSD experts to diagnose Finn and explain much of what he had been going through as typical effects of the disorder. He had then said that if Finn had been carrying a serious injury to his leg or his arm, he would waste no time in seeking treatment to avoid further injury and get back to full health, wouldn't he? The brain was no different he had gone on to say. It suffers injuries, it buckles under stress, but it can be repaired with the correct help and treatment. After this discussion, Finn recognised the validity of the expert's statements and engaged whole-heartedly with their program.

For the first time in his life, he had spoken in detail about the boy. He relived the incident, breaking it down at the doctor's instruction, his body wracked with heaving sobs as the horror returned. He was then asked to justify every single movement and action he had carried out on that awful day. This was read back to him and he was then requested to suggest what alternative actions he could have carried out that would have changed the outcome. This in turn was also read back to him by the doctor and he was then asked why he hadn't taken these alternative actions.

Over the weeks and months Finn learned that there was nothing that he could have done differently that would have altered the outcome. Indeed, when examined in detail, most of his suggestions for alternative courses of action would have resulted in more deaths or injuries to his troop.

Although Finn wasn't sure why, he found this type of therapy worked well for him. By applying logic and analysis to his actions that day, he found that his professional mind examined and discarded all the emotional judgements that he had made upon himself, leaving only rational decision making and justification. On one of their final sessions, the doctor had asked Finn if he still dreamt about the boy. Finn had told him that he didn't and shared his experience on the mountain just before he had lost consciousness. The doctor had smiled knowingly and made a cryptic remark about the Taylors being pleased to hear that.

Mhairi had visited Finn regularly while he was convalescing and brought the newspaper articles that had hit the press. They read the reports together, starting with Rory's front-page headline. *The Times'* article while factual, was also entertaining and Mhairi and Finn had been making fun of some of the passages until they realised that they actually had been through the incredible situations Rory had written about. This first article prompted a media frenzy with reporters, journalists, television news crews and even PR agents descending on the hospital. Finn and Mhairi were of course, prohibited from speaking to the media while the investigation into the incidents on the island was on going.

Mr Campbell however, proved very adept at ensuring the press were in receipt of any information that pointed to Finn's trauma and consequently, how Finn could not be held accountable for his actions.

Rory's colleague had also been as good as his word and had dug up lots of details about the poachers. Even this article read like a work of fiction: South African mercenaries, Russian oligarchs, a wildlife smuggling plot, and murder. The bodies of André Voster's colleagues had been found, one in the woods and one brought up by a trawler net to the west of Frobost. Mhairi and Finn had found this background to the poachers the most interesting aspect of the whole affair considering how close they had come to being killed by them.

The public interest in the story exceeded all expectations. Finn read the newspapers and watched the television and was stunned to see the surge of support for all that he had gone through. On *Newsnight* a mother spoke of her son's suicide on his return from Afghanistan, a result of his PTSD not being diagnosed in time to help him. Another couple spoke of their son's descent into depression and alcohol after losing three of his best friends in an IED attack in Libya. It was clear from the many programmes and articles Finn saw, that the general public viewed him as a casualty of war rather than a criminal. He had Rory Starkey and the Taylors to thank for that.

A military police Colonel and Warrant Officer showed up with Mr Campbell one day and gave Finn the best news he could have wished for: There would be no Court Martial and no dishonourable discharge. Finn was found to have been suffering extreme PTSD at the time of his actions and could not be held legally responsible for them. As he had been officially diagnosed and treated for PTSD, he would be given a medical discharge and retain his military pension. The news had stunned Finn, his emotions a cocktail of joy, disbelief and uncertainty for his future. A bout of paperwork signing had then ensued overseen by Mr Campbell's keen eye then the military men had left, shaking hands with Finn before they went.

Mhairi had visited Finn the day after he the military policemen's visit. She had hugged him hard and had tears in her eyes at the good news. He had enquired about her leg and she told him that it was much better, the physiotherapy painful but effective and that she expected to be back at work within the month. There had been a moment of silence until she asked Finn: *And what about you?*

56

Rory Starkey grinned as he entered the room, seeing Finn waiting and ready to go. The marine looked up and smiled at the reporter, standing up to greet him.

"Mr Starkey. So good to see you again! To what do I owe the honour?"

Rory sat on the edge of the bed and looked around the room. "Nice place, but I'll wager it feels more like a cell than a hospital."

Finn raised his eyebrows at the journalist's observation. "Bang on Rory. It's an amazing place to have been allowed to recover but I've been going out of my brain with being cooped up."

"Yes, I can imagine you've been dreaming about getting out of here for some time."

"Can't come quick enough. The doc should be here any minute to give me the final clearance and then I'm gone."

The journalist nodded. "So glad it has all worked out for you Finn, and I mean that sincerely. You deserve a decent break my friend."

"Well to be honest, it's really you that I have to thank for most of it Rory. Your story set the ball rolling, put the truth out there and gave the public the information they needed. I'd have had none of that support if it wasn't for you."

Rory reached his long arm across the bed and patted the marine on the shoulder. "Well, it was earned Finn: You saved my life if you remember."

Finn looked into the reporter's eyes. "To be fair, it was Angus and me that helped keep you alive. The old man did well. And again, I still feel that none of this would have happened if you all hadn't been looking for me." Seeing the journalist begin to shake his head, Finn shushed him with a raised finger. "No, I know I wasn't in control of my faculties when I went AWOL to the island but the fact remains that people were killed and injured because of me. I know I'm not to blame for what I did, but I will always feel like I was the catalyst for those tragedies. Does that make sense?"

Rory regarded the younger man's intense expression for a moment before replying. "Finn, a crazed South African mercenary hurt and killed those people, not you. And more people would be dead if it wasn't for you. Yes, we were on that island looking for you, but that Finn Douglas was a different man from the one sitting here today. *That* Finn Douglas was seriously injured but didn't know it and he was doing the only thing he thought would help; staying as far away from people as he could, where he would do the least harm. Yes, in the course of this laws were broken that meant people were sent to find you and bring you to justice. But that wasn't your fault Finn. Your brain was broken. It needed fixing but you didn't know there was anything

329

wrong with it in the first place so you just followed its impulses, like all of us do every single day."

Finn stood and turned to the window. "It's okay Rory, really. I'm completely at peace with everything. The docs have been amazing and I finally understand what's been happening to me. There's no magic pill or solution for this and it's an on-going condition that I have to monitor but I'm getting there. I'll never get over it, it just doesn't work that way, but I will get through it, bit by bit."

Rory stood and joined Finn at the window, placing his arm around the marine's shoulders. "You'll be fine Finn, absolutely fine. You're a good man with a good heart and people can see that."

"I hope so Rory because I've got no idea what I'm going to do now. I keep getting requests from agents about book deals, magazine articles, TV appearances and I'm just not interested. I know there's money to be made that way but I have no interest in it whatsoever." He gave a lopsided grin to the reporter. "So, if you see me selling *The Big Issue* outside a train station in the near future, I fully expect you to stop and buy a copy, okay?"

Rory Starkey laughed and held his hand up in front of him. "Slow down tiger, what's all this talk of jobs and money? Sorry to be the bearer of bad news but you don't have those options anymore." Puzzled, Finn turned to face the reporter as Rory swept his arm, encompassing the room with his gesture.

"You didn't think you were getting all of this for nothing did you? No, no, nothing for free in this life my friend. Once you get the all clear from the doc, you belong to me: That's why I'm here today, to get you started in your new job."

Finn sighed. "Rory, I really appreciate the offer mate but I know nothing about newspapers or writing articles. And if it's a book you have in mind, I really don't think I have it in me to bring up old wars and conflicts, not when I'm doing so well with my therapy."

Rory was about to reply when the doctor and a team of nurses and junior doctors entered the room. Rory turned to Finn. "Right, I'll leave you in these fine professionals' capable hands. When you're done, meet me outside, I'll be in the black Rover waiting for you. As I said Finn, you don't have those options anymore so let's get you up and running on the job as soon as we can eh?" With that the lanky journalist nodded to the medical team and left the room. Finn stood in silence as he processed Rory's statements. *A book; definitely a book. Rory must have made an agreement with his editor to get a book deal out of our relationship. Well, I do owe him for a lot, can't really walk away from that.* Sighing Finn looked up and met the doctor's eyes as he handed Finn another folder of papers and documents for signing.

57

Angus watched the Range Rover approach and put down the sandpaper block he had been rubbing the oar with. The vehicle's tyres crunched on the gravel driveway of the old man's croft and he shielded his eyes from the sun's glare reflecting off the car's windscreen. The vehicle came to a halt and Angus walked over to it, a smile lighting up his face as the occupants alighted.

"Sergeant Stewart, what a pleasure it is to see you on such a beautiful day."

Mhairi smiled and removed her glasses, moving closer to accept the old man's embrace. "Hello Angus, how have you been keeping?"

The old man pulled back and smiled. "Oh grand, just grand. And you? How's that leg holding up?"

Mhairi patted her thigh. "Good as new Angus, good as new."

The driver's door opened and closed and Angus walked around the vehicle. "Well, well, well, the new Wolf Management Assistant graces me with his presence."

Finn laughed aloud at the old man's jibe and hugged him tight, clapping his back softly. "Hello Angus, good to see you old man."

Angus led them to the back of the croft where they sat in the sunshine and drank tea and ate biscuits. They were silent for some time, enjoying the stunning view over the beach and the sea. The blue of the sky and sea broken only by the white feathering of small waves, breaking softly over the rocks of the headland. The old man squinted in the sunlight and turned to Finn.

"And how are you liking the job Sergeant Douglas?"

Finn laughed. "There's no Sergeant Douglas anymore Angus; I'm a civilian, just like you. Just plain old Finn Douglas now. As for the job, it's perfect. I still can't quite believe it's real."

Angus nodded. "Well, I think it's a grand thing, having you back here. I really think you belong on the island Finn Douglas."

Finn smiled back at the old man then tilted his head back, revelling in the warmth of the sun. He still couldn't believe his luck. That day at the hospital he had concluded his leaving paperwork and walked outside where he met Rory, as arranged. The pair had travelled in silence and it was only when Finn noticed that they were heading west instead of south that he had questioned the journalist. Finn had assumed that they would be going to the newspaper offices in Glasgow or Edinburgh and was curious about the western direction they were taking. Rory had burst out laughing and explained the whole thing to Finn, unable to keep up the charade any longer.

Paul and Fiona Taylor had approached Rory and asked him to keep them abreast of Finn's future plans. They confided in the reporter that, if Finn did not have a secure position open to him, they would be very keen to employ him on the estate. They had ample cottages available for accommodation and he had proved himself eminently capable of working in the mountains and forests. Rory had informed them that Finn would jump at the chance to live and work in the islands and the wolf program but that he would not say anything until he learned what the former marine's plans were.

Rory had driven Finn to Ullapool and the pair had taken the Ferry to Stornoway. The Taylor's pilot was waiting with the helicopter and had flown the men to Monach Hall where they were greeted by the Paul and Fiona. The Taylors welcomed Finn and along with Rory, drank coffee in the drawing room while they briefed Finn on the aspects of the job, if he chose to accept it. A modest salary, a cottage of his own, food provided from the main kitchen, the use of the estate vehicles and helicopter transfers to Stornoway whenever he wanted to use his holiday allocations.

Finn had been moved to the point where his eyes watered and his voice became husky with emotion. He had started to attempt to voice his gratitude for their generosity when Paul had interrupted in a pseudo masculine attempt to convince Finn that they would be working him to the bone, offering him nothing less than a life of servitude. Everyone had laughed and the mood lightened as Finn was introduced to Bruce, the Wolf Program Manager. Bruce had helped him with his belongings then taken Finn to his new home; a small, detached cottage a few hundred metres from the hall. He had given Finn the tour, showing him how the boiler worked, where the stopcocks were, spare linen, washing machine, tumble dryer. He had grinned as he'd thrown Finn the keys and welcomed him to his new job, telling Finn that they had one of the best jobs on the planet and that he was going to love it. And he did.

Mhairi stretched and leaned forward, sighing with contentment. "You have a beautiful spot here Angus. I could look at that view all day."

The old man placed his mug on the grass at his feet. "Aye, it's a great spot to be and no mistake. It's just as beautiful in winter but in a different way: Wild, angry, powerful. Reminds us that as men, we are really just wee insignificant things in comparison."

Finn nodded his agreement. "That's very deep Angus. Didn't think an old soldier would have enough brains to come out with something like that!"

The old man turned to face Finn, a raised eyebrow and a mischievous glint in his eye. "That, from a man who thought it would be a great idea to take on an armed psychopath with a bit of climbing rope?"

Mhairi burst out laughing as Finn's mouth dropped open, then he too was chuckling at the old man's wit. "Well, when you put it like that Angus..."

Finn stood and looked at the mountains behind them. The day was clear and he studied the peaks that only several months ago had almost been their final resting place. *Amazing,* he thought, *how your life could change so drastically from one moment to the next.* Angus stood beside him and followed his gaze.

"What are you doing today Finn?"

"Well, Mhairi's got a few days off so we're going to take the tent up to Hecla and spend the next two days keeping an eye out for the Spean pack. I just want to document their condition and numbers, look for any changes in the pack relationships."

Angus cleared his throat. "You have picked a good time for it lad. I heard your beasts howling last night and the weather is stable for the next few days."

Mhairi stood and patted Angus on the shoulder. "Right Angus, we'll love you and leave you. We'll be back down for the car on Thursday so see you for a cup of tea then?"

Angus nodded and accompanied them to the Range Rover where they collected and shrugged on their large backpacks. With a final wave they set off down the rough driveway and the old man watched as they crossed the weed-covered road. He smiled as he saw Finn reach and take hold of the policewoman's hand. *Good for you. A young man or a woman should have someone. Not right to be alone, that's for old rogues like me.*

As Finn and Mhairi entered the saplings at the base of the forest a furtive shadow moved among the firs near the top of the mountain. The shadow melted into the darkness of the forest's interior but kept its gaze focussed on the area where the two people had been walking. Amber eyes stared, unblinking at the lower reaches of the treeline for some time before becoming distracted by the activity by its side. Looking down at her cub, Freya lowered her head and nudged the small, grey animal, gaining its attention. Freya turned back towards the edge of the forest and raised her head, sniffing and searching for scent on the wind. Beside her, the cub mimicked her actions, its small head turning from side to side as it interrogated the soft breeze for information with comical intensity. With a low growl Freya dropped her head and nudged the cub's flank once again before loping into the cover of the dark woods. The cub stumbled along behind her, lacking any of her mother's grace before it caught up to Freya and the pair moved silently through the hush of the forest to return to the den.

THE END

Thank you for reading and I truly hope you enjoyed this book. Please, if you have enjoyed it, take the time to leave a review and let others know how much you liked it.

Thank you once again.

James

www.jamesemack.com

www.facebook.com/authorjamesemack

THE KILLING AGENT

The worst terrorist attacks that the UK has seen. A country in turmoil, a government in disarray. Intelligence agencies with no leads or suspects.

Lovat Reid, a veteran covert operator with the Special Intelligence Group, is tasked to help track down the mastermind behind the attacks. With his partner Nadia, an officer from the Special Reconnaissance Regiment, they soon realise that they are dealing with an individual the likes of which they have not seen before.

When another atrocity is carried out, the entire weight of the Intelligence agencies and Special Forces is thrown behind the effort to find the terrorist responsible. But for Lovat, something isn't quite right. Suspecting a dangerous power-play between the agencies, Lovat digs a little deeper into the background of the terrorist suspect.

And is stunned by what he finds.

With a race against time to halt the next attack, Lovat and Nadia find themselves fighting a war on two fronts as they strive to uncover the depth of deception while hunting the master terrorist.

From the killing fields of Kandahar to the back streets of London, the consequences of a secret assassination program are brutally levelled against an unsuspecting British public.

FEAR OF THE DARK

An idyllic Scottish village...

A small team of rural Police Officers...

A man who won't talk...

When a violent stranger is arrested and refuses to give his name, it is only the beginning. Digging further into the background of their mysterious prisoner, Police Constable Tess Cameron finds that he is a disgraced former Special Forces soldier with a chequered past.

As the worst storm of winter hits the village and communications and electricity are cut, the severe weather is blamed. Tess, however, feels that something more sinister may be responsible for their isolation.

Because the stranger has friends.

And they want him back.

Whatever it takes.

In the darkest night of winter, Tess and her fellow police officers find themselves facing an elite team of killers determined to rescue their leader. And Tess knows that if they are to survive the night, they have only one choice:

Fight.

First Blood meets *The Bill* in this exciting new thriller from the author of Only the Dead.

Printed in Great Britain
by Amazon